SWAT: Special Wolf Alpha Team

X-Ops

WOLF HUNGER

PAIGE TYLER

sourcebooks
casablanca

Published by Sourcebooks Casablanca, an imprint of Sourcebooks, Inc.
P.O. Box 4410, Naperville, Illinois 60567-4410
(630) 961-3900
Fax: (630) 961-2168
sourcebooks.com

Printed and bound in United States of America.
OPM 10 9 8 7 6 5 4 3 2 1

With special thanks to my extremely patient and under-standing husband. Without your help and support, I couldn't have pursued my dream job of becoming a writer. You're my sounding board, my idea man, my critique partner, and the absolute best research assistant any girl could ask for.

Love you!

Prologue

MAX LOWRY HEARD SHOUTING COMING FROM INSIDE THE house before he stepped onto the porch. It didn't matter that all the windows and doors were buttoned up tight in an attempt to keep the barely cool air from the cheap air conditioner inside the run-down north side apartment. He could still hear his father's hoarse voice clear as day. It wasn't even noon yet, but from the sounds of it, his old man was already in one of his foul moods.

That wasn't surprising. A kneecapper for one of the off-strip bookmakers downtown, Carl Lowry was a mean, nasty SOB at the best of times. But when the weather got hot, his temper took an even more violent turn. Which kind of sucked for Max, his younger sister, and his mother, since they lived in Las Vegas. It was over a hundred degrees, and summer was officially still a few days away.

Max almost turned and walked away, even if that meant staying out in the stifling heat. Since graduating from high school two weeks ago, he'd been working as much as he could simply to stay out of his old man's sight. His father had always enjoyed taking his anger out on Max and had been beating on him as far back as Max could remember. That's why Max had pulled a twelve-hour shift at the convenience store last night, then worked another six hours this morning. He hated going home. But he was exhausted and needed to crash for a few hours or he was going to pass out. Of course, with his father acting like the a-hole he was, Max doubted he'd get any sleep—unless one of his old man's haymakers knocked him out cold.

Max took a deep breath and grabbed the doorknob. If his dad was in the mood to punch someone, better it was him than his mom or Sarah. His sister was only fourteen and on the small side. When their father hit her, it was usually pretty bad.

As he opened the door, Max heard his mom tearfully begging his dad to calm down. Max didn't know why she bothered. He'd pleaded with his mother to take him and his sister and leave his abusive father for years. The three of them could stay in a local shelter or even move to Oklahoma, where his mom's family lived. Someone out there would put them up until they could get their lives together, he was sure of it. His mother wouldn't even consider it, though. She kept thinking her bastard of a husband would change and stop smacking them around if she simply loved him enough.

The moment Max walked into the living room, he could tell his dad had been drinking. He wasn't drunk yet. Well over six feet tall and more than 250 pounds, his father was a big man, and it took a lot of alcohol to get him smashed, but he was obviously well on his way.

His father was standing in front of his old, worn-out recliner, waving his arms around and sloshing beer from his half-full bottle all over the place, yelling something about not telling him what to do in his own damn house. Fortunately, while he seemed pretty pissed, his eyes didn't have that red-rimmed, insane look he got when he was about to explode. This was just his normal, every-day kind of pissed.

Max's mother didn't even look his way. Instead, she stood there wringing her hands as her husband ranted like a madman. But his little sister saw him and flashed a quick smile to let him know she, at least, was happy to see him. It had always been the two of them against the world—or at least against their dad.

Max didn't make it more than a few feet into the room when his father turned bloodshot eyes on him. "Where the hell have you been?"

Max almost sighed but stopped himself just in time. Sighing, rolling his eyes, hell, even looking like he had a pulse were all things his father would beat him for, and he was too damn tired to put up with that crap this morning.

"I was at work, Dad," Max said, subtly moving closer and putting himself between his old man and Sarah, just in case.

His mom still hovered off to the side, her hands clenching and twisting together in front of her even more anxiously.

"I pulled a double shift...for a little extra money," Max added when his father didn't say anything.

His father's lip curled in a sneer. "You think you're the shit now that you're making minimum wage down at the local Gas-and-Go? You think you're better than me because you have a little change in your pocket?"

Max shook his head, hoping he could somehow defuse the situation, but when he saw his dad's face turn red and his eyes get that crazy look, he knew it was too late. Dad had been looking for an excuse, and he'd found it.

Max didn't bother trying to avoid the blow coming his way. It would just enrage his old man more than he already was, which would make the beating that much worse.

His father's fist caught him square on the jaw, knocking his head sideways so hard little strobe lights exploded behind his eyes. There were times in the past when a shot like that would have put him out cold. But he wasn't a little kid anymore. He wasn't as big as his dad, of course, but he was nearly 190 pounds, most of it muscle. It still hurt to get punched in the face, but he could take it a lot better than when he was younger. Max ignored the pain, refusing to reach up and wipe away the blood running down his chin. Instead, he glared at the piece of crap in front of him, unwilling to retreat even when his old man took a threatening step toward him.

"You think you're tough now because you finished high school and got a job? I'll show you tough, you little punk."

Maybe that was why his father hated him so much. Maybe he was pissed at Max because Max had graduated high school. Something the big, tough Carl Lowry had never done. His dad had always crowed about never finishing fifth grade, like he was proud of it, but now Max guessed that wasn't so true.

His dad cocked his fist back, and Max knew he was probably going to be pissing blood after this one—if he lived through it.

A flash of movement out of the corner of his eye

caught his attention; then Sarah was latching on to their father's right arm. "Daddy, stop it! Please, just stop it!"

Max wasn't sure how it was possible, but everything slowed down right then. At first, his old man seemed shocked, but then his face darkened, and Max realized this situation had suddenly taken a very bad turn.

His mother must have figured that out, too, because she lifted her hand and placed it on his dad's shoulder, tugging at him tentatively. "Baby, don't…"

But it was too late for any of that. His father yanked his arm away from Sarah and backhanded her across the face. She flew backward, bouncing off the living room wall with a cry of pain. Eyes full of tears, she reached up to cover her bloody nose with her hand, sinking to the floor.

Their father grabbed her by the shirt and yanked her back to her feet, his face a mask of rage. "Don't you ever try that shit again, you hear me?"

His voice was so loud Max was sure the neighbors heard. Not that they'd do anything. Shouting was a common occurrence around here.

His mother swallowed hard, her trembling hands tightly clasped in front of her now like she was praying.

Max refused to wait for God to come down to stop his dad. He'd said those same prayers often enough to know that no help was coming—heavenly or otherwise.

Hooking one arm around his old man's shoulders, he yanked him away from his sister, slinging him as far across the room as he could manage. His father almost stumbled over the recliner but caught his balance quickly. Eyes wild, he charged at Max with a yell.

Max might have been scared as hell, but he stood his ground. He couldn't let his dad hurt Sarah, not again.

His father swung first. Max jerked back so the blow barely grazed his chin, then went on the offensive. He'd never hit his dad before, and when his fist connected with his old man's face, pain shot through his wrist and up his arm. He ignored it and swung again, then again. He kept swinging, forcing his dad back toward the recliner.

Max wasn't sure how many times he hit his father, but when he finally felt someone clutching his shoulder, he looked over to see his mom standing there, tears streaming down her face. Breathing as hard as if he'd run a race, Max slowly turned his attention back to his father. His old man was half-sprawled on the recliner, his ugly face a bloody mess.

Max stared down at him, wondering what the hell to do now. It wasn't like he could act like none of this had ever happened. He'd just beat the shit out of his old man.

His mother pushed past him with a sob, dropping to her knees beside the chair to check on his dad. His father shoved her away, knocking her back on the floor. Climbing to his feet, he pushed past Max and headed toward the bedroom.

Max sidestepped his mother, where she knelt on the floor, looking lost and confused, and hurried over to check on Sarah.

His sister was sitting back against the wall, pinching her nose closed as she tried to stop the bleeding. Damn, her nose was almost certainly broken. He was going to have to get her to a hospital, though he had no idea how to explain why she'd ended up this way. There was an outreach clinic over on Owens Avenue. Maybe they wouldn't ask too many questions.

"Can you stand?" he whispered. "I have to get you out of here."

Sarah nodded, letting him help her up. He'd just slipped his arm around her waist and turned to lead her to the door when the look of terror on his mother's face made him freeze.

Max snapped his head around in time to see his father coming into the room, his face still covered in blood and a big gun in his hand. It took Max a second to comprehend what the hell was happening, and by then, his old man was pulling the trigger.

Max shoved Sarah aside, then lunged at his father. He had to get the gun away from his old man before he shot his sister.

Two bullets zipped past Max before the third hit him in the stomach. All the air went out of him, and he stumbled, forcing himself to keep moving, churning his feet and refusing to think about what the pain in his gut meant.

As he tackled his father, Max felt another round clip his right hip. He ignored that stab of pain, too, focusing every bit of energy on getting his hands on the gun. They struggled on the floor, slamming into the walls, the furniture, and each other. His father cursed, promising Max he was going to kill him.

The gun went off twice while they were grappling over it. Max had no idea where the bullets went. One or both of them could have hit him for all he knew. He only prayed Sarah had gotten out of the way.

Max grit his teeth, feeling the strength leaking out of him along with his blood. Before long, his father started wearing him down. Then his old man was on top of him, crushing him to the floor and twisting the gun out of Max's grasp and aiming it at Max's head.

Max lashed out with his right fist, his left hand reaching for the barrel of the gun at the same time. He didn't realize he'd hit his father in the throat until his old man started coughing. But none of that mattered. The only thing Max cared about was getting the barrel of the weapon away from his head. Max grabbed the gun with both hands and shoved it away from him just as it went off again.

His father collapsed on top of him, crushing out what little air remained in his lungs. Max tried to gasp for more, but his chest wasn't working right, and no air would come. His fingers were numb and slippery with blood, and he couldn't hold on to the gun anymore. He braced himself, sure his father would jerk the pistol free and put a bullet in his head, but there was absolutely nothing he could do about it.

Instead, his father rolled off him, onto the dirty carpet with a loud thud, blood staining the front of his shirt.

As he lay there on the floor gasping for air, Max realized the nightmare was finally over. Well, as over as it could be, considering he'd killed his own father and was slowly bleeding out on the living room rug.

Then he heard the pitiful sounds of his mother crying in that same gut-wrenching way she always did after Dad had beaten her, Sarah, and him. At least the piece of shit would never be able to do that to any of them ever again.

Max tried to call Sarah's name, but he didn't have enough air to get his throat to work. Having no other choice, he slowly rolled over, grunting as pain that hadn't been there before ripped through his body. Ignoring the dizziness, he pushed himself up on his hands and knees, then closed his eyes as blackness washed back and forth across his vision, teasing him with the possibility of passing out. When the wave of weakness finally receded, he opened his eyes again. What he saw stopped him cold.

Sarah lay on the floor unmoving, blood running down the side of her head.

Their mother kneeled beside her, hands clasped together as she rocked back and forth, sobbing. When she wasn't staring blindly at his sister, she was glancing over at Max's father.

Tears filling his eyes, Max forced himself forward, needing to check on his sister. Sarah was only a few feet away, but it still seemed to take forever to get to her.

"Call the police," he told his mother, the words barely audible.

She turned her gaze on him but didn't move. "What have you done?" she whispered over and over.

Max wasn't sure whom she was referring to with that question. It could have been him, his father, maybe even herself.

Even though he knew it was too late, Max took Sarah's slender wrist in his hand and felt for a pulse. One of their father's stray bullets had hit her in the temple. Sarah had never had a chance.

One moment, Max was holding her wrist, wondering what chance either of them ever had. The next, he collapsed to the floor beside her. Everything around him was getting fuzzy when the police kicked open the door and charged in, weapons swinging back and forth in search of a threat.

Max would have laughed if he could. One of the neighbors must have called when they heard the fighting getting loud. If the cops had gotten there a few minutes earlier, maybe it would have mattered. Now they were just here for the cleanup.

Max was still marveling at how rare it was for the cops to show up in this part of town at all when the blackness folded in on him and he hurried to catch up to his sister.

Chapter 1

Dallas, Texas, Present Day

"THIS FOOD TASTES LIKE CRAP," MAX SAID AS HE SHOVED another tiny spinach quiche into his mouth and chewed. If it weren't for the fact that werewolves could eat anything they wanted without it messing with their weight, he'd have been worried about the wasted calories.

"Stop complaining," fellow werewolf and SWAT officer Jayden Brooks said. A senior corporal on the team, Brooks was a former college star running back, and while he was the biggest werewolf in the Pack, he was also the most soft-spoken. "Besides, it's free. That makes it taste better."

With a grin, Brooks popped some kind of fancy hors d'oeuvre in his mouth. His plate was piled so high with them Max was surprised they didn't fall on the floor of the large banquet area that had been set up outside the main auditorium in the Dallas Police Department Headquarters. Max wasn't a fan of coming here, regardless of the event. In his opinion, the place was made for lawyers and politicians, not cops. Having to wear his dress uniform made it even worse. If it wasn't for the fact that some of his fellow SWAT teammates were being recognized, he wouldn't have come at all.

"Free doesn't always mean good," werewolf/SWAT

officer Diego Martinez pointed out as he and another of
Max's teammates, Zane Kendrick, joined them.

The late afternoon award ceremony was packed with
people, so it had taken a while for them to work their
way through the buffet line and come over to the cocktail table in the corner they'd staked out. Clearly, Diego
and Zane shared Max's opinion of the food. They'd
barely put anything on their plates.

"We should try and convince Chief Curtis to hold
these events at the SWAT compound," Max said. "Then
we could grill some real food."

Brooks chuckled at the suggestion. "I don't see that
happening. Chief Curtis isn't a fan of ours these days.
We're never going to get him out to the compound
unless it's so he can arrest one of us."

He was probably right about that, Max thought. Chief
Curtis had suspended Max, Brooks, and their teammate
Alex Trevino after they'd been caught breaking into a
private research facility while looking for some girls
who'd gone missing from Regional Texas College a
few months ago. It wasn't that they had gone into the
place without a warrant that had pissed Curtis off. It was
the fact that the facility had been owned by Councilman
McDonald, one of the chief's biggest political support-
ers. It hadn't helped when they'd later disobeyed the
chief's orders to stay away from the case and continued their investigation into the girls' disappearance,
ultimately proving McDonald had been the one who'd
kidnapped them. To save face, Chief Curtis had to pretend the suspension was a smokescreen, so Max and the
others could expose the corrupt politician.

"It must have really chafed the chief's ass to stand

up in front of nearly half the DPD and give Alex a commendation for rescuing those college girls," Diego said with a grin, his teeth a flash of white against his tan skin.

Max glanced at Diego. At six foot even, he was the shortest werewolf in the SWAT Pack, but what the guy lacked in height, he more than made up for in brawn. He was flat-out built like a fireplug. "You think he's that petty?"

Diego snorted.

"No doubt about it," Zane agreed in that British accent of his everyone in the Pack loved teasing him about, including Max. "I thought the chief was going to toss the award at Alex and tell him to pin the damn thing on himself."

Max chuckled. He'd thought the same thing.

"It probably didn't help that he had to pin medals on Khaki and Xander, too," Brooks added. "Three commendations for SWAT in one night—that's gotta burn."

"Speaking of Khaki and Xander, where are they?" Max asked, looking around for his two pack mates Khaki Blake and Xander Riggs. "I thought they were going to join us as soon as they grabbed some food."

Brooks picked up a crab puff that looked way too tiny for his gigantic hand. "Khaki was too burned out from spending most of the day at the courthouse for Jeremy's sentencing hearing. She and Xander went home so she could chill out."

Diego shook his head, mouth tight. "I still can't believe that asshole wiggled out of the death penalty. He murdered one man and almost killed Khaki and Xander. Hell, he even shot a frigging dog. If that isn't enough to get a guy a needle in the arm, I don't know what is."

It was a subject that had been rehashed a thousand times over the past year, both at the SWAT compound and in the local newspapers. It was hard to believe the trial had taken a year. It felt like only a few months since Jeremy Engler, a cop from Khaki's past, had shown up in Dallas looking to settle a score with her and, by extension, her new boyfriend, Xander. To say things had gotten nasty was an understatement.

Khaki and Xander, as well as the dog—SWAT mascot, Tuffie—had thankfully made it through okay, but the case had dragged on endlessly in the courts. Jeremy's lawyer had first gone with an insanity defense, which actually might have worked since Jeremy swore up and down that the entire Dallas SWAT team was filled with bloodthirsty monsters who had claws and fangs and would murder them all.

When the doctors and the judge had rejected that defense, his lawyer went with plan B—make Jeremy as sympathetic as possible. While Jeremy had been found guilty on all charges, the jury had bought the claims that his "episode" had been brought on by the stress of being a police officer out in Washington State and "losing the woman he loved to another man." Today, he'd been sentenced to life without parole instead of the death penalty.

"I heard they're sending him down to the Coffield Unit just south of here," Zane said, picking at the food on his plate with disinterest. "That means he'll be in the same prison as Frasheri and his crew of omegas."

Max shook his head. Armend Frasheri was an Albanian mobster they'd put in prison a while back who'd used omega werewolves as muscle. Omegas were similar to alphas like Max and the other werewolves on the SWAT team in size and aggression, but unlike alphas, they had almost no control over their inner wolves.

"Serves the asshole right," Brooks muttered. "If we're lucky, maybe they'll put Jeremy in a cell with an omega."

Max was picturing Jeremy screaming his damn head off in the middle of the night as he realized he was bunking with a "monster" when his nose picked up an intriguing scent he'd never smelled before. Max didn't have the best nose in the Pack, not by a long shot, but he was usually good at identifying scents. He turned his head this way and that, sniffing the air as he tried to figure out which part of the large room it was coming from. But it was no good. It seemed to be everywhere at once, surrounding him.

"Do you guys smell that?" he asked his teammates, interrupting a conversation they were having about making a run to the store for steaks and taking them back to the SWAT compound to grill.

"Smell what?" Diego asked, lifting his nose slightly and testing the air.

"I'm not sure how to describe it." Max sniffed again, surprised none of the other guys had picked up on the delectable scent. "It's sweet and spicy at the same time, like…I don't know…maybe cinnamon and flowers?"

Diego and Zane stared blankly at him while Brooks shook his head.

"I don't smell anything," the big man said. "There are a lot of people in here. Maybe you're picking up a combination of their scents."

"Maybe," Max said softly, though he didn't think so. This was one very specific scent, not a blend of several. It was hard to explain how he knew that, but he did. All he could say for sure was that the scent had come out of nowhere. Like someone who hadn't been there before had just walked into the room.

Not just anyone. A woman.

"I'm going to check it out," Max said, setting his plate on the table.

He didn't get more than two steps before Brooks put a hand on his shoulder. "Track down this scent if you're that curious, but your eyes are already getting a yellow glow to them, so you need to keep it under control, okay?"

"Shit," Max muttered. "Thanks."

He hadn't known he was so geeked up, but now that Brooks had pointed it out to him, he realized his heart was beating a little faster than normal. He wasn't sure why his inner wolf was suddenly restless. Then again, he rarely understood why he lost control so easily. Even though he'd been a werewolf for more than four years, he still had issues with it.

After seeing how omega werewolves behaved, he was beginning to think he might not be an alpha at all but a whacked-out omega instead. Gage Dixon, the SWAT team commander and alpha of their pack of alpha werewolves, said that was bull. He insisted Max was an alpha through and through and that Max's control issues were most likely related to the fact that he was barely eighteen when he turned—which made him the youngest alpha in the Pack—or to the traumatic circumstances surrounding his change. Max didn't have any experience with the first explanation and preferred not to think about the second. He'd spent a good portion of his adult life trying to put that part of his past behind him. But since everyone in the Pack had gone through a traumatic experience when they'd changed into werewolves in the first place, that didn't make much sense, either.

Whatever the reason, Max had to expend a lot more energy than anyone else in the Pack on keeping his fangs and claws retracted, his anger in check, and his eyes from flashing yellow at the worst possible times—like now.

Resorting to the lessons Gage and Brooks had taught him, Max closed his eyes and took slow, deep, calming breaths, turning his attention inward and consciously getting a handle on his excitement, heart rate, and breathing. When he opened his eyes again, Brooks was still standing there.

"Good?" Max asked.

"You're good," Brooks said.

Giving Brooks a nod, he turned and slowly made his way through the crowd. There had been over thirty commendations given out this afternoon, so the place was still packed with those police officers, their families, and their coworkers. Max had to be careful as he wove in and out of them while trying to let his nose guide him.

As he moved across the room, the woman's scent grew stronger and even more intriguing. There were some aspects of her pheromones that seemed familiar, though it took him a while to pin down exactly what he was keying in on. Then it struck him—she was a werewolf.

He stopped and took a deep breath, letting her scent wash over him as he tried to figure out if she was an alpha, a beta, or an omega. Outside of Gage, most of the Pack hadn't learned about the complexities of the werewolf world until recently. While they'd been surprised to find out there were different breeds of werewolves, they were even more stunned to discover there were female werewolves.

Max took another sniff and frowned. If the woman was a beta, she was different than any beta he'd ever met. And with all the werewolves showing up in Dallas lately looking for protection from hunters, he'd smelled a lot of betas.

As he continued across the lobby area in search of the woman, Max couldn't help wondering if maybe there was a fourth kind of werewolf out there that none of them knew about. It would be kind of cool running into a completely new breed. Had she come here looking specifically for him and the other members of the SWAT Pack, to ask for protection from the hunters who'd been killing werewolves all over the country? If so, this could be an epic first meeting.

Max was almost on the far side of the room and quickly running out of places to search when he walked around a group of people talking about how amazing the Cowboys were playing this season and finally found her.

After spending so much time trying to track her down, he probably should have walked right up and introduced himself, but instead, Max found himself standing there, transfixed. She was turned away from him so he couldn't see her face, but she was wearing a seriously sexy cocktail dress, her long, honey-blond hair trailing haphazardly over her shoulders and halfway down her back. The dress was one of those short, black numbers that hugged her slender curves and showed off her long legs. There was a crisscross, strappy thing going on in the back, too, which gave him teasing glimpses of smooth, creamy skin as well as confirming she wasn't wearing a bra under there.

He followed the curve of her butt until he locked on her legs. What could he say? He'd always been a leg man, and this woman had legs for days! Between the glimpse of toned thighs the dress afforded him and the display of shapely calves accentuated by the high heels she wore, it was all he could do not to drop to his knees and nibble his way up and down those gorgeous legs.

Though it would surely be fun, that probably wouldn't be the best way to make a first impression.

He wasn't sure how he knew, but something about her demeanor made Max think she'd rather be somewhere else at the moment. Since she was alone, he wondered if someone had stood her up. If so, the guy must have been stupid as well as a jerk. But then she shifted her weight back and forth from one high heel to the other. Ah, that explained it.

Max waited, expecting the female werewolf to smell him and turn around. Even though he was close enough for her to pick up his scent easily, she never looked his way. Finally, he gave up and walked over to her, moving around to stand in front of her.

He hoped he didn't actually gasp out loud—that would have been cheesy—but he couldn't help it. Saying she was gorgeous would have been an injustice. With smiling, blue-green eyes, the poutiest lips he'd ever seen, and a button nose that begged to be kissed, she came about as close to physical perfection as a person could get.

He gave her a grin. "You know, you'd probably be a

lot more comfortable if you kicked off those heels and walked around in bare feet."

She laughed, and the sound of it was as beautiful as she was. "Is it that obvious?"

"I'm afraid so." He made a show of looking left and right, as if he didn't want anyone to hear, then lowered his voice conspiratorially. "I get the same look on my face when I wear uncomfortable shoes."

Her eyes danced with amusement. "Funny, you don't strike me as the high-heel type."

He chuckled. He loved a woman with a quippy sense of humor. "I go more for the strappy wedge kind."

She nodded knowingly. "Makes sense. Someone your height would look much better in a wedge."

"Good to have my fashion sense confirmed." He smiled. "My name's Max. Nice to meet you."

Returning his smile, she took the hand he offered and shook it firmly. "Lana."

This close, her scent enveloped him so completely it was almost intoxicating. She held on to his hand a little longer than was customary, too. Not that he was complaining. He glanced casually at her other hand, checking for a wedding ring. He didn't see one. Before he could go ahead and do something completely crazy, like propose marriage right then and there, a dark-haired woman in a short, red dress joined them, two plates of hors d'oeuvres in her hands.

"They were all out of spinach puffs, so I got you these instead. I think they're squash blossoms with some kind of cheese," she said, handing one of the plates to Lana before giving Max a smile. "Who's this?"

"This is Max," Lana said. "We were just discussing the comfort benefits of wedges over heels."

The dark-haired woman took the strange topic in stride. "Did you reach any conclusions?"

Lana shook her head. "Not really. We both decided going barefoot would probably be the best idea."

"I totally agree," the woman said, then offered Max her hand. "By the way, my name is Brandy Perez."

"One of my best friends in the world," Lana added. "In fact, these heels actually belong to her."

Brandy shrugged. "They look better on you than me anyway. And before you ask, no, they don't have a bar set up—I looked everywhere. I don't know why I believed you when you said this would be a great place to party."

"Because you're gullible?" Lana suggested.

"Actually," Max said, "I did see some servers walking around with trays of white wine a few minutes ago on the other side of the room."

Brandy lifted a perfectly arched brow. "Seriously? You aren't just saying that to get rid of me so you can be alone with Lana, are you?"

Max's mouth twitched. "I am trying to get time alone with Lana, but I promise I'm not lying about the wine. They always have it at these award ceremonies."

Brandy glanced at Lana.

"Go ahead," Lana told her. "I'll be fine with Max."

Brandy's lips curved as she looked Max up and down. "I'm sure you will. I'll be back in a few—unless I run into some fine specimen of male hunkiness of my own. In which case, I might not be back for a while."

Lana laughed as Brandy disappeared into the crowd. "Speaking of award ceremonies," she said to Max, "I didn't see you on the stage getting a commendation,

so I'm guessing you must be here to support someone
who did?"

He nodded. "Yeah. Some of the members of my team
got recognized today. How about you? Your boyfriend
getting a commendation?"

Max thought he was being pretty damn smooth, but
the smile tugging at Lana's lips told him she saw right
through his deception.

"Nope, no boyfriend," she said. "Actually, it was
my dad. Brandy took forever getting dressed. Then we
got stuck in traffic. We barely made it here in time to
see him get the award. I had to watch from the back of
the auditorium."

That explained why Max hadn't picked up Lana's
luscious scent earlier. And while he was relieved she
didn't have a boyfriend, it made him wonder which of
his fellow cops getting a commendation this afternoon
could possibly have a daughter this smokin' hot.

Max opened his mouth to ask her who her father
was when another DPD officer walked by with a plate
filled with a collection of various hors d'oeuvres. While
Max wasn't impressed with the selection of food, Lana
looked at the appetizers longingly, even though she still
had the ones her friend had given her. Maybe she wasn't
big on squash blossoms. He didn't blame her.

"Would you like me to get you something else to
eat?" he asked.

She glanced down at her plate, then shook her head.
"Thanks, but unfortunately, the spinach puffs were
the only thing remotely edible, which is probably why
they're all gone. I can't believe they're trying to pass
this stuff off as food."

He grinned. "I was just thinking the same thing a little while ago. I'm planning to head out as soon as this thing is over so I can get some real food."

She leaned in close and gave him a conspiratorial wink. "Maybe we can slip out now while no one is looking. I can drop my car keys off with Brandy and we can disappear into the night. I'd just about kill for a slice of pizza."

Any other time, Max would have been stoked to hear that. In his opinion, there wasn't anything sexier than a woman who loved pizza. But right then, all he could think about was how his body was reacting to Lana's nearness. Not only was his pulse racing, but his claws and fangs were dangerously close to coming out. He only hoped his eyes weren't turning gold.

On the upside, at least he now knew for sure she was a werewolf. He could smell it in her pheromones. That was probably why they hit it off so well. Well, there was another reason, but he wasn't about to go there—even if a little wolf voice in the back of his head whispered maybe he should.

Lana was telling him about an awesome pizza place that wasn't too far away, wondering if he'd be interested in checking it out, but instead of answering her, he went in a completely different direction.

"It's so cool finding another of our kind here," he said. "I totally didn't expect it."

She didn't seem to mind that he'd changed the subject, but she looked a bit confused. "Another of our kind? Are you a pescatarian, too?"

Max chuckled. That body and those looks combined with a wicked sense of humor? It was like she was made for him. A werewolf who didn't eat meat? Now that was epically funny.

Unless it was true, in which case it was a little strange.

Before he could say anything, Lana leaned over to look at something behind him, her lips curving into a smile. Max turned to see who she was looking at and was a little surprised to find Deputy Chief Hal Mason. The deputy chief was in charge of the police department's specialized Tactical Division, which included the mounted police, canine unit, helicopter support, EOD, and SWAT. As a high-ranking officer in the department, Mason had to attend every award ceremony, but this time he'd been recognized for his commitment to developing his entire division, especially SWAT.

"Hey, Dad." Lana stepped around Max to give Mason a hug. "I was looking for you and Mom earlier, but you were deep in conversation with some people and I didn't want to interrupt."

Max picked his jaw up from the floor and shoved it back into place. Lana was Mason's daughter? How the hell was that even possible? They didn't look anything alike. Maybe she was adopted.

Mason pulled away to regard her fondly. "You didn't have to come to this thing. I know how much this kind of stuff bores you."

Lana made a face. "Of course I did. It's not every day my dad gets a big, prestigious award." She grinned. "You looked quite dashing up there, by the way."

"Thank you." Mason smiled…for all of two seconds. Then his face took on its signature serious expression that seemed to be glued there permanently. "Since you're here, there's someone I want you to meet."

Giving Max the stink eye, Mason gently took his daughter's arm, clearly intending to lead her away. But apparently Lana wasn't the kind of woman who liked to be led around by anyone. She firmly disengaged her arm from her father's grip, arching a brow that would have done the commander of the SWAT team proud.

"Dad, I'm talking to Max," she said. "Maybe I could meet your friend later?"

Mason scowled at his daughter like she was one of his junior officers. "I know you were talking to him. That's why I came over. Officer Lowry has to go back to work immediately, if not sooner. He's on the SWAT team and he's always quite busy."

Lana gave Max a shrug and a smile. "Later perhaps?"

"Officer Lowry will be busy later, too," Mason said. "In fact, he's going to be busy every day for the next month or so."

Damn, Max thought as the deputy chief led Lana away. Mason didn't want him anywhere near his daughter—that much was obvious. Cockblocked by the deputy chief of the Dallas PD. Could it get any worse? As Max watched Mason introduce his beautiful daughter to some good-looking lawyer type in an expensive suit with metrosexual hair and Italian leather shoes that probably cost as much as the payments on Max's new Camaro, he decided it could indeed get worse. Max felt the hackles on the back of his neck rise as the pretty boy reached out and put a possessive hand on Lana's arm.

"Watch where you're putting your hands, jackass, or you'll draw back a nub," Max growled under his breath.

Shit.

Max closed his eyes and took a deep breath. It was harder to get a handle on his inner wolf this time, mostly because he was so pissed at Mason for interrupting his conversion with Lana. The fact that her scent lingered in the air didn't help. It made it difficult to think about anything but her curves, smile, and creamy skin. Not the kind of thoughts he wanted to have in his head when he was attempting to find his calm place.

He had no idea how long it took him to tame his wolf half, but by the time he opened his eyes, Lana was nowhere to be seen. Unfortunately, neither was pretty boy. Why the hell would someone like Lana run off with a guy like that? Besides the nice hair, fancy suit, and expensive shoes, not to mention the money.

Max considered looking for her, but then realized he probably didn't want to find her, not if it turned out she was hanging on pretty boy's arm. Cursing, he headed across the room to rejoin his teammates.

Brooks, Diego, Zane, and Gage were standing around the same small cocktail table, a sheet of paper in front of them with a shopping list for what look like a serious cookout on it. Max glanced at his watch. By the time they got out of here, bought all the food on that list, and grilled the stuff, it'd be eight o'clock. Not that it mattered. Steak tasted good no matter what time of night it was, especially when followed by a game of volleyball.

Gage looked up from the list, his dark eyes curious. "Brooks said you were off looking for some scent that caught your attention. Any luck?"

Max glanced around to make sure no one was within earshot—no one with normal human ears at least. "Yeah. It was a female werewolf."

The other guys stopped debating whether to get hot dogs or not and stared at him.

"Seriously?" Brooks did a double take. "You sure she's another werewolf? I didn't smell her."

Max shrugged, refusing to ponder why he seemed to be the only one who recognized Lana for what she was. "I'm sure. Or pretty sure. She smells a little like a beta, but totally different than a beta at the same time. She's like no werewolf I've ever smelled before." He looked at Gage. "There's not some other kind of were-wolf out there you haven't told us about, is there? One that doesn't fall into the three categories we already know about."

"Not that I know of." Gage frowned. "What makes her so special?"

"You mean besides her unique scent?" Max asked.

Gage nodded.

Max refrained from revealing the part about Lana being the most amazing woman he'd ever met in his life and that she could mess with his control over his were-wolf half simply by standing too close to him. Instead, he focused on the serious stuff.

"She never gave me a single indication she recognized me as a werewolf the whole time we were talking. I swear, it's like she didn't even notice," Max said. "There's something else, though, that definitely doesn't fit with anything we know about werewolves?"

"What's that?" Brooks prompted.

"She's a pescatarian."

It was Zane's turn to frown. "What's that?"

"A vegetarian who eats fish, eggs, and dairy, but not meat," Max explained. "I thought she was joking at the time, but now that I think about it, I'm pretty sure she wasn't."

That seemed to shake the guys more than his announcement that there was a werewolf in the room they couldn't smell. Max could understand why. Regardless of the kind of werewolf they'd run into, two basic facts had always held true: Werewolves ate a lot of food to make up for the speed at which their bodies burned calories. And the majority of their diet was composed of meat. Gage had told them it had something to do with a werewolf needing a lot of protein to repair all the damage they were constantly sustaining. Which was why Lana probably wasn't a strict vegetarian.

"A werewolf who doesn't eat meat?" Zane looked at Gage. "Is that even possible?"

Before that question could lead to a long, meaningless argument that had nothing to do with the current situation, Max figured he should tell them the big news.

"Oh, and while we're talking about what makes her different," he said, "I should probably mention she's Deputy Chief Mason's daughter."

His teammates stared at him, stunned. Gage in particular looked as though Max had just smacked him with an axe handle.

"What makes you so sure Mason is her father?" Gage asked hesitantly, not like he doubted Max, but as if he was praying Max was wrong.

"Well, there was the part where she said, 'Hey, Dad,' when he came over to us. That was sort of a dead giveaway," Max said dryly. "Then there was the part where Mason told Lana he wanted to introduce her to some pretty boy lawyer and suggested I was going to be too busy with overtime for the next month to even think about seeing her again. That kind of screamed *overprotective father* to me."

Gage blew out a breath. "Okay, I didn't see that coming."

"You think Mason knows we're werewolves?" Brooks asked quietly. "If his own daughter is one, he has to be able to recognize the signs."

His teammates looked at each other, concern written plainly on their faces. It was one thing having people like Jeremy Engler or Armend Frasheri know about their identities. Those guys were psychopaths no one was likely to ever believe. But a deputy chief in the Dallas PD was someone people would take seriously.

"If you'd asked me five minutes ago, I would have said there's no way in hell Mason knows," Gage said. "But now? It would be pressing the limits of credibility to assume he doesn't."

"What do we do?" Diego asked softly. Crap, he looked ready to bolt.

"For now, nothing," Gage said. "If Max is right about this, it's likely Mason has known about us for years. If he'd wanted to do something with that information, he already would have done it. He's probably just as worried about this secret getting out as we are. He wouldn't want it coming back on his daughter."

Brooks nodded. "Makes sense. Are you going to talk to him about it?"

"When the time is right, yes," Gage said. "It's not like I can walk into his office and bring it up."

Max snorted. No kidding.

He was just wondering if he should circle the room

looking for Lana again when a now-familiar scent drifted across his nose. His pack mates forgotten for the moment, Max turned to see Lana coming his way, her hips swaying suggestively and doing crazy things to his pulse. He was so focused on the dazzling smile Lana gave him that he didn't even realize Brandy was with her until both women were right in front of him.

"I was worried you'd already left," Lana said, her intoxicating scent washing over him like a gentle wave. "I wanted to apologize for my father. I don't know why he was acting like that. Sometimes I think he forgets I'm twenty-three years old and can take care of myself."

"Don't worry about it." Max grinned. "I'm glad you found me. I thought you might have run off with that guy in the fancy suit."

Lana laughed. "Oh, the suit definitely tried to get me to leave with him. He even said he'd take me out to some fancy French restaurant named Chambre Française that everybody raves about. I told him I wasn't interested because I already had another offer for dinner." She gave him a sexy smile. "You *were* going to take me out for that slice of pizza, weren't you?"

"Definitely. I love pizza." He grinned, about to suggest they split right then until he remembered he was wearing his dress uniform. "I need to stop by my place and change first, if you don't mind?"

"Not at all," she said. "In fact, I was going to mention that I need to get out of this dress."

"I could help you with that, if you need a hand," Max said before he could stop himself.

Lana gave him an appraising look, her lips curving. "Thanks for the offer, but I think I can manage…just this once. Why don't you pick me up at my parents' house? That's where I'm staying while I'm in town. I can be ready to go in forty minutes."

Max didn't like the sound of that. If she was staying at her parents' house while she was in Dallas, that meant she didn't live here and was only visiting. *Crap, dude, slow down and take this one step at a time.* They hadn't even gone on a date yet and he was already worrying about the future.

"That works for me," he said. "Let me get the address from you."

He was just reaching for his phone when one of his teammates—Diego, he thought—cleared his throat. Crap, he'd totally forgotten they were standing there. Turning, he quickly made introductions.

While Lana typed her address into his phone, Brandy glanced at the grocery list on the table, her eyes widening.

"You must be feeding an army with all that stuff," she remarked.

Diego flashed her a grin. "Just us and the rest of our team. We're having a party tonight out at the SWAT compound with some of our friends."

Brandy returned his smile. "Is that right?"

Max would be the first to admit he didn't know a whole hell of a lot about this kind of stuff, but there definitely seemed to be some sparks between Lana's friend and Diego.

"I sent myself a text so I'd have your number," Lana said, handing Max his phone. "See you in forty minutes? Actually, better make it an hour. I have to drop Brandy off at her place on the way."

Brandy shook her head, never taking her eyes off
Diego. "I think I'm good, Lana. If you guys don't mind
me crashing your party?"

"Not at all," Diego said, his grin broadening.

Brandy licked her lips. "Let me make a quick run to
the ladies' room and I'll be ready to go."

Lana looked at Max. "So, forty minutes?"

He nodded. "I'll be there."

As Lana walked away, Max had a hard time figuring
out where to look—her sexy legs or her equally sexy
butt. Both were amazing. Only when she'd completely
disappeared from sight did he turn back to the guys to
find them grinning at him.

"What?" he demanded.

"Nothing," Brooks said. "I'm guessing you're not
going to make it to the cookout tonight, huh?"

Like Brooks even needed to ask. "What do you think
of Lana? She smells like some kind of beta, right?"

Brook shrugged. "She definitely smells like some
kind of werewolf, but the scent is faint. I wouldn't have
picked it up if she wasn't standing right in front of me."
He eyed Max thoughtfully. "I'm surprised you were able
to pick it up from across the room. You don't have the
greatest of noses."

"Maybe it's because she's *The One* for Max," Zane,
the Pack's one and only werewolf of London, pointed out.

"Maybe," Max said noncommittally.

If Zane expected him to deny it, he was going to be
disappointed. The idea of every werewolf having one
perfect soul mate for him, or her, wasn't a big deal to
Max. None of the guys in the Pack who'd already met
their one-in-a-billion significant other were complaining,

but some of his other pack mates had started wondering if they had a say in any of it.

The legend that there was a woman out there for each of them who would accept them for what they were sounded cool at first. Who didn't want to meet an awesome woman and be in a relationship that didn't require you to hide what the hell you really were? But then it started happening over and over again, against all possible odds, and after a while, it seemed like the guys were falling in love whether they were ready for it or not. Hell, for ridiculous reasons of his own, Remy Boudreaux had tried to fight his attraction to his mate, Triana Bellamy, and he'd made himself physically ill from trying to resist her.

While it wasn't something any of them would admit out loud, Max knew a few of the currently unattached guys in the Pack were scared the same genetic mutation that had turned them into werewolves in the first place was now mating them up with women of its choosing simply to make the Pack stronger for what everyone assumed was a coming war with the hunters.

If there was some kind of undeniable force out there pairing them up with the first suitable woman who came along, Max could understand why they might be freaked out. No one wanted to think their free will was being stripped away and replaced by pack instinct. But the whole idea of finding that one perfect woman he was meant to be with had never worried him, which was probably why he'd been one of the first werewolves in the Pack to embrace the idea of finding a soul mate.

Of course, if he was being honest with himself, he'd admit it was because he never truly thought it could happen to him. After all the crap that had happened with his old man, he knew he was a little messed up. What woman would want to deal with all his baggage?

But maybe he'd been wrong. Maybe Lana was *The One* for him. It was an appealing—and scary—thought.

Okay, that was enough introspection for now.

"I'm going to get out of here," Max said. "Take good care of Brandy, huh?"

He glanced at his watch, quickening his step as he headed for the exit. He was going to have to hurry if he wanted to change clothes and pick up Lana on time.

Max was halfway across the parking lot when he smelled Gage behind him. He stopped and turned to see his boss eyeing him with obvious concern.

"What's up, Sarge?"

"Nothing. I just wanted to talk to you about Lana," Gage said. "You know Zane's probably right about her being *The One*, don't you? The fact that you picked up her scent all the way across the room when Brooks, of all people, didn't has to mean something. It sounds a hell of a lot like what happened to Remy when he met Triana."

"Yeah, I know," Max said, trying to sound casual. "It's not a big deal."

Gage lifted a brow. "Not a big deal? Really?"

Max wasn't surprised his commander had followed him out here. Gage was the alpha of the Pack. He worried about all of his guys. But since pulling Max out of the downward spiral that his life had become after his family's death, Gage had become more than his pack alpha. He was like a father to him.

Being the leader of a pack of headstrong alphas meant Gage frequently had to get physical with them.

In some cases, there was simply no other way to get a jacked-up werewolf back in line. But because of Max's background, Gage tended to be more proactive than reactive, putting a little extra effort into watching out for him and trying to make sure he didn't get too out of control in the first place.

Not that Gage didn't have to get physical with Max on occasion. Sometimes there was no way to avoid it. But Max knew that, unlike his real father, the SWAT team commander would never lay a hand on him if it wasn't a crisis situation, and that made all the difference.

While this situation was nowhere near crisis mode, Gage was obviously worried about how Max would handle finding *The One*. Max supposed he couldn't blame him. Some of the other members of the Pack who'd already found their soul mates had gotten themselves in a buttload of trouble in the process.

Xander had almost been kicked out of the Pack when he'd fallen for Khaki. Eric Becker had inherited an entire beta pack along with his mate, Jayna Winston. Landry Cooper had been blown out of a high-rise building for his wife, Everly. Alex Trevino had gotten suspended for his girlfriend, Lacey Barton. And Remy had run through the streets of New Orleans in wolf form in order to be with Triana. Hell, even Gage's relationship with his wife, Mackenzie, had nearly ended in catastrophe, almost sending the entire Pack on the run to South America.

Up to this point, finding *The One* had come with a lot of problems for almost all the members of the Pack. It made sense Gage would want to keep the same thing from happening to Max. Then again, maybe Gage simply wanted to protect Max from getting hurt emotionally.

Since Max hadn't been in a serious relationship with a woman in his life—booty calls and one-night stands didn't count—it wasn't an irrational concern.

Max appreciated that, but it wasn't necessary.

"Seriously, Sarge, it's really not a big deal. I'm not a player like Remy used to be or an adrenaline junkie like Cooper, and I'm not going to do anything crazy like Alex and get suspended. I'm going to take my time with Lana and make sure the Pack is protected."

"And if she is *The One* for you?" Gage prompted, a smile turning up the corners of his lips. "What then?"

Max almost said that any woman would have to be crazy to tie herself to him, but he stopped himself. "If someone as amazing as Lana is the woman I'm supposed to be with for the rest of my life, you're not going to see me turning my nose up at her, if that's what you're asking. If Lana is *The One*, I'll take it step by step, slow and easy."

Gage let out a sound that was half snort, half growl. "Take it from someone who's been there: if Lana turns out to be your soul mate, going step by step, not to mention slow and easy, might be tougher than you think. Make sure you focus on staying in control of yourself, for Lana's sake if nothing else."

His commander had a point there. Keeping his shift under control around Lana was going to be tough. But he'd do it.

"I will," Max said. "I won't do anything to risk the Pack."

"I know," Gage said. "One more thing before you go. Worrying about *The One* and how you'll deal with that isn't the only thing you need to think about. Keep in mind the woman you find so fascinating happens to be Deputy Chief Mason's daughter. You screw this up, and you won't just lose *The One*. You might end up losing your career, too."

Chapter 2

"MAN, THIS IS GOOD." MAX GROANED AS HE TOOK A BIG BITE of his pepperoni pizza and chewed happily. "I can't believe I never knew this place was here."

Lana smiled as she took a much daintier bite of her slice of cheese pizza. She'd never thought watching a man eat could be sexy, but Max was proving her wrong. Then again, maybe it was the simple fact that everything about Max was sexy, from his handsome face to his mesmerizing blue eyes, to his muscular body and casually tousled, dark hair. The man was sinfully attractive and apparently had no idea. It also didn't hurt that Max had a gorgeous smile that got her going every time he threw it her way. There was a bad boy hiding behind that disarming grin, she was sure of it. And while she thought he'd looked devastating in his dress uniform, he looked even better in jeans, work boots, a casual button-down shirt, and a leather jacket. In a word, he was smoking!

Max had picked her up right on time and they'd headed straight to Piggie Pies. Within minutes of getting in his Camaro, it felt like they'd been dating for months. Lana couldn't believe how well they clicked. She'd been attracted to Max the moment she saw him at the awards ceremony, but it wasn't until they'd started bantering and flirting that she knew she'd struck gold. If she'd known there were cute, athletic, interesting guys like him on the police force, she would have made the three-and-a-half-hour drive from Austin for every awards ceremony. Max and his fellow SWAT team-mates alone represented more hunks per square inch than she'd seen in her lifetime. Then again, she'd spent the past five years going to college for science. There weren't a lot of alpha types in the classes she'd taken.

Still, she had to wonder why her dad had always steered her away from any and all police functions. He had to know she'd be interested in guys who were as fit and charming as Max. But every time she'd come home during semester breaks, he'd made sure she stayed away from his office.

Well, she was going to make up for all that lost time now—with Max.

"I stumbled across Piggie Pies Pizza and Pasta a few years ago, and now I eat here whenever I'm back in town," she said. "Their crust is so good, I think I could eat it plain. The pasta is awesome, too. And their veggie primavera is to die for."

Max wiped his mouth with his napkin, then lifted his nose and sniffed the air. It was kind of an odd thing to do but also extremely cute. He'd asked her several times what she thought about certain aromas coming out of the kitchen, none of which she could pick up. He must have one heck of a good sense of smell.

"You're right," he said. "It smells delicious. Maybe I'll try some of their carbonara, too."

She couldn't help laughing. For a guy as trim and well built as Max, he certainly ate a lot. While she'd ordered two slices of cheese pizza, he'd gotten an entire large pepperoni for himself and had already polished off three slices. She had no idea where he put it, but she had no doubt he could probably polish off a plate of carbonara with no problem.

"You probably can't give me your recommendation on the carbonara, though, huh?" he asked. "Not with the whole bacon thing?"

She shook her head. "Nope, no bacon for me. But I'm sure it's good."

"You know, when you first made that crack about us both being pescatarian, I thought you were kidding. I hope I didn't offend you."

Lana smiled. This guy simply kept getting better and better. She vaguely remembered that part of the conversation they'd had back at DPD headquarters. She also remembered being a little confused, wondering what he'd meant by *another of our kind*. But then her dad had shown up, and she'd forgotten all about it. She considered asking Max about the comment now but decided against it. She'd probably misunderstood what he'd meant.

"No, I wasn't offended," she said. "Most people are caught off guard when I tell them I don't eat meat."

"Have you always been a pescatarian?" he asked, reaching for another slice of pepperoni. "Or is it a decision you made recently?"

"I've been one pretty much my whole life," she admitted, taking another nibble of her cheese pizza. "Mom is a pescatarian and I picked it up from her."

"It doesn't bother you that I eat meat, does it?"

"No, not at all. It's not like a religious thing. I simply never developed the taste for meat."

Max lifted a brow, making Lana wonder what she had said that was so shocking. When she abruptly realized the way her words had sounded, she laughed to keep from blushing. "I was not talking about that kind of meat and you know it! Don't even go there, or I'm going to smack you."

He held up his free hand in a gesture of surrender, his mouth twitching. "I wasn't going to say a word, but thanks for confirming the fact that your mind will head straight for the gutter at the drop of a hat."

"You are so bad," she laughed.

He was right. Her mind had immediately gone to the naughtiest place possible when he looked at her like that. It wasn't her fault—Max was so damn hunky.

Max chuckled and went back to eating his pizza. Just like that, her embarrassment disappeared. She got the feeling they could say anything to each other and it would work.

"You said earlier that you're staying at your parents' place while you're in town," he said in between bites of pizza. "You don't live in Dallas then?"

It was a casual question, but Lana sensed a little tension in Max's voice. She tried not to read too much into it, but dare she hope he already felt the same chemistry she did?

"I'm sort of between living arrangements at the moment," she said.

He frowned, his slice of pizza halfway to his mouth.

Lana laughed. "It's not as bad as it sounds, I promise. I just finished my master's program in organic chemistry at the University of Texas at Austin. I'm living with my parents while I'm lining up job interviews." She thought a moment. "This is going to sound weird, but I felt this crazy urge to come back home, like I had to be here."

"Well, I'm glad you paid attention to those urges, or we wouldn't have met," Max said.

"Must be fate."

"Must be." His eyes held hers. "Any of those job interviews in Dallas?"

"Some," she said. "I also have several set up in New York, Boston, San Francisco, and Seattle. Even a few in France."

He did a double take. "France—wow. That sounds exciting."

She shrugged. "I'm just keeping my options open. I haven't decided where I want to work yet. It could be anywhere."

"Like Dallas?" he mused.

Max's heated expression suggested that was the option he'd prefer. Considering the fact that they'd known each other for all of two hours, Lana was shocked at how open she was to the idea of working much closer to her childhood home than she'd ever planned.

"Dallas is certainly in the running," she murmured, licking some Parmesan cheese off her fingers.

Max's eyes locked on her tongue, and she would have had to be clueless not to notice the way those beautiful blue eyes of his practically sparkled in the dim light of the restaurant as he watched her. Actually, his eyes lit up like a pair of Christmas tree lights. Damn, that was sexy as hell.

She felt a little tremor of excitement in her belly and had to wonder how a simple gaze from a guy she'd just met could get her going so fast. She'd never experienced this kind of immediate sexual intensity with anyone, but with Max, it was like she'd caught lightning in a bottle.

"So," he said softly, his voice deeper, rougher.

Apparently, Max was as into this date as she was. The knowledge made her feel warm and gooey all over.

"So," he said again, his voice a bit more in control this time, "a master's in organic chemistry. Does that mean you'll be creating new foods, like mashed-potato-flavored soda and veggies that taste like Doritos?"

Lana laughed. "Unfortunately, while I could do that with an organic chemistry degree, it's not the particular discipline I'm involved with."

"No cool nacho cheese–flavored green beans then?"

She shook her head. "Sorry. My background is in pharmaceutical R&D. I'll be developing new medications and drug-testing protocols."

He nodded. "That's pretty cool, too. I mean, if you can't put mashed potatoes in a bottle, saving lives is a good backup plan."

"I know. I was bummed, too." She smiled. "But we can't all make snack-flavored veggies for a living."

"Too bad. More kids would eat their vegetables if they tasted like Doritos," he pointed out. "Hell, the vending machine possibilities alone are staggering."

As they ate, they discussed the best veggie-chip combinations for a while, with Max suggesting he might even try the vegetarian lifestyle if someone could make broccoli taste like Fritos.

By the time Max had polished off his entire pizza, they'd talked about her classes at the university, the long nights studying in her apartment, the stress of wanting to get good grades for both herself and her parents. He listened to all of it, asking serious questions and showing more interest in her college experience than any guy she'd ever talked to, and that included some guys she'd dated at the university. She'd be the first to admit that organic chemistry wasn't exactly thrilling to anyone other than another organic chemistry major, but Max seemed to be genuinely interested.

"You could study for three days straight without sleep?" he asked, apparently impressed. "Seriously?"

She nodded. "Yeah. I don't seem to need as much sleep as other people. After seeing me pull all-nighters for the whole five years we went to school together, my roommate, Denise, is convinced I must be from another planet."

He frowned. "You lived with the same roommate the entire time you were in school? You two must be really good friends."

She nodded as she sipped her iced tea. "We are. Normally, roomies start to get on each other's nerves at some point, but Denise is an organic chemistry major who came in the same semester I did. We hit it off right away, so when we were lucky enough to get into off-campus housing together, we jumped at the chance. I don't think either of us would have done as well in school if we hadn't had each other to lean on."

Lana set down her glass, then looked longingly at her empty plate. She should have ordered three slices instead of two. She was still hungry. Max must have seen the way she was gazing unhappily at her plate, because he laughed and asked if she wanted dessert.

"I smelled some killer cheesecake when we walked in."

She laughed, marveling at him and his super-sniffer as she considered dessert. "I probably shouldn't."

He regarded her thoughtfully. "I hope this doesn't sound rude, but you don't strike me as someone who's prone to putting on weight."

Lana opened her mouth to tell him that was only because she worked out so much, but then decided simply to be honest. "I'm not. In fact, I weigh the same thing I did in high school, and I hardly ever work out. It drives Denise crazy. I can eat anything I want and never gain a pound. She stands too close to a bowl of ice cream and has to go straight to the gym."

Max smiled. "It's probably in your DNA. Fast metabolism, you know?"

She pushed back her plate and rested her forearms on the table, returning his smile. "Any chance that you have a fast metabolism like that, too?"

He nodded, his grin broadening. "As a matter of fact, I do. So, how about that cheesecake?"

"Definitely," she said with a laugh as he caught their server's eye.

After the cheesecake showed up, Lana decided they'd done enough talking about her. It was time to find out a little about this amazing guy across the table from her.

"Now that you know everything there is to know about me," she said, licking cheesecake off her fork with a little show of tongue simply because she liked Max watching her do it, "let's talk about you."

His smile wilted a little, much to her disappointment. "My life isn't nearly as interesting as yours. Definitely nothing worth talking about."

"That's silly," she scolded. "I bet you have a lot of fascinating stuff to talk about. I mean, for starters, did you grow up in a cop family here in Dallas?"

Max didn't say anything, and for a moment, she wasn't sure he'd heard her. Instead, he focused on his slice of cheesecake, like he was more interested in that than he was in her. Finally, he looked up and gave her another smile—only this time, it lacked humor.

"No, I didn't grow up in Texas. I was born in Las Vegas and lived there until I was eighteen," he said quietly. "My family was…well, let's just say it was about as far as you can get from a cop family. To put things in proper perspective, if one or two events in my life had gone slightly different, you'd be sitting at the table with a guy who works at a Gas-and-Go."

With his looks, confidence, and knee-weakening charm, Lana had a hard time believing Max could ever be anything but amazing. "But growing up in Vegas must have been cool, with all the lights and excitement?"

Max shook his head, though, turning his attention back to his cheesecake, taking a small bite. "I didn't grow up on that side of Vegas." He lifted his head to look at her again. "I lived in what you might call the projects—the low-rent housing section of North Vegas."

"Rough neighborhood?" she prompted, trying to imagine Max in a place like that. The image just wouldn't stick. He looked like he could take care of himself in a fight, but the idea of him dealing with that kind of life as a kid bothered her.

"Sometimes it could be," he admitted. "A lot of my friends ended up in jail or dead. I always considered myself lucky to have gotten out."

"What about the rest of your family?" she asked, curious despite herself. "Did they get out, too?"

"Not so much," he murmured.

Lana saw the flash of pain that crossed his face, no matter how hard he tried to hide it, and was immediately sorry she'd asked the question. She waited, expecting

Max to say more. When he didn't, she was smart enough to know it was time to back off that particular subject. There was something bad lurking in his past, something he didn't want to talk about.

"I'm sorry," she said, reaching across the table to rest her hand on his heavily muscled forearm. "I didn't mean to dredge up bad memories."

He looked at her, a slow smile spreading across his face. Setting down his fork, he placed his hand on top of hers. "You don't have to be sorry. I had a tough life growing up, and I did a few stupid things. But while the events in my past will always be with me, they don't necessarily define me. In a lot of ways, although some of it really sucked, that life also made me stronger."

Lana gazed at him, lost for a moment in those vivid-blue eyes, wondering if maybe the past Max was referring to was the reason her father seemed so resistant to the idea of her hanging out with him. She tried to imagine what he could have done but stopped herself. If Max had done something that terrible, he would never have been allowed to become a cop, especially one on the SWAT team. She knew enough about her dad's job to know that SWAT only took the very best.

They sat there quietly for a while, eating cheesecake and enjoying each other's company. Just another indication there was something special going on between them. In her experience, dead air in the middle of a first date was a sure a sign that she wasn't compatible with a guy. But with Max, she felt completely comfortable with it.

When her dessert plate was clean—short of licking it, of course—she found herself curious about one thing and hoped it was something Max wouldn't mind talking about.

"If you don't mind me asking, how did you get from that bad place in North Vegas, with the tough life you had and the stupid things you did, and into the Dallas PD SWAT Team? That's got to be a complicated story."

His mouth quirked mischievously. "Yeah, complicated would be a good word for it. I'm just not sure I should tell you about it."

"Why not?" she asked, surprised.

"Because, like I said, I did some stupid stuff. Stuff I'm not so proud of. I don't mind telling you, but I'd hate to give you a bad opinion of me."

"Is my opinion of you that important already?" she asked coyly.

He smiled again. "Actually, it is. As crazy as that may be."

She didn't think it was crazy at all. Probably because the connection between them was growing stronger by the second. She couldn't imagine anything he told her would affect what they had.

"I hereby solemnly promise not to judge," she said. "Lay it on me."

He laughed and reached into the pocket of his jeans. A moment later, he came out with a poker chip and set it down on the table between them. She picked it up to read the logo. It was a fancy ten-dollar chip from a casino in Reno that she'd never heard of. Then again, she didn't know much about casinos in general, much less those in Reno. She flipped it over, expecting to see something on the backside that would help her understand what she was looking at, but there was nothing special there, either.

"What's this?" she asked, bouncing the chip in her hand and feeling the weight of it before handing it back to him. "Did you win it while you were in Reno?"

He took the chip back and gazed at it, a slight smile curving the corners of his lips. "No, I didn't win it. I paid for it out of my own pocket. I keep it as a reminder of the day my entire life changed."

Lana waited, knowing more was coming.

"It was a Friday." Max rubbed his thumb back and forth across the front of the chip as he spoke. "It was four in the morning, and I was sitting at a blackjack table with a stack of chips just like this one in front of me. I was too young to be in there, but I was tall enough and big enough, so no one questioned me."

She shook her head, having a hard time imagining staying up that late for any reason that didn't involve studying for an exam—or getting naked with a hot guy. "Four a.m.? Were you there on a gambling binge or something?"

He looked up and smiled. "Actually, I was there to rob the place."

Max said the words so casually that, at first, they went right over her head. Then, when she realized what he'd just said, she was sure he was kidding.

But he wasn't laughing.

"Seriously?" she asked, then lowered her voice, terrified someone nearby would hear, even though there weren't many people in the place at the moment. "You were going to rob a casino?"

He chuckled. "I did say I grew up on the wrong side of town and did some stupid stuff, remember? I'll be the first to admit that when I left home at eighteen, I was pretty screwed up. I got involved with a group of idiots who'd been doing small-time burglary jobs all across the Southwest — pawnshops, electronics warehouses, mom-and-pop jewelry stores. I was stupid as hell to get mixed up with them, but back then, being with them looked about as good as it was going to get."

"Did you ever hurt anyone?" Lana asked, afraid to ask but needing to know. "Or carry a gun?"

Max shook his head, looking down at the chip in his hand again. "I carried a gun, but I never had a need to use it. We hit small places without security guards, usually late at night. If a situation had ever occurred where I had to pull that gun, I'm not sure what the hell I would have done. I never wanted to hurt anyone."

"So what happened?" she asked hesitantly, fervently wanting to believe this story had a happy ending.

"The guys running our little crew got greedy and set their sights on a much bigger payoff. One of them had a cousin who worked in a casino in Reno, and they got it in their heads that we could pull off a smash-and-grab job there early in the morning, just as the security company that serviced the place was taking the evening's winnings to the bank. They figured we could get away with two hundred thousand, easy."

Max stopped talking, flipping the poker chip over and around his fingers so fast Lana could hardly follow it. She tried to be patient, but it was all she could do to not lean over and smack the chip out of his hand. She needed him to hurry up and tell her what happened.

"I was the biggest guy in the crew, so it was my

job to follow the four-person security team through the casino and take out the two in the back as they were pushing the money cart out the rear exit. Then the other members of the crew would sweep in, deal with the two guards up front, and grab the cart full of cash. It was a horrible plan, but in theory, no one was supposed to get hurt."

"But?" she prompted, her stomach tightening.

"But as I was sitting there at the blackjack table, this big guy sat down beside me. He looked me straight in the eyes as the security guards started to move and casually told me that if I got out of my chair, he was going to put me in jail for the rest of my life."

O-kay. Lana wasn't sure what she thought had been coming next, but it hadn't been that. "He was a cop? They knew you were there to rob the place?"

"He wasn't just any cop." Max's mouth edged up. "He was Gage Dixon, the commander of the Dallas SWAT Team you met at headquarters tonight. And yeah, he knew I was there to rob the place."

Lana only had a vague recollection of the men with Max at the awards ceremony because she'd been so focused on him. Her mind spun as she imagined the scene he'd described at the casino.

"How the heck did he know you were about to rob the place? Why was he even in Reno?" She waved her hand. "No, wait. Skip all that for now. Tell me the important part first—what the heck did you do?"

Max chuckled. "Well, I wish I could say I did something brilliant and daring, but in reality, I freaked out. The casino guards were already moving past me, and I knew that if I didn't do something quick, the whole plan would implode. So I did the only thing I could think to do—I tried to punch him."

Lana stared, her jaw dropping.

"Remember that part where I said I'd done some stupid stuff?" Max said. "Well, me—at nineteen years old—trying to take a swing at a fully trained SWAT officer is definitely in that category."

"It didn't work?"

He shook his head with another laugh. "Understatement there. I won't bore you with the details, mostly because it's so damn embarrassing to have to remember them. Suffice it to say, Gage had no problem keeping me in that chair."

"Did the rest of your crew get arrested?" she asked.

He nodded. "Yeah, there were a dozen cops waiting for the job to go down. The moment it did, they swarmed in and grabbed everyone. It was over in seconds."

"You were arrested?" she asked, but then realized that couldn't be right. If he'd been arrested for attempted robbery, how the heck could he be in SWAT right now?

"No, I wasn't arrested," Max said. "While everyone else was paying attention to all the excitement on the far side of the casino, Gage yanked me to my feet and we walked right out the front door. We got in his rental car and drove straight for the California state line. Then he pulled over and told me I could get out if I wanted to."

This story was becoming stranger by the second, and if it wasn't for the deadly serious expression on Max's face, Lana would have thought he was making the whole thing up.

"Wait a minute," she said. "Your future commander

went all the way from Dallas to stop you from robbing a casino, then let you go?"

"Not quite." Max's mouth quirked again. "He was ready to let me walk, but first he wanted to talk to me. I had nowhere better to go, so I listened. We ended up sitting there in his car talking until the sun came up. For reasons that are too complicated to get into, Gage had tracked me to Reno and figured out what I was doing. He got some of his friends from the local PD involved, and in exchange for the tip on the casino robbery, they agreed to look the other way while he got me out of the state."

Lana frowned. "Why would he go all the way to Reno to do something like that? Is he family?"

Max thought about that a moment, then smiled. "Yeah, I guess that in some ways, he is family. He knew what I was going through and went out of his way to find me. He helped me understand a lot of the things that were going on in my life at that time. He got me straightened out and kept me from totally destroying my life."

"And he got you into SWAT?"

Max chuckled. "It wasn't quite that easy. He brought me to Dallas and got me a place to stay, then helped me get into a community college to get enough schooling to meet the minimum DPD requirements. After that, I had to get through thirty-five weeks of training at the police academy, then another twenty-four weeks of field training. Only after all that was he able to get me on the team, and even that was tough. The department wasn't thrilled at the idea of putting a rookie on the SWAT team. He had to really work to make it happen."

Lana traced her fingers up and down his forearm. "He must have seen something very special in you to go through all that effort."

Max shrugged. "I guess. Sometimes I have to admit I don't know what he saw in me back in the beginning. I was a soup sandwich."

She laughed. She'd never heard that expression before, but she liked it. "Oh, I don't know. I think I can see some of the special qualities he might have seen."

Max raised a brow. "I'm pretty sure the two of you see completely different things when you look at me."

"I guess that's possible," she agreed.

As she continued to run her fingers along his arm, the light caught Max's eyes again, making them glimmer. Lana was about to remark on it when their server suddenly appeared at their table.

"Sorry to interrupt," the woman said softly as she put the folio with the bill on the table between them. "But we're going to be closing soon. Is there anything else I can get for you before you leave?"

Lana glanced at her watch, blinking in surprise when she saw it was almost one o'clock in the morning. She looked around and realized they were the only ones still in the place. Piggie Pies was supposed to close at midnight. No wonder the server was itching to push them out the door. The poor woman was ready to go home.

"No, we're good," Max said, slipping a few twenties into the folio. "Thanks for everything."

The woman gave them a smile and told them to have a good night.

Max looked at Lana, his eyes still full of heat. "So, where to?"

—~~~—

Lana caught Max giving her a curious look as they slowly walked hand in hand up to the front door of her parents' two-story house. She would have asked him what was so interesting, but the truth was, she was enjoying herself too much to bother.

It had been difficult to head home after leaving the restaurant. When Max had asked where they should go next, her first thought had been his place. But she'd controlled her urges. Max had to work tomorrow and she definitely didn't want him being tired the next day, not with the kind of job he had.

"I'm glad we had a chance to go out," Max said when they reached the porch. "I had an amazing night, and I'm not just talking about the pizza, though that was pretty outstanding, too."

Lana turned to face him, moving a little closer for warmth against the chilly November air. Not that she was cold. In fact, she rarely ever got cold. But she didn't mind sharing some of his body heat since he seemed to have so much of it. The cold didn't seem to bother him, either. He had his jacket hanging open.

"I had a good time, too." She smiled up at him. "Maybe we can do it again sometime?"

Lana tried her best to not appear too overeager. She didn't want Max to think she was desperate. Although she was eager to see him again, she couldn't let him know that. A woman had to play it cool.

"How about tomorrow night?" he asked, his grin suggesting he knew exactly what she was up to. "If you're not doing anything else?"

Lana didn't even bother playing silly games anymore. Laughing, she went up on tiptoe and hooked her arms around his neck. "I'm completely free tomorrow night. What do you have in mind?"

Max wrapped his arms around her, tugging her even closer than she already was and snuggling her up against his chest nice and tight. Wow. She already knew that Max was well built, but leaning up against him like this confirmed that she'd underestimated just how fit he was. He had some serious Adonis-like muscles going on under that shirt.

Max slipped his hands under her jacket and settled them comfortably on her lower back. The move was so natural and nonchalant, she might not have noticed it if it wasn't for the crazy tingles of arousal that wiggled through her body simply at his touch.

"We could go to a club and do some dancing," he suggested, so close now that she could feel his warm breath on her face. "Or we could have dinner at one of those dine-in movie theaters."

She was so distracted by knowing Max was about to kiss her that it took a supreme effort of will to even think about what he'd just said. The idea of the dine-in movie sounded cool. She'd seen theaters like that before but had never gone to one. As fun as that would almost certainly be, the thought of getting Max out on a dance floor sounded even better. She'd have a chance to let her hands roam all over his amazing body and not even have to feel guilty about it.

"I'd love to go dancing. I didn't get a chance to do much of it in school. I need to catch up," she said, tipping her head back a little more and sending the clearest signal possible that she was ready and waiting for a kiss.

He flashed her that mischievous smile, his lips grazing the curve of her jaw in the most delightful way. "Dancing it is. I'll pick you up tomorrow around seven and we can get something to eat first."

"Sounds good," she murmured.

She turned her head to the side in an attempt to capture his mouth. He let his warm lips briefly touch hers before gliding away to tease one of her earlobes. She groaned in frustration, which only earned her a chuckle from Max.

Deciding she'd had enough teasing, she slipped one hand up to weave her fingers into Max's short, spiky hair and got a good grip. Then she turned his face to hers and gave him a pointed look. He got the idea. Yanking her tightly to him, he covered her mouth with his. She opened hers, letting his tongue in with a groan of pleasure this time. Mmm, he tasted good.

She tightened her hand in Max's hair, urging him on, wanting more. He slid his hands down her back, resting them on the top of her jean-clad ass, sparking lightning through her body.

Lana didn't know what came over her. Since this was a first date, she'd intended to give him a good-night kiss to thank him for a wonderful evening, but she could barely breathe she was getting so excited. As if it had a mind of its own, her free hand ran up and down Max's strong chest, her fingernails digging into the material of his shirt to trace every bulge and ripple of the heavy muscles underneath. Her body immediately responded, heating up faster than it ever had in her life.

Then she felt his hard-on pressing into her quivering stomach and knew he was as turned on as she was. That knowledge fired her imagination, and ideas of slipping up to her old bedroom without her parents knowing, or even back out to Max's Camaro, flooded her mind with scenes that she'd never had about any guy she'd ever dated—first date or beyond.

She was close to stripping his clothes off right there on the front porch when the door suddenly jerked open. Startled, she jerked her mouth away from Max's.

"Lana," her father said in that flat, emotionless tone he used when he was angry. "I didn't realize you were going out this evening."

She looked up at Max to find his face turned toward the street, his eyes closed and his mouth set in a tense line. Though whether he was doing it to keep from cursing at her dad or laughing at him, she had no idea.

She carefully and slowly disengaged herself from Max's embrace, feeling colder the moment she was out of his arms. Turning, she frowned at her father. "Seriously, Dad? Were you standing there watching me through the window?"

Her father didn't answer. Instead, he opened the door wider and gestured her in. "You should come in. It's cold out."

Lana immediately felt Max start to move away.

Oh, hell no!

She caught his hand and walked into the house, tugging Max in after her. Her father scowled, but Lana ignored him. What did he expect, that she'd leave her date out on the doorstep so he could slam the door in the guy's face?

Lana's mother was standing in the middle of the living room, wearing slippers and a cozy-looking robe over her pajamas. But rather than glowering like her father, her mother was smiling warmly at them. Her mom had always been a rebel of sorts and clearly approved of Lana figuratively tweaking her father's nose.

"Mom, this is Max Lowry, one of Dad's SWAT officers. We met at the awards ceremony, and he was nice enough to take me out to dinner," Lana said. "Max, my mother, Nora."

Her mother offered Max her hand. "Very nice to meet you, Max. Where did you two kids go for dinner?"

"Piggie Pies Pizza and Pasta," he told her, and Lana saw her mother practically melt at the charming smile Max threw her way. "Lana recommended the place, and I've discovered she has excellent taste in restaurants."

Her mother nodded, her smile broadening as she glanced over at Lana. "Yes…I'd have to agree with you on that. She definitely has excellent taste."

"Piggie Pies closes at midnight," her father said. He was still standing over by the open door as if he expected Max to leave now that he'd met her mother. "Where have you been since then?"

It was Lana's turn to scowl this time. "They were nice enough to stay open a little late for us because we were having such a good time."

"I see." Her dad's mouth tightened. "Well, it's getting late. Officer Lowry should be going since he has to be up early for work tomorrow."

Lana might have thrown her purse at her father if her mother hadn't come to the rescue. "Oh, don't be silly, Hal. Max has time for a cup of coffee at least. And it's decaf, so it won't keep him up the rest of the night. Now, close the door and come into the living room. You're letting all the heat out."

Her father hesitated for a moment, but at another stern look from her mother, he finally closed the door and came into the living room.

Lana's mother looked at her. "Would you help me in the kitchen, dear?"

Lana hesitated, not sure she should leave her dad alone with Max, but her mother took her hand. She gave Max a helpless look as her mom pulled her toward the kitchen. Max grinned, his eyes twinkling with amusement until her father moved to his side and glared at him again.

"Max is adorable," Lana's mom said the moment they were in the big eat-in kitchen. While still slightly open to the living room, the upper cabinets made it private enough to talk without Max or her dad hearing. "Is he nice?"

Lana smiled. "Yes, Mom. He's very nice. And before you ask, yes, we had a very good time and hit it off really well."

Her mother filled the coffeepot with water from the sink and quickly got the machine going. Then she turned and leaned back against the counter, her blue eyes bright with interest. "You two definitely make a cute couple. Are you going out with him again soon?"

Lana almost laughed. Her mother would be thrilled if she got into a serious relationship with Max simply so she wouldn't be tempted to take a job far away. She'd even gone so far as to encourage Lana to drop her résumé off at companies in Dallas—and by *encouraged*, Lana meant her mother had sent the résumés in for her.

"We're going out to dinner, then dancing tomorrow night." Lana sighed. "Dad will love that."

Her mother waved a dismissive hand. "Forget your father. He's just being obtuse because he doesn't want you getting involved with a cop. That's the stupidest thing I've ever heard. If a cop was good enough for me, a cop is good enough for our daughter. Especially when he's as nice as Max."

That made complete sense to Lana. Even so, she felt the need to point out the obvious. "Mom, we've only been on one date. Maybe you should wait a little while before you start shopping for china patterns."

Her mother rolled her eyes. "Please. Unlike your father, I refused to spy on you and Max once you reached the porch. But I saw you two walking up to the house together hand in hand. It's obvious to me there's some serious chemistry between you two. A mother knows these things."

Lana didn't bother to deny it since it was true. "We'll see, Mom. Is the coffee ready yet?"

"Just about. Grab some sweetener and cream, would you?"

Lana did as asked, even though she was pretty sure Max probably took his coffee black.

Her mother filled the mugs, then put them on a tray along with the sugar and cream. "Come on. Let's see what the boys are talking about."

It turned out that Max and her father weren't talking about anything. Instead, Max was sitting on the couch while her father sat in one of the matching stuffed chairs, glaring at each other. The tension was so thick Lana almost choked on it.

Ignoring her father, Lana took a seat beside Max and handed him one of the mugs. As she suspected, he drank it black. As Max and her mother talked about how long he'd lived in Dallas and when he'd joined the SWAT team, her father sat there, staring holes into Max the entire time, not saying a word and generally being a jerk. Her mother definitely noticed and stared daggers right back at him.

Even though Lana hated to see him go, she didn't blame Max for chugging his steaming-hot coffee quickly, then getting to his feet.

"I really do have to get up early tomorrow," he said. "I should be going."

Lana felt like smacking her father, but she wasn't going to make a fuss in front of Max. So, she stood and followed him over to the door. Her father made a move as if to follow, but at the fierce look her mother gave him, he sat down again.

"I really did have an amazing time tonight," Max said when they got to the door. "Better than I could have imagined."

Lana rose up on tiptoe and gave him a quick kiss. Even that little peck made her heart beat faster than normal. Wow, this guy really did it for her.

"Ditto," she told him with a smile. "Can't wait until tomorrow night."

She trailed her hand along his big shoulder and down his arm as he turned to go, wishing she could give him a real kiss before he left but not wanting to get him into any trouble with her father. She didn't like to think her dad would be so petty as to mess with Max's job, but as the deputy chief, he could make it happen.

As she closed the door behind Max, her father's

heavy footsteps echoed in the entryway. "I don't want you seeing him anymore, Lana."

She spun around and stared at him in disbelief. Behind her father, her mother looked livid.

"What did you say?" Lana asked.

Her father's expression softened a little. Like he thought that would help the situation. "Honey, don't take this the wrong way. Max and the other guys on the SWAT team are good cops—the best. But you just finished your program at the university and have your whole life ahead of you. You can do so much better than a cop."

Anger welled up inside her. *She could do better?* She was interested in dating Max, not getting a good deal on a new car. The urge to tell her father exactly what he could do with his opinion was difficult to ignore, and she had to fight hard to calm down. That shocked her a little. She couldn't remember ever being this furious, especially at her father. But the idea of anyone telling her to stay away from Max goaded her like nothing she'd ever felt.

She closed her eyes and breathed through the anger, slowly tamping the emotions back down. When she had herself back under control, she opened her eyes and leveled her gaze at her father.

"Dad, I appreciate your concern. But I'm twenty-three years old and have been living on my own for five years. If I choose to see Max again, then I will. And I won't ask for your permission or opinion."

Her father opened his mouth to say something, but Lana held up her hand, forestalling him.

"It's late, Dad. We're done talking about the subject. I'm going to bed."

Stepping around her father, she kissed her mother on the cheek, then headed for the stairs, refusing to even look in his direction.

Chapter 3

"MASON FLAT-OUT TOLD ME TO STAY AWAY FROM HIS DAUGHTER." Max and some of the other guys on the team were in the equipment room cleaning their weapons. They really weren't dirty, but that's the way it was in SWAT. If you had everything else done and found yourself with a few free minutes, Gage put you to work. "He actually said she's out of my league and that I need to back off. I felt like I was in some kind of frigging Taylor Swift music video."

Cooper looked up from the pistol he was cleaning, mouth set in his trademark smirk. "What the heck does Taylor Swift have to do with you and Lana?"

Max looked at Becker, who wasn't much older than he was, knowing he'd get the reference. They both laughed, while Brooks, Diego, Zane, and Senior Corporal Trey Duncan, one of the Pack's two medics, stared at them like pigs looking at a Rolex. At least Tuffie seemed to understand the analogy. The adorable pit bull mix the SWAT team had adopted regarded the older werewolves in the room like they were dense before giving Max a doggy grin.

"Forget it, dude," Max told the team's explosives expert. "You're too old to get the cultural reference, Cooper. The important thing is that Mason is damn serious about keeping me away from his daughter."

Cooper shrugged. "Can't really blame the man. If I

had a daughter, I wouldn't want you near her, either."
He ran a brush over the barrel of his Sig Sauer automatic. "It's nothing personal. The deputy chief probably
took one look at you and imagined how hideous your
children would be. No one wants ugly grandchildren."

Max snorted, giving his fellow werewolf the finger.
"Nice."

Cooper laughed. "Tell me again what it is Lana sup-
posedly sees in you?"

He and Cooper might be buddies, but that didn't stop
Max from picking up a bottle of gun cleaner so he could
throw it at him. Brooks stopped him with a look.

"Forget Cooper," Brooks said. "What are you
going to do about Mason? Are you planning to keep
your distance?"

Max shook his head, not shocked Brooks had changed
the subject. The senior corporal was one of the peace-
makers in the Pack, always making sure things didn't get
out of hand, which could happen easily enough. They
were a close pack, but with a team full of alphas, fights
could break out at any time. In fact, they frequently did.

"Hell no," Max said. "Lana and I are going out
tonight."

Everyone stopped what they were doing to look at
him in surprise. Even Tuffie seemed shocked.

"Two dates back to back with the deputy chief's
daughter?" Trey let out a low whistle. "Lana must be
pretty frigging special."

Max's mouth edged up. Saying Lana was special was
an understatement. When they'd kissed last night, it had
been hard to keep from completely losing it. He'd never
had the urge to bite a woman's neck while making out,

but with her, the desire was definitely there. She tasted so good he wanted to eat her up.

Then there was the way his body had reacted to those kisses. It almost bordered on scary. He'd gotten hard as a rock within seconds and stayed like that until taking a cold shower this morning before leaving for work. He'd laid awake the entire night staring at the ceiling and reliving how amazing it felt to have Lana in his arms. He was getting excited all over again just thinking about it.

"I don't think you need to reply to that question," Cooper said with a laugh. "I'm pretty sure we already know the answer."

Max looked at his pack mates in confusion. "What do you mean?"

Around him, his teammates chuckled and shook their heads.

"Your eyes are glowing and your canines just popped out," Brooks finally explained, still grinning. "And if those two things weren't a dead giveaway, your phero-mones would be. It smells like you're close to blowing a gasket."

Zane squirted more gun cleaner on the rag in his hand. "Don't be embarrassed. You're still young. You'll learn more control once you've finished going through puberty."

Max grunted, opening his mouth to come back with a witty reply and nearly sliced off his tongue on his fangs. Damn, he hadn't even felt them extend. Abruptly, what Brooks had said about him being excited hit him.

"Shit," he muttered.

Embarrassed, he tried to shift the major boner in his uniform pants into a more comfortable position. That worked about as well as could be expected. There really

wasn't any way to get comfortable when your dick
was as hard as a crowbar. When the guys only laughed
harder, he bared his fangs at them and growled.

Brooks glanced up from the M4 he was cleaning.
"So, this thing with Lana must be serious if she's getting
to you this fast."

Max nodded since denying it would have been a waste
of time. "Yeah, I guess it is. I've never met anyone like
Lana before. All it takes is a smile from her and my heart
starts to beat out of control."

"You make any headway on figuring out what kind
of werewolf she is?" Trey asked, curious.

This morning, Max had filled in the team medic on
the conversation he and the other guys had at DPD headquarters last night, specifically the part about Lana not
smelling quite like any beta they'd ever run into before.

"Unfortunately, no," Max said. "I started to doubt my
nose, so I asked her some questions to see if I was right
about her being a werewolf at all. She admitted she can
eat whatever she wants and not gain weight and that she
can stay awake for days at a time and not get tired. Then,
just when I was sure she's a werewolf, other evidence
contradicted the theory."

"What do you mean?" Brooks asked, slapping his M4
back together and putting it through a function check so
fast Max could barely follow his hands.

Max tossed his rag on the table, then carefully began
reassembling his own weapon. He didn't want to be so
distracted by thoughts of Lana that he ended up putting his carbine back together without the firing pin
installed correctly.

"Her nose doesn't work right," he said. "Three or four

times during the date, she admitted she couldn't pick up scents that were blatantly obvious to me. She has the same sense of smell any normal human would have."

"Maybe her nose was damaged at some point, like Hale's," Brooks suggested. "That might explain it."

Max doubted that. Hale Delaney had the most god-awful sniffer in the Pack. His nose really served no other function than to separate his eyes and give his cool sunglasses someplace to rest. But his nose was nonfunctional because he'd had his face smashed in by someone's fist before he went through his first change. The damage had been so extreme that even being turned into a werewolf hadn't healed it.

"I didn't see scars to make me think that might be the case. Besides, like I said, she can smell stuff. She said the pizza smelled good, and the cheesecake, too. She simply doesn't have a werewolf's ability to pick up subtle scents or anything at a distance."

"I'm guessing she didn't flash any fangs or claws either, right?" Diego asked.

Max shook his head. "Definitely not. A werewolf's sense of smell isn't the only thing she's missing, either. She also can't see in the dark."

That earned him a few raised brows and a head tilt from Tuffie. Sometimes it seemed like that dog understood English better than Max did.

"We were walking toward the front door of her house last night and a skunk scurried across the lawn a few dozen feet away," Max explained. "It was dark, but you couldn't miss it. Lana didn't see it at all."

"How do you know?" Zane said. "Maybe she saw it and didn't react."

Max frowned. "It was a skunk, dude. It's genetically impossible for a woman to see a skunk in the dark and not freak out. I'm telling you, she can't see in the dark."

"Did you ever get the impression she might be faking it?" Trey asked. "Maybe she's hiding it from you."

"Why would she do that?" Max asked. "I'm another werewolf. She has to know she's safe with me."

"Think about where your head was when you and Gage first met," Brooks said. "Back before you knew there were others like you in the world. Did you recognize Gage for what he was the first time you met him?"

Max considered that and realized Brooks was right. He'd been able to see and smell things he shouldn't have been able to back then, but none of it had made sense to him. When Gage had shown up, he'd been too freaked to analyze his scent.

"I see your point," he said.

"Lana may have no idea what she is or that there are other people like her," Brooks added. "If so, it's not like she's going to run right out and admit she's different."

Max was mulling that over when Cooper lifted his head from the handgun he was cleaning. "There's another option we haven't considered. What if Max is right, and Lana is simply a werewolf who never learned how to use her nose or her eyes?"

Zane snorted. "That's bloody barmy, Cooper. What kind of werewolf can't use their nose and eyes?"

Cooper shrugged. "How about the kind that doesn't know they *are* a werewolf."

Everyone—including Max—stared at Cooper. Leave it to Cooper to head to left field. Max blamed it on all those years his fellow werewolf spent sniffing explosive fumes in the army. Or maybe it was all those times he'd been blown up by those same explosives.

"What are you saying?" Brooks asked, apparently taking Cooper seriously, which was never a good idea in Max's opinion.

"Is it so difficult to believe that at some point we'd run into a werewolf we know absolutely nothing about?" Cooper asked. "Until a year ago, no one but Gage knew there were such things as alpha, beta, and omega werewolves. Maybe Lana is a completely different kind of werewolf. One who doesn't have the same abilities we do or whose abilities are stunted for some reason. Brooks, you're the one who said she smelled slightly different than the other betas we've run into lately. My theory would explain that. It's like she's a latent beta."

Max wanted to say that was crazy, but the more he thought about it, the more sense it made. Lana was a werewolf who had no clue what she was. Moreover, she had no idea Max was a werewolf, either. It explained why she hadn't reacted to his scent at all.

"Should I tell her what she is?" he asked.

Brooks, Zane, Diego, and Trey all shook their heads, indicating they thought that would be a bad idea. Cooper, on the other hand, seemed to be considering it.

"I think you should tell her," the explosives expert said. "Take it from me, women don't like it when you hide stuff from them. They can get pretty pissed. And don't even try that for-your-own-good crap. That never works."

Brooks frowned. "Don't listen to Cooper. Take your time and work up to the truth slowly. If you're right, and Lana doesn't realize what she is, telling her too soon could freak her out."

Cooper snorted. "Working up to it slowly won't freak her out any less." He looked at Max. "So, are you going to follow my advice since I actually have experience dealing with a woman who turned out to be *The One* in my life? Or do you go with Brooks's approach? Keep in mind that he tackles moving cars for fun."

Max looked back and forth between Brooks and Cooper, wishing one of the other guys would give him his opinion on the subject, but Zane, Diego, and Trey stayed silent.

Finally, he shook his head. "Sorry, dude. I have to go with Brooks on this one. He might tackle cars now and then, but at least he's never gotten himself blown out of a ten-story window."

Cooper shrugged. "Have it your way. But when Brooks's approach blows up in your face, come on back and I'll tell you how to fix everything."

They were still talking about whether this latest theory on Lana meant Deputy Chief Mason didn't know about werewolves when Gage stuck his head in the door.

"We got a call for support," he said. "Brooks, Zane, Diego—I need you to provide backup on a rollout to Northwest Dallas, near the apartment complex off Webb Chapel and Park Lane."

Brooks, Diego, and Zane immediately jumped up, weapons in hand.

Even though his boss hadn't said his name, Max was next on the rotation along with the other guys, so he automatically moved to join them.

"You don't need to take this one, Max," Gage said. "It's a domestic violence call."

The other guys didn't slow as they headed for the

building's exit that led to the parking lot with the response trucks. Their gear would already be loaded and waiting for them.

Max hated DV calls for obvious reasons. Gage and the rest of the team knew it, too, and did their best to keep him off those calls. But he couldn't avoid them forever. It was a major part of SWAT's job to help out uniformed officers on DV calls when things looked like they might get out of hand.

"Sarge, I appreciate you trying to protect me from this stuff, but I'm going to have to go on a domestic violence call at some point. They're like thirty or forty percent of our workload. I can deal with it."

Gage didn't say anything. Cooper and Trey were studiously focusing on the weapons they were cleaning. They didn't like the idea of Max going out on these calls, either.

"Okay," Gage finally said. "Go on the call, but keep yourself detached from the situation. Stay in control and follow Brooks's lead, understand me?"

Max nodded once and headed for the door at a run to catch up with the other guys. While he was glad Gage had relented, he was a little worried about whether it had been a good idea to push the issue. If there was one situation that messed with his control of his inner wolf more than any other, it was DV calls.

Tuffie gave him a look when he sprinted past, as if she was a little worried about him, too.

━━∼∼∼━━

They got to the apartment complex on Park Lane at the same time two DPD cruisers from the Northwest

Division rolled in. According to dispatch, this address had been the subject of over a dozen domestic violence and noise complaint calls over the past two years and everything pointed to the situation escalating each time—hence the request for SWAT backup.

Max had personal experience with how these things tended to escalate and how they usually ended. He hoped it wasn't the case this time, but he wasn't holding his breath.

The two patrol cars stopped in front of a single-family dwelling on the other side of the street from the apartment building. While it had obviously been built in the same manner as the other houses around it, there was something about this particular house that made it stand out. Max wasn't prone to being melodramatic, but it was like the house itself was sad. It was a stupid thing to think, but how else did you describe a home that seemed a little bit dimmer and less alive than the other houses around it? Max couldn't help but wonder if this was how his apartment in Vegas had looked to others in the neighborhood.

An officer from one of the cruisers headed toward the house next door to talk to the person who'd called the police about the disturbance. The second cop, Senior Corporal Alvarez, walked over to Max and the other guys.

"We've been out here four times over the past few weeks," he explained. "The guy's a real son of a bitch, but the wife and kids are too afraid to say anything to us. It could get ugly in there."

"We'll keep that in mind," Brooks said.

Giving them a nod, Alvarez headed up the walkway

toward the front door of the ranch-style home, his back stiff and straight, one hand resting on the top of his holstered weapon. No doubt the patrolman had been called out to this address before and was assuming the worse.

Brooks motioned to Zane and Diego, indicating they should go around to the back of the house while he and Max followed the uniformed officer onto the front porch. Senior Corporal Alvarez gave Max and Brooks a quick glance, confirming they were there and ready, then knocked on the door. It looked like there had been a doorbell on the exterior at some point, but the gaping hole that appeared to have been filled with old bubblegum was the only thing there now. A well-used aluminum screen door protected the heavy wood inner door, but even with those two barriers, Max still picked up the scent of fresh blood coming from inside the house. He was glancing at Brooks to see if he smelled it when the inner door jerked open.

The metallic odor of blood hit Max all at once, and his fangs slid out as a big man in a mechanic's uniform filled the doorway, a pissed-off look on his face. The urge to grab the man by the shirtfront and rip him through the screen door was tough to ignore. He might have done it if it hadn't been for Brooks. His fellow werewolf gave him a warning look and a nudge. Max used the distraction to shut out the scent and get his pulse under control.

"What the hell do you want?" the man demanded.

"We've received a call about a disturbance at this address, Mr. Wallace," Officer Alvarez responded calmly, clearly familiar enough to know the man's name. "An altercation involving one or more of the residents."

The man's face twisted into a scowl. "It was that damn old fart next door, wasn't it? He's full of shit and needs to mind his own damn business."

Max had to hand it to Alvarez. The patrol officer didn't so much as bat an eye. "Sir, we'll have to come inside and check to make sure everyone in the house is safe, so I'm going to need you to open the screen door and step back."

The big man didn't move. "This is bullshit. Not to mention harassment. There's nothing going on here and you have no right to come in this house!"

Max was all too familiar with the lines Wallace was spouting. It was the same kind of shit his old man used to say on those very rare occasions when the LVPD had bothered to show up.

Max took a step forward, ready to kick in the door and flatten this jerk on his way to figuring out where the scent of blood was coming from, but Brooks reached out and put a hand on his shoulder, stopping him. Max almost turned and snarled at Brooks. His teammate had to be able to smell the blood. Someone in the house was hurt.

But Brooks didn't move his hand. He didn't look at Max, either. Instead, he kept his gaze locked on the piece of crap blocking their entrance.

"Mr. Wallace, I've been out here enough times to know you're aware of how this works," Alvarez said. "If you don't voluntarily let us into your house, I'm going to ask the two officers with me to open it instead. It's up to you."

As they waited for Wallace to decide, Diego's voice came through the earpiece Max wore. "I'm looking through the kitchen window right now and can see four people sitting in the living room—a woman, a teen boy, and two younger girls. The boy has a bloody towel wrapped around his hand."

Beside Max, Brooks clenched his jaw. "We need to get inside," he said softly to Alvarez.

The uniformed officer didn't look back or ask what was going on. In fact, he never took his eyes off the man on the other side of the screen door. "Three seconds, Mr. Wallace."

Wallace cursed and pushed open the screen door, stepping aside to let them in.

"This is bullshit!" he said as Max and Brooks led the way inside the house. Two seconds later, Max heard Zane and Diego come in through the back door.

"Where the hell did they come from?" Wallace groused as the pair walked into the living room.

Max ignored the man, focusing his attention on the four scared people sitting on the couch. The woman was probably in her midforties, but the lines of stress and tension around her face made her seem older. Her face was pale and her eyes unfocused as she gazed distantly at a spot on the carpet in front of her. Even with everything going on around her, she never looked up.

The two girls, one maybe thirteen, the other a little younger—ten or eleven—were sitting close together, clinging to each other in a heartaching gesture of mutual support. The younger one had her face buried in her sister's shoulder, refusing to look at anyone around her. The older girl was gazing around the room at all of them but refusing to make eye contact. It looked like she'd been crying recently and had dried her tears only seconds before Max and the others had come in.

The boy, who couldn't be more than fifteen or sixteen years old, sat there with a bloody dishrag wrapped
around his right hand, his face tight with pain. Like
his sister, he refused to make eye contact with anyone
around him. Max had worn that same look on his face
when he was a kid back in Vegas. It was the look of
someone who believed he was all alone in the painful
world he was living in.

Max knew right then that the woman and her kids
weren't going to say a word about what had gone on
here today. But as he slung his M4 over his shoulder and headed for the injured boy on the couch, it
wasn't difficult to figure out what the hell had happened. The boy's bleeding hand and the broken top
of the glass coffee table in front of the couch said it
all. Something—or someone—had knocked the boy
down hard enough to put him through the glass. The
boy's hand had almost certainly been damaged as he
attempted to stop his fall.

Max stopped to glare at Wallace over his shoulder,
rage that he hadn't felt in a very long time building up
inside him again. His heart hammered in his chest and
he felt his fangs slide out a little. As if on cue, his claws
began to force their way out, too.

Turning, he strode toward the big man before he even
realized what he was doing. He had no idea what he was
going to do when he reached the piece of shit in front of
him, but he promised it wasn't going to be pleasant for
the bullying asshole. He knew he'd told Gage that he'd
keep it under control, but he couldn't. Not after seeing
this scene that was so achingly familiar to him.

The asshole was oblivious to Max, instead telling

Alvarez that his son was a klutz who'd stumbled over his own feet and fallen onto the coffee table. Max barely suppressed a growl. He didn't care that he was on the verge of losing it completely. Someone had to do something to stop this.

Suddenly, Brooks was in front of Max, forming a wall he'd never be able to get around while at the same time providing a calming presence to allow him time to get it together. Max fought down the rage, forcing his body to retract his claws and fangs before anyone saw them.

"Go check on the boy," Brooks said softly. "I need to know if we have to call the paramedics."

Max took a deep breath and nodded. Based on the blood seeping through that rag around the boy's hand, some kind of medical attention would be needed. He threw one more look at Wallace, then walked over to the boy. He shoved the remains of the glass coffee table aside with his boot, noting blood on some of the larger shards. Yeah, the kid had definitely gone through the table hand first.

"The kid's fine," Wallace complained as Max moved closer. "Don't coddle him."

The look Max threw the man was enough to make the guy go pale. Even Officer Alvarez lifted a brow.

Dropping to one knee in front of the boy, Max caught his eye. "Hey," he said softly. "My name is Max Lowry. I'm going to take a look at your hand and see how bad it is. You okay with that?"

The boy didn't meet his gaze. Max understood that. If you never looked people in the eye, they could never see the pain you were in. Max didn't push but simply waited patiently.

After a few seconds, the kid finally looked up only long enough to shake his head. "I'm good. It's not that bad."

"Mind if I look anyway?" Max asked.

The boy shrugged but held out his hand.

Max slowly and carefully unwrapped the towel. Why weren't Trey or Alex here? Everyone on the SWAT team had basic first-aid training, but those two were certified paramedics who were qualified for crap like this.

There was one long gash across the boy's palm and another starting at the heel of his hand, running up the inside of the wrist for a good three or four inches. The older girl leaned over to peek, but then quickly looked away, tears pooling in her eyes. The boy's mother never looked up from the imaginary spot on the floor she was focused on. Max had seen that expression before, too. It was that of a woman who had given up on everything and everyone.

Max cautiously moved the boy's hand this way and that, checking for severe bleeding, as well as ligament, tendon, or muscle damage. That slash along the wrist worried Max, but even though fresh blood seeped out, there was nothing to indicate any arterial damage. The cuts didn't look deep enough to affect the use of the kid's fingers, but Max wasn't a medic. He knew one thing for sure, though. The boy would definitely need to see a doctor to treat these.

"He's going to need stitches," Max told Alvarez.

"That's bullshit!" Wallace bellowed. "It's just a scratch."

Max ignored him and turned back to the boy. "What's your name?"

He tried to be as gentle as he could as he rewrapped the

kid's hand, but pressure was the best thing for the wound right now, even if it hurt. The boy didn't flinch regardless of what Max did. That was a sure sign of a kid who'd been hurt so many times he barely felt pain anymore.

"Terence," the boy said quietly, his voice giving nothing away as he answered the question. No pain, no feelings, no hope.

"These are my sisters, Nina and Natasha," Terence said, motioning with his chin at the two girls.

The older girl, Nina, locked gazes with Max for a second, her eyes a mix of hope and curiosity. Unlike her mother, she hadn't completely given up on the world yet and retained some hope that maybe something would happen one day to stop all this.

"How did you hurt yourself, Terence?" Max asked in a low voice.

"I told you already," Wallace bellowed. "The stupid kid fell over his own feet. Tell them, Eileen," he added, looking at his wife.

Max caught Terence's eyes and held them. "Is that what happened? Did you fall down? Or did someone push you?"

Wallace was making a fuss about the cops talking to his underage son, but Max stayed focused on Terence. The kid returned Max's gaze, his face distrustful. Max's heart almost tore in half. He'd been in Terence's shoes, hoping things would change but never believing it would happen. In that kind of place, you'd be an idiot to trust anyone.

"Terence, nothing is going to change unless you help it change," Max murmured. "I can't help you if I don't know what happened. Did you fall down, or were you pushed?"

Terence stared at him, and out of the corner of his eye, he saw Nina gazing almost hopefully at her brother. Terence opened his mouth, and for a moment, Max thought the boy would tell them everything. That for once, the ending would be different.

But before Terence could say anything, his mother snapped her head around to look at him, her face full of pure terror as she shook her head. Just like that, the slight glimpse of hope Max had seen building in the boy's eyes disappeared, snuffed out like a candle.

"I tripped and fell, just like Dad said," Terence told Max in a voice so flat and emotionless it was almost robotic.

"Your father didn't touch you?" Max prompted.

The kid shook his head, refusing to look at Max.

Biting back a curse, Max reached out and gently pressed two fingers against the boy's stomach, right below the sternum. Terence winced in pain, involuntarily pulling back a little. Max moved his hand away even as the boy tried to recover and act like nothing had happened. Blows to the stomach hurt like hell, but they rarely ever left a mark. Wallace was a smart, twisted, sadistic son of a bitch. Just like Max's father had been.

Max glanced at the kids' mother. She'd seen her son get beaten by the man who was supposed to love and protect him. Maybe he could plead his case with her. But there was nothing in the woman's eyes to make him think there was any reason to bother. The woman was gazing at her husband the same way his own mother had looked at his father. Eileen Wallace was thinking her husband would finally realize how much he'd hurt their children and then everything would be better.

But it never worked out that way. The violence would

stop for a time. Maybe a few days, maybe even a few weeks. But at some point, it always started up again.

Sighing, Max stood. On the other side of the room, Wallace gave him a smug smile. The urge to rip the man a new asshole surged inside Max, bringing fangs and claws with it. He probably would have gone at the bastard right then, but once again, Brooks stepped in front of Max. Taking Max by the arm, Brooks led him outside, blocking both Alvarez's and Wallace's view of Max as he did.

Out on the front steps, Max inhaled deeply, fighting for control over his inner wolf and tamping down the desire to kill that piece of shit Wallace regardless of how stupid it might be. Zane came out a few moments later.

"Alvarez will make sure the kid gets medical attention," Zane said. "He's in there right now laying into that wanker, promising to come back tomorrow to check the kid's stitches himself."

"For all the good it will do the kid," Max muttered. "His hand will heal, but what about the next time, when his father puts his head through a wall?"

Zane didn't say anything. There was only so much a cop could do in situations like this. SWAT cops could do even less. This wasn't their patrol area, and it wasn't like they'd be coming out here again anytime soon on official duty, unless it was to deal with another DV call that went even worse than this one.

"Go talk to the neighbor who called 9-1-1," Brooks suggested. "See if he can tell you anything."

Max nodded. If he stayed on the steps any longer, he was going to end up walking into the house and ripping out Wallace's throat.

He and Zane found the old man sitting on his porch with the patrolman, filling out paperwork.

"This is Ernest Miller," the officer said. "He's the one who keeps calling us out here. He's also the only one who cares enough to fill out the reports."

Ernest was a crusty-looking guy who sported shorts and a T-shirt, chilly November weather be damned. He had faded naval tattoos covering both forearms and an irritated look on his face.

"Those poor kids okay in there?" Ernest asked, his voice coming out in a gravelly, two-pack-a-day gargle. "Or did that bastard finally kill one of them?"

"They're all alive…barely," Max said. "You hear them fighting in there a lot?"

Ernest snorted. "Three or four times a week. Normally I'm not one to put my nose into another man's business, but I can't stand by while that man beats up his wife and children. What kind of bastard does that and still calls himself a man?" The guy turned and spit over the side of the porch, as if just talking about his neighbor made him sick. "You going to be able to finally arrest that piece of garbage?"

Max shook his head. "Unfortunately, no."

Ernest cursed. "If I were ten years younger, I'd take that jackass behind the woodshed and beat him within an inch of his life."

Max couldn't argue with that. Next door, Brooks and Diego came out of the Wallace house. Reaching into his pocket, Max pulled out a business card, handing it to Ernest. He'd never had a reason to give anyone his card before, but this seemed like a good use of one.

"My personal cell phone number is on there," he said.

"Call me if you hear anything from the Wallace house. Day or night."

Ernest assured Max he would. "Not that I imagine I'll have to wait too long. You might have put the fear of God into that bastard for a little while, but I wouldn't be surprised to hear the screaming and hollering start up again before long."

Max knew the man was right, which made getting back in their SWAT vehicle to leave damn hard. But not nearly as tough as when he looked back and saw Terence gazing out the front window at them, his face a mask of anguish.

Chapter 4

"I CAN'T BELIEVE YOU DIDN'T CALL AND TELL ME YOU WERE going to a party," Miriam said, looking pointedly at Brandy. "You left me here sleeping in my bed without a clue. What kind of wingwoman are you?"

Brandy laughed as she reached into the fridge for another round of diet soda for the three of them. Lana had stopped by her friends' apartment hoping to catch up with them before her date with Max that night.

"The kind that never would have tried to get you out of bed after you'd pulled a twelve-hour shift at the ER," Brandy said, handing one of the cans to her red-haired roommate. "You would have been stumbling around like a zombie in high heels."

Lana smiled as her two friends continued to bicker about the fact that Brandy had gone to the SWAT cook-out and spent the entire night hanging out with a team full of hunky cops without mentioning it to her room-mate. It didn't help that Brandy had taken selfies with all the hot, single guys who'd been at the SWAT compound last night—and there had definitely been a lot of them. Lana swiped through the pictures on Brandy's phone, noticing there were quite a few of her with Diego. But as Lana got further along in the photo album, she realized there were even more pictures of Brandy with a smaller guy with dark-blond hair, a trace of stubble, and a smile that never seemed to leave his face.

"Hey, Brandy. Who's this guy with you in all these pictures?" she asked, holding the phone up so her friend could see it. "I thought you had the hots for Diego?"

Brandy stopped arguing with Miriam and walked over to the couch where Lana was sitting. Setting the two cans she was holding on the coffee table, she took the phone with a smile. "Oh, I do have the hots for Diego Miguel Martinez. God, the way that name rolls off the tongue!" Still grinning, she swiped through the pictures. "But I also have the hots for Zane and Hale and Trey," Brandy said, showing Lana pictures of each guy as she spoke.

Lana had to admit they were all super attractive. They couldn't compare with Max, of course, but they were nothing to turn your nose up at.

"In fact, I have the hots for pretty much the entire SWAT team—including the ones already taken by someone else," Brandy continued. "There's not a man on that team I wouldn't wrap in a tortilla and eat up like a burrito." She stopped swiping, gazing longingly at one particular photo, her dark eyes suddenly dreamy. "But then I met Chris Hughes, one of their friends, and something funny happened."

Miriam pushed her curly, red hair behind her ear and leaned over Bandy's shoulder to look at her phone. "He's cute, but I don't think I'd put him in the same class as the SWAT guys."

Brandy shrugged. "Normally, I'd say the same thing. But there's just something about him…maybe the way he made me laugh with that Mississippi accent of his. Whatever it was, I ended up sitting at a picnic table with him until the sun came up this morning."

Lana lifted a brow, then looked at Miriam to see that she was just as stunned. It wasn't that Chris wasn't attractive—he definitely was. It was simply that Brandy had always—as in *always*—been a party girl. She would go for the hottest guy in the room, get what she wanted from him, and then move on. She'd never been serious about a man as long as Lana had known her—and Lana knew her since middle school.

"Wow," Miriam said. "So I guess you're going to see Chris again, then?"

Brandy thought a moment, then shook her head. "I don't think so."

"Why not?" Lana asked.

Brandy shrugged. "I'm not looking to get involved with anyone seriously, so there wouldn't be any point in seeing him again."

Her friend said the words lightly, but it sounded a little forced to Lana. One glance at Miriam told Lana she thought the same thing.

Throwing up her hands, Miriam flopped down on the opposite couch, popped the top on her diet soda, and looked at Lana. "Okay, how about you? Brandy said you ran into a hunk of your own last night. Please tell me you're smart enough to hold on to him."

Lana laughed. "Definitely. Max and I had an awesome time. We went out for pizza and ended up talking for hours. We didn't get to my parents' place until well after one o'clock."

Miriam jumped up and hurried around the coffee table to sit beside Lana, her green eyes bright with excitement. "Dish on the details. And don't leave anything out."

Brandy sat down on the other side of Lana, a little more subdued than normal but apparently more interested in talking about Lana's evening than her own.

"For starters, Max is extremely attractive but doesn't seem to know it." Lana sat back, wrapping her arms around a throw pillow and hugging it to her chest with a smile. "He's funny and really easy to talk to. He didn't come close to falling asleep when I told him about my organic chemistry classes. He even gets that I'm a pescatarian."

Brandy sipped her soda. "If you guys hit it off that well, I'm surprised you didn't go back to his place and make out."

Lana laughed. "Oh, trust me, I wanted to. But it was late, and I didn't want to keep Max up all night, not with the kind of work he does. We did make out on the front doorstep like a couple of teenagers, though, and that was smoking hot. If my dad hadn't jerked open the door when he did, I'm not sure we would have stopped."

Miriam did a double take. "Why the heck did your dad open the door? Didn't you say it was after one in the morning? Isn't that way past your dad's bedtime?"

Lana made a face. "Apparently he's not thrilled with the idea of me dating a police officer. He acted like a complete ass in front of Max and flat-out told me to stop seeing him, like I'm sixteen years old."

"I hope you're not putting up with that crap," Brandy said hotly.

She couldn't help but smile at how vehement Brandy was at the thought of someone trying to stand between Lana and Max, especially when she didn't seem interested in putting nearly that much energy into the relationship she could have with Chris.

"No, I'm not going to put up with that crap," Lana assured her friends. "I made no secret of the fact that I plan on seeing Max again. We're going out tonight, actually. I asked him to pick me up here. We're grabbing something to eat, then going dancing."

She was about to add that she'd asked Max to pick her up here instead of her parents' house so she wouldn't have to deal with her dad's stupidity when her cell phone rang. Hopping up, she hurried over to the chair where she'd tossed her purse when she'd first come in. She hoped it wasn't Max calling to say he had to work late.

But Max's name didn't pop up on her phone. Instead, it was a number she didn't recognize. She almost let the call go to voicemail, then changed her mind. It was a 512 area code, which meant Austin. It could be someone from the university calling.

She thumbed the green button and put the phone to her ear. "Hello?"

"Ms. Mason, this is Detective Gabriel Peterson, Austin Police Department. I was wondering if you could come to the station. I need to speak to you about your roommate, Denise Sullivan."

It took a few seconds for the words to filter through, but when they did, the first emotion that hit Lana was panic. "Oh God! Is Denise okay?"

"This is really something I'd prefer to talk to you about in person, Ms. Mason. Would you be able to come to the station? I could meet you somewhere else if you prefer."

"I'm not in Austin right now," she said. "I graduated

from college a few weeks ago and I'm back home in Dallas. Please tell me Denise is okay."

Lana's breathing came faster and faster, her whole body buzzing like she'd put her finger in a light socket. Even her gums were tingling.

"Detective?" she prompted.

Brandy and Miriam must have figured out there was something wrong because they got up and gathered around her. They looked as nervous as she felt.

What is it? Brandy mouthed.

Lana ignored her. She couldn't focus on Brandy and the phone at the same time. "Detective?" she said again, almost begging this time.

There was a pause and then a slight cough, like Peterson was clearing his throat. "Ms. Mason, your roommate was found murdered in your apartment this morning. Would it be possible for you to come to Austin so we can ask you a few questions? We could really use your help."

Lana heard Brandy and Miriam asking her what was wrong, and the detective asking if she was still on the line, but she was so stunned she couldn't think of how to answer. All she could think about was the last time she'd seen Denise.

That had been only three days ago. How could her friend possibly be dead?

"What happened to her?" Lana asked Peterson softly.

"It would really be best if you could come down to the station," the detective said. "I can tell you more then."

Lana stuttered out that she'd be there, though she wasn't sure how the heck she'd make the three-hour drive south on I-35. Her hands were shaking so badly she could barely hold her phone. How could she possibly drive?

She hung up, then somehow stumbled across the room until she found the couch and sat down. Brandy and Miriam followed, taking a seat on either side of her, each of them putting an arm around her.

"It's my roommate from school, Denise," Lana murmured. "She was murdered. The police found her dead in the apartment we used to share in Austin. They want me to come down there so they can ask me some questions."

"There's no way we're letting you drive all the way down to Austin on your own," Miriam said. "Not in the condition you're in right now."

Lana nodded as her phone rang again. She sat there, too numb to answer it.

Brandy took the phone gently out of her hand and answered it. Lana tried to listen in on the conversation, but she was too out of it to focus on anything. Instead, she leaned against Miriam, tears in her eyes.

"Honey," Brandy said, taking her hand and giving it a squeeze. "That was Max. He's on his way. I told him what happened and he said he'll take you down to Austin to talk to the police. Okay, Lana?"

Lana nodded, a little bit of the weight crushing her chest easing up at the mention of his name. Max would be here soon. He'd help her get through this.

———

"This is going to be hard for you to see, Ms. Mason," Detective Peterson said as he placed a closed folder on the table in front of her, his hand resting on the cover as if he thought Lana would open the thing on her own. "But I need you to look at the pictures we took at your apartment and see if anything is missing or out of place, or whether there's something there that doesn't belong."

Lana nodded, trying not to hyperventilate. The long drive from Dallas with Max had helped calm her down, but the moment they'd gotten to the police station and Peterson had brought them into the small conference room, the reality of what she was doing there all came rushing back. She'd felt like she might be ill, and something told her that looking at these pictures was only going to make it worse.

Beside her, Max's big hand enveloped hers. "I'm right here, Lana."

She gave him a small smile, thanking God he'd come with her. She wasn't sure she'd be able to do this without him. For some crazy reason, she felt like she could take on the world when she was with him.

Taking a deep breath, she flipped open the folder, prepared for the worst, relaxing when she saw that the first photo was a picture of the front door of the apartment she used to share with Denise. Her lips curved a little at the fall-themed welcome sign hanging from the little hook under the peephole, the one with the pumpkins she and Denise had gotten at a local flea market.

"The door wasn't damaged, so we thought Denise must have known her attacker and let him in," Peterson said. "But earlier today, we had a locksmith take a look, and it's his opinion that the lock was picked by someone who knew what they were doing."

Lana transferred the photo to the other side of the

folder, then looked at the next picture. Any relief she'd felt at the sight of the front door disappeared as she took in the living room. The couch and matching chairs looked like someone had taken a knife to them, the coffee table had been smashed, the TV had been completely destroyed, and the built-ins that made up the entertainment center had been demolished.

The rest of the photos were just as bad. The kitchen, bathroom, and bedrooms looked like a tornado had hit them. Lana could only stare in disbelief. Who would do something like this?

Peterson asked her one question after another. Was there anything missing? Did Denise have a boyfriend? Did she sleep around? Was there anyone Denise had problems with lately, anyone who hated her enough to want to hurt her? Was Denise doing well in her classes? Did she take drugs? Did she hang out with anyone off campus?

Lana answered the questions the best she could, telling the detective Denise wasn't like that. "Seriously. She was fanatically focused on her classes. If it wasn't for the occasional times I'd drag her out to go see a movie after an exam or big project, she probably wouldn't have left the apartment other than to go to school."

She looked through the photos again, stopping when she got to the picture of one of their kitchen chairs. There were pieces of what looked like duct tape attached to the wooden arms and dark smears that could only be blood. Lana knew Peterson was talking because she could hear the sound of his voice in the background, but he was saying stuff that made no sense, using words like *gagged*, *beaten*, and *tortured*.

Denise had been a beautiful person who'd never hurt a soul in her life, and never given anyone reason to hurt her in return.

Lana pushed the pictures away and got to her feet, then walked over to stand on the far side of the small conference room to look at the photos on the wall. They were of various Austin PD police functions, from chili cook-offs to commendation ceremonies. They weren't all that interesting to her, but she needed something to get the images she'd just seen out of her head.

Max ended up becoming a translator for her, talking to Peterson, then gently prodding answers out of Lana a little at a time. The fact that someone had not only killed Denise, but had also tortured her was simply too much to deal with.

Detective Peterson was of the opinion that this hadn't been random. It was too violent to be anything other than personal, but Lana refused to believe that. No one who'd ever met Denise could have hated her this much. This had to be some kind of horrible case of mistaken identity.

After Peterson was done with his questions, Lana forced herself to ask one of her own.

"Have you reached Denise's parents yet?" she asked, sitting down beside Max again.

It might seem like an odd question, but Denise had grown up in the wilds of Alaska. When Denise sent packages to her parents, they took weeks to get there, and calling her parents had always been an adventure too.

Peterson nodded, his face bleak. "They're on the way down from Alaska now. They're arranging to take her home at the end of the week or early next week—after the ME's office has done their job."

Lana couldn't imagine how hard this was for Denise's parents. She'd been an only child. Lana would need to call and find out what arrangements they were making, so she could pay her respects. Alaska…that was going to be complicated.

Finally, after what seemed like forever, Max asked Peterson to keep in touch in case anything turned up, and then they left. For her part, Lana hoped she never heard anything more about this case unless it was to say that they'd caught the person responsible and put them away forever.

She wasn't aware of much of anything after leaving beyond Max helping her into his car. When he started his Camaro, she leaned back in the seat and lost herself in the soothing rumble of the muscle car's engine. She probably would have stayed like that all the way back to Dallas, but halfway there, Max pulled off the interstate and into the parking lot of an all-night diner.

"What are we doing?" she asked in confusion.

He shut off the engine, then looked at her. "When's the last time you ate anything?"

She shook her head. "I don't know. Lunchtime, I guess. I'm not really hungry."

"Lana, it's almost midnight, which means lunch was probably twelve hours ago," he said gently. "We still have two more hours on the road before we get back to Dallas, so I'm going to take you in there and get you something to eat. And while we're eating, you're going to tell me about all the funny stuff you and Denise did while you were roomies."

That sounded like the most insane thing Lana had ever heard. She didn't have any desire to eat or talk about Denise. But it wasn't like Max was giving her an option. Getting out of the car, he came around and opened her door, then stood there, hand outstretched. She took it simply because she didn't know what else to do.

When the server came over, Max ordered grilled cheese sandwiches and bowls of tomato soup, then started prodding her with questions about Denise. At first it was hard talking about her friend, but after a while, she told him more and more, including all the funny stuff he wanted to know—the way they'd met, the way they'd borrowed each other's clothes, the way they'd passed notes in organic chemistry class about the cute guy in the front row.

Lana cried some, but she laughed a lot, too. Before long, the soup and sandwich were gone and Lana could barely stop the stories that kept pouring out. She wasn't sure how long they stayed in the diner, but the waitress kept refilling their coffee and bringing Lana more tissues, so she supposed it must have been a while. It was then that Lana realized she'd stumbled across one hell of a man. There weren't many guys in the world who'd sit with a woman half the night listening to her stories about a friend who'd just been murdered—not when they'd known each other for less than two days.

But Max was that kind of guy. She decided then and there that she was going to do everything she could to keep him around for as long as possible.

Chapter 5

MAX SAT IN HIS CAR ON PARK LANE, HIS GAZE TRAINED ON the Wallace house as he strained his ears to hear even a peep of a noise that meant Terence and his sisters were in trouble. If he heard anything to suggest that Wallace was hurting those kids or their mother, he'd go in and worry about the consequences later.

Ernest Miller, the crusty, old neighbor, had called Max a couple hours ago, saying Wallace was up to his old ways, shouting like a madman less than a day after the cops had been there. Ernest had called the police, but by the time the uniformed officers had shown up, everything had calmed down. Eileen Wallace claimed everything was fine and that the kids had been watching TV too loud or some crap like that.

Max had wanted to haul ass for the Wallace house the moment Ernest called, but unfortunately, he and a few of his pack mates had been stuck outside a convenience store in midtown, waiting while negotiators convinced a guy with a gun to come out with his hands empty, instead of clutched around a hostage. The city negotiators, with more than a little help from the team's hostage negotiators, Zane and Diego, had gotten the guy to give himself up, but waiting around had been agonizing.

To make things worse, Max couldn't simply take off the moment they'd gotten back to the SWAT compound. Since it was the middle of the afternoon and he was still on duty, he had to ask his squad leader, Xander, for a couple hours off so he could take care of some personal business, all the while praying his fellow werewolf didn't question it—or worse, know he was lying. But Xander had told him to take off.

Max had wanted to march right up to the front door of the Wallace house the moment he got there, but he was smart enough to know that wasn't going to work. As much as he hated the idea, since the kids and their mother were too scared to talk to anyone, the only way to put a stop to the abuse was to catch Wallace in the act.

He tilted his head a little when he heard a loud noise coming from the house, his fangs and claws extending. He was already reaching for the door handle before he realized the sound he was hearing *was* a TV playing too loud. Some kind of cop show or something.

He pulled his hand away from the door and put it back on the steering wheel, staring at his claws. He'd never been great at keeping his claws and fangs where they belonged, but lately, it seemed like he was losing control at the drop of a hat. It didn't escape his notice that it coincided with Lana's appearance in his life. Not that he was complaining. Lana was an incredible woman, and if having her in his life meant he had to put in extra effort keeping himself focused when he was with her, then it was worth it.

Max almost laughed. He was beginning to think there wasn't anything he wouldn't do to be with Lana, which was a little scary when he thought about it.

It was obvious that Lana was *The One* for him. Still, he'd have been lying if he didn't admit the intensity of this whole thing had him a little...unsettled. Sure, he'd

heard the guys talk about what it had been like when
they'd met their mates—"catching lightning in a bottle,"
"strapping yourself to a tornado," and "riding a nonstop
roller coaster" were some of the ways his pack mates
had described it. But even after hearing all that, he was
only now starting to realize exactly what Gage had
meant when he'd said taking it slow and easy might be
tougher than Max thought. Max was falling for Lana so
fast it made his head spin. He'd known her for less than
forty-eight hours, and she was already the only thing he
could think about. He just wished he had a clue whether
Lana felt the same.

He knew she was attracted to him. From the way she
leaned into him when they walked and looked at him
when they talked, it was obvious. This thing with her not
behaving like any other werewolf he and his pack mates
had ever met was tossing him for a loop, though. What if
Lana was so different that the legend of *The One* didn't
apply to her? What if she liked him the way any woman
would like a guy she'd just met? What if she didn't feel
the same magical connection he felt?

Max cursed. There were bigger issues to worry
about here than whether he and Lana were meant to be
together, and it all had to do with her roommate's murder
in Austin. He wasn't sure what the hell had happened,
but whatever it was, it was more than just a simple home
invasion gone bad. His gut told him that somehow Lana
was at the center of all of it.

After Lana had gotten up and walked to the other side
of the conference room, Detective Peterson had gone
through the rest of the photos with him. Max was glad
Lana hadn't seen them because they were all pictures

of Denise. Lana's roommate had been badly beaten, worse than Max had ever seen—and he'd seen a lot since becoming a cop. She had been brutally tortured for an extended period of time before she'd been shot in the head.

After hearing Lana talk about Denise for nearly three hours in the diner, Max couldn't imagine what the girl could have done to inspire that kind of treatment. The fact that no one heard anything during the night meant Denise Sullivan had been gagged for much of the beating.

The expert lock picking, the methodical way Denise had been beaten, and the silenced gunshot to finish her off implied this had been a professional looking for information. But what information? It wasn't like Denise had been sitting on a wad of money or a drug stash.

Max could see where Detective Peterson was trying to take his investigation. All the questions about boyfriends, whether Denise had slept around, and who she might have hung out with when she wasn't with Lana told Max the man was looking at this as a simple crime of passion. Denise had gotten on some guy's bad side, and he'd gotten back at her.

That didn't feel right to Max.

He knew his worries about Lana's safety might be clouding his judgment, but with all the hunter crap they'd heard lately, it was difficult not thinking this might be connected to them. They'd learned a few months ago in New Orleans that the hunters were a vicious bunch who didn't shy away from hurting people, and they tended to go for a head shot when it came to taking out werewolves.

Max was tempted to believe Lana was hiding that she was a werewolf because she knew hunters were on her trail and thought if she kept her true nature a secret, it would be safer for everyone. But when he started picking at the individual threads of that argument, the logic kind of unraveled. If she knew she was in danger from hunters, why wouldn't she reach out to Max for help, since he was a werewolf, too? Hell, if she knew there were hunters around, wouldn't she want to warn other werewolves about them? Max was pretty sure he knew Lana well enough to suggest she'd never put another person—or werewolf—at risk to save her own skin.

Of course, there was always the possibility that Cooper was right and Lana wasn't aware she was a werewolf, in which case running home to Dallas before the hunters arrived in Austin might have been an instinctive thing. That idea kind of made sense. Lana said she'd felt like she needed to come home the second she'd finished college. A lot of the werewolves who'd shown up in Dallas lately had admitted they'd been drawn here without knowing why, like pure survival instinct telling them to get close to a strong alpha pack.

Max had mentioned these ideas to Gage this morning, and while his commander promised he'd talk to some people about the possibility, he was of the opinion that Max was twisting the facts in an attempt to connect dots that were simply too far apart. Denise getting tortured and shot, as horrible as it was, didn't automatically mean hunters were involved. Sometimes, it was merely regular psychos out there killing people. Heaven knew there were enough of them.

While that all sounded very logical, it didn't keep Max from worrying. Lana was a werewolf, even if she didn't act like one. His gut told him if anyone was coming after her, it would be a hunter. With that in mind, it was damn difficult not seeing hunters in every shadow.

He was still contemplating that when he heard shouting coming from the Wallace house.

Max didn't stop to think. Shoving open the car door, he jumped out and sprinted down the block just as a little girl's scream echoed in the air. The terror in it made his inner wolf howl.

He was wearing his backup piece in a holster around his right lower leg, but as he hit the porch steps, Max didn't bother slowing down to grab it. Another high-pitched scream came from inside the house, forcing his fangs to extend even as he swung open the screen door.

"Dallas Police Department...I'm coming in!" he shouted before twisting the knob and shoving the inner door open.

The scent of fresh blood hit his nose as he rushed inside, ripping a growl from his throat and pushing him within an inch of totally losing control. But if Max thought the scent of blood had him close to the edge, that was nothing compared to how bad it got when he saw the scene spread out in front of him.

Little Natasha kneeled behind the arm of the couch, her eyes almost completely glazed over in fear. Nina stood in the middle of the living room, her face tight with defiance as she stood between her father and brother. Terence was in the kitchen doorway, standing defensively in front of his mother as if trying to protect her. There was a thick layer of white gauze wrapped around his right hand, from fingertips to the middle of his forearm. Red stains were already seeping through the bandages, and Terence wrapped the fingers of his other hand around them, squeezing hard as if trying to stop the bleeding—or the pain.

Max didn't know exactly what had happened, but it seemed obvious that Wallace had been going after his wife and Terence had put himself in the middle of it. No doubt Wallace had decided to take his anger out on the boy instead, doing something to bust open the stitches in the kid's bandaged hand.

Max growled low and deep as he moved across the living room, every instinct in his body screaming at him to kill the son of bitch where he stood.

"You can't just come in here like this!" Wallace yelled, taking a single step in his direction. "This is my house!"

The jackass probably would have said more if Max hadn't picked him up and slammed him forcefully against the wall. The urge to punch the piece of shit was nearly overwhelming, but he settled for shoving a forearm against Wallace's throat and holding him a few inches off the floor as he looked over his shoulder at the boy.

"Did he hurt you?" Max asked, trying his best to keep the question from coming out as a snarl...and pretty much failing. "I heard screaming from outside. Was he attacking your mother?"

Even though he was obviously still in pain, Terence opened his mouth to answer. But then his mother was at his side, shaking her head as she put her hand on her son's shoulder.

"That's not what happened," she said, her voice trembling. "Terence stumbled and hit his hand on the doorjamb. He's doing that all the time. Natasha was scared when she saw the blood and screamed. That's all that happened... I swear. Tell him, Terence. Tell the officer what happened."

Wallace struggled against Max's forearm, but Max pinned him with a single cold stare. Still holding on to Wallace, Max shifted his gaze to stare at the wall as he slowly got control of himself. Regaining control was much harder this time than it ever had been in the past. He was *this close* to killing this son of a bitch. Wallace might have deserved it, but that wasn't the way Gage expected him to operate.

When he finally forced his fangs and claws to retract, he turned to look at Terence, hoping the kid would be brave enough to tell the truth. But the small amount of hope and strength that had been there earlier drained away, leaving the boy's face an expressionless mask, devoid of emotion.

"That's what happened," the boy said softly. "I stumbled and hit my hand... That's all."

Max's heart broke for the kid. Seeing a light go out in the boy's soul was almost too much. He glanced at Eileen Wallace.

"You know this won't stop until you make it stop," he said. "Trust me, I know how this ends. If you don't stand up to him, this will keep happening until one of your children is dead."

For a moment, it looked like Eileen Wallace might actually do the right thing, but then she shook her head. "It won't. Nick wouldn't do that. Just let him go. Please. It's all going to be okay now."

"That's right, asshole," Wallace snarled. "Let me go!"

Max cursed. It was over. He could call the local division house, file a report, and give a statement about the shouts he'd heard, but it wouldn't do any good, not with everyone in here singing this well-rehearsed routine.

He let Wallace go so suddenly the man fell to the floor like the bag of crap he was. Max didn't leave right away, but locked eyes with each of the kids in turn, seeing their fear and resignation. He knew the feeling. It was the emotion that came when you truly realized nothing was ever going to change. When that last little bit of faith you had left in the world disappeared.

Turning, Max strode out of the house, not bothering to close the door behind him. That just made it easier to hear Wallace shouting about hiring a lawyer and suing the city, the police department, and him.

Given how little Chief Curtis thought of SWAT these days, there wasn't much chance of the city or the police department paying for any of this. They were going to fire his ass the minute word reached DPD headquarters and let him take the heat for this all on his own.

Ernest Miller was standing in his yard next door, shaking his head in disappointment as Max walked down the street and climbed in his Camaro. Max couldn't disagree with the man. He'd well and truly screwed the pooch this time. Instead of helping those kids, he'd likely made it worse. He'd embarrassed Wallace in front of his family. The bastard would be taking it out on one of them soon enough.

Max put the car in gear and pulled away from the

curb, more drained and exhausted than he'd ever been in his life. Right now, getting drunk would have been nice, but it was nearly impossible for a werewolf to get inebriated, so he guessed there was no point in trying. Not that he'd get the chance, because something told him he'd probably be spending the rest of the day and most of the night explaining himself to internal affairs.

Shit.

An IA investigation. That would be fun.

"Still thinking about Denise?"

Lana looked up from her menu and across the table at her mother. Crap, how long had she'd been zoning out? Her mom had suggested coming to the Galleria Mall hoping it would help take Lana's mind off what had happened to Denise, but so far, it wasn't working. Lana opened her mouth to fib and tell her mother she was simply trying to decide what to order for lunch, but realized it would be a waste of time. Her mom knew her too well.

"Sorry," Lana apologized, giving her mother a small smile. "Was it that obvious?"

Her mother's lips curved. "Well, the fact that you've been looking at your menu upside down for the past few minutes was sort of a dead giveaway that you're distracted. And considering you just found out about Denise last night, it wasn't difficult to figure out what you were thinking about."

Lana glanced down at her menu and realized her mom was right. Good grief, Charlie Brown, where was her head at? She flipped her menu right side up and saw it was still going to be hard to decide what to order. The restaurant had a lot of great-looking choices. Not that her mind was very focused on food right then.

"It's hard not thinking about Denise," she admitted. "A few days ago, we were talking about renting an apartment together and trying to get a job at the same company."

"Were you able to get in touch with Denise's parents?" her mom asked.

"Yeah, but it took a while. As you can imagine, it's been a tough couple of days for them."

"Are you going up to Alaska for the service?"

Lana nodded.

Her mom reached across the table and gave Lana's hand a squeeze. "I can go with you if you want."

Lana smiled. Her mother had always been there for her whenever she'd needed support the most. Offering to drop everything and go to Alaska with her was just one of the reasons Lana loved her so much.

"I appreciate that, Mom," she said. "But Max already offered to go with me. You don't mind, do you?"

Her mother smiled, but before she could say anything, their server interrupted to take their order. Lana glanced down at her menu and chose the first thing she saw: salad with a chili-lime vinaigrette and a cheese enchilada on the side.

The waiter, a blond guy she probably would have thought was attractive until she'd met Max and had her entire definition of the word changed forever, gave her a smile. "Orders are usually two enchiladas, but I can put in a good word with the chef, see if I can get him to hook me up with a single one."

"I wouldn't want you to waste any of your favors on

me," she said as she handed him her menu. "You can go ahead and bring two. I'll share with my mom."

Realizing his charm wasn't working on Lana, the waiter turned his attention on her mother. Her mom lifted a brow, shutting him down before he started and sending the would-be Romeo off for their food.

"There was a time not too long ago when you would have been thrilled to have a cute guy like that trying to charm you," her mother observed as she sipped her iced tea.

Lana shrugged, wishing she still had her menu so she'd have somewhere else to look other than at her mom, who was currently regarding her with a knowing expression. For once, she'd rather her mother didn't know her so well.

"I'm not eighteen anymore, Mom."

"Uh-huh." Her mother regarded her thoughtfully, apparently not convinced. "You sure it doesn't have something more to do with a certain SWAT officer?"

"Maybe," Lana conceded. "You don't mind if Max takes me up to Alaska, do you?"

Mom waved her hand. "Don't be silly. I can't imagine anyone I'd rather you go up there with."

Lana had spent the morning telling her mom about what had happened down in Austin, from finding out all the horrible details surrounding Denise's murder to the hours she'd spent at the diner with Max afterward. It wasn't an exaggeration to say he'd saved her sanity.

"He is rather amazing," she admitted with a smile.

"You like him a lot, don't you?"

"Yeah, I do."

Lana would have said more, but their server appeared

with their food. He was less charming and all business this time, she noticed. She picked up her fork and speared a tomato.

"I know this is going to sound crazy. We just met, but I already feel like we're perfect together." She glanced at her mother. "You don't think I'm crazy, do you?"

"Not at all. Sometimes, we really do fall fast for the person we're meant to be with. If Max is that person for you, there's nothing wrong with admitting it."

Lana sighed. "But how do I know for sure if Max is that person? What if my feelings for him are being affected by all this stuff with Denise? That makes a lot more sense than the idea I've stumbled over my soul mate."

Her mother shook her head and dipped her spoon in her soup. "You really are your father's daughter, aren't you? Always trying to logic your way through a situation. Maybe just this once, you should put your head on cruise control and let your heart lead the way."

Lana smiled at the analogy. "I think I can do that. Though I don't think Dad is going to be too thrilled with any of this. He's especially not going to like the idea of me going up to Alaska with Max." She snorted as a sudden thought occurred to her. "I can just imagine him wanting to go up there with us, so he can chaperone and make sure we don't get too close."

"You let me worry about your father," her mom said.

Lana was only too happy to do that. She ate a bite of her enchilada, chewing thoughtfully. "There's something I've been meaning to ask you, Mom."

"What's that?"

"The other night, you said Dad didn't want me to get

involved with a cop. Why not? I would think he'd be all for it, especially since Max is on his SWAT team."

Her mother sighed. "Who knows how your father thinks? He can be stubborn as hell sometimes for no apparent reason. If it's any consolation, my father never wanted me getting involved with a cop, either."

Lana's jaw dropped. This was the first she'd heard of that. "What? But Grandpa was a cop, too. Why didn't he like Dad?"

Her mother sighed. "Your grandfather wanted me to marry a doctor. He even had a guy picked out for me. But then your father pulled me over for speeding one day and it was love at first sight. We got married three weeks later. Your grandfather had an absolute cow, of course. He threatened to disown me if I went through with the wedding."

Lana wasn't sure if she was more shocked that her mom had been speeding or that she'd gotten married so fast.

"They get along great now," Lana pointed out.

Mom smirked. "Sure they do—now. But back then, it was awful, especially when your dad told your grand-father we'd elope and run off to Vegas to get married if my family didn't get on board."

Lana gaped. "He didn't!"

"Oh yes, he did. Your father was a real rebel back then, which is why I think he's so against you dating Max. I think he's terrified of Max doing the exact same thing to him that he did to my father."

"That is so whack it almost makes sense," Lana said.

She tried to wrap her head around the idea that her father, the deputy chief of the DPD Tactical Division, had been a bad boy in his youth, but she couldn't imagine it, even after she and her mother spent the rest of the meal talking about all the crazy things he'd done before Lana was born. Lana was almost looking forward to him trying to cause trouble between her and Max just so she could throw some of it in his face.

"You ready to do some more shopping?" her mother asked as they waited for their server to bring their check, which might take a while since the guy was currently at a table full of college girls, plying them with his charm.

"I never turn my nose up at shopping," Lana said.

She left her mom to deal with the waiter and made a quick run for the restroom, glad she'd let her mom talk her into coming to the Galleria. Nothing was going to make her forget that Denise was gone, but being with her mother made the sorrow a little easier to bear.

Lana was still thinking about that when she walked out of the ladies' room into the long hallway that led toward the main part of the restaurant, and almost ran smack into some poor guy heading toward the men's restroom. The man put his hands on her shoulders to steady her as she stumbled back. She opened her mouth to apologize, only to stop as the most bizarre sensation she'd ever felt ran all the way up from the base of her spine to the back of her neck, making her shudder. All at once, her teeth and gums began to tingle like crazy. If that wasn't odd enough, her fingers began to throb. Crap, it felt like someone was trying to yank her fingernails out.

She quickly took a step back. "Sorry."

"It was my fault completely," the man said in a deep voice.

She looked up at him. Damn, he was tall. And big. Almost as big as Max. No wonder she'd walked into him. There was no way to get past him in the narrow hallway without running into him. He had a face to match his body—intense and kind of scary.

She nodded, thinking she should acknowledge his apology. But then she had this sudden unexplainable urge to be anywhere but in that narrow hallway. She didn't understand why she was feeling so weird. It was like a snake or something else equally slithery had appeared right in front of her.

"Lana Mason?" he said, making her stop her attempt to squeeze around him and look up at him again.

She almost told him he was mistaken and pushed past him, but then her manners—and her curiosity—won out.

"Do I know you?" she asked even though there was no possible way she did.

"I doubt it. But I think I know you," he said. "Weren't you at the DPD awards ceremony the other day? I swear I saw you with Deputy Chief Mason."

Lana's jaw almost hit the floor. Today was definitely full of surprises. "You're on the DPD?"

How could she have missed him at the ceremony? He had the kind of face a person would tend to remember. Then again, she'd only had eyes for Max that day.

"Yeah, central division." A smile cracked his face, making him look a little less intimidating. "I've worked with your father's tactical divisions a few times."

Lana was tempted to ask the man if he'd ever worked with Max, but the impulse to get the hell away from him overwhelmed any desire for polite conversation.

She said to hell with politeness and moved to step around the walking roadblock. "Nice to meet you."

He moved to intercept her, reaching into the pocket of his jacket and pulling out something. She backpedaled quickly, sure he had a gun.

It wasn't a weapon but a perfume bottle.

"I hate to be a bother," he said, apparently not aware he'd already surpassed that point some way back. "But I just bought this perfume for my girlfriend and have no idea if it's any good. The woman at the counter swore up and down it was the scent of the season, but I could really use an unbiased opinion."

Lana shook her head, suddenly light-headed.

"Please," the guy pleaded. "My girlfriend is really difficult to please. If I give her a perfume that smells bad, she'll probably break the bottle over my head."

Lana couldn't blame the woman—she wanted to do the same thing. She resisted the urge and forced herself to nod. Anything to get out of this hallway faster.

It took everything in her to extend her wrist so he could spritz her with the perfume. Part of her wanted to push past him and run, but another part begged her to stay and...do something, though she didn't know what.

She lifted her wrist to her nose to take a sniff and almost gagged as an awful stench hit her. The part of her skin where he'd sprayed the perfume began to sting even as her nose started to burn from inhaling the stuff. *What the hell?*

She wrinkled her nose and made a face. "Ugh! What kind of crap did they sell you?"

"It isn't any good?" he asked in a tone that almost sounded amused.

"Hell no, it's not any good. It stinks. Plus, it burns. If I were you, I'd return it and get my money back."

Turning, she shoved open the door of the ladies' room and hurried inside, rushing over to the sink. Over the water, she swore she heard the man laugh, but she was too intent on washing the perfume off her wrist and couldn't be sure.

It took a long time and a lot of soap to get the worst of the stuff off her skin. Even after that, her nose still burned so badly her eyes watered. She splashed water on her face, hoping that would help. When she did the best she could, she dried her hands and face, grimacing as she looked in the mirror and realized her makeup was a complete disaster. She dug into her purse for her cosmetic bag and quickly put on some mascara and a touch of lipstick.

As she was putting her makeup back in her purse, she realized the funny sensations she'd experienced earlier were gone now.

Weird.

Lana stepped out of the bathroom to find the big man still standing in the hallway, blocking the way to the restaurant. That was when she noticed something that made her gums tingle and fingertips ache all over again—a second man standing at the far end of the hallway, near the emergency exit.

The first man took a step her way, smiling without any humor.

A metallic taste filled her mouth like she'd bitten her tongue, and a tremor of something halfway between anger and fear rumbled up her throat.

"Lana, there you are!" her mother said, coming

toward them from the restaurant. "What the heck is taking you so long?"

Relief washed over Lana as the big man who'd sprayed her wrist with perfume earlier brushed past her and headed for the emergency exit. The second man shoved it open, and they disappeared outside.

Why hadn't the alarm gone off?

She had no answer to that question, just like she had no way to explain why her body stopped buzzing and tweaking the moment the door had closed behind the two men.

"Who was that?" her mother asked.

"He said he was an officer from central division," Lana said, not wanting to alarm her mom or attempt to describe all the weird stuff that had just happened.

Her mother frowned. "Really? I didn't recognize him. What's his name?"

That's when Lana realized the man had never told her. "He didn't say."

Max was parked on the couch in his apartment, staring at the TV, hoping Wallace was full of hot air and wouldn't go through with his threats to file a complaint against him, when his phone rang. He grabbed it from the coffee table, cursing when he saw Gage's name on the screen. Thumbing the green button, he put it to his ear.

"What's up, Sarge?"

"Get your ass down to the compound. Now," Gage said in that tone he used right before he usually exploded and started throwing werewolves around the office like rag dolls.

Shit.

Even though it was well after 6:00 p.m. when Max got to the compound, there were still quite a few vehicles in the parking lot keeping Gage's Charger company. In addition to Xander's, Brooks's, and Cooper's vehicles, there were two others he didn't recognize. He wasn't so concerned about the late-model piece of shit with rust spots and a pervasive burnt-oil smell about it that suggested the thing was on its last legs, but the generic white Chevy Caprice sedan worried him. It screamed *DPD unmarked car*, which meant it was someone from internal affairs or headquarters.

Double shit.

Brooks was there to meet him, a concerned look on his face. "What the hell did you do, Max? Gage and Xander are in there with IA, and none of them look happy."

Max shook his head. He'd never felt more like a complete frigging idiot than he did right now. "I got a call earlier from that old guy on Park Lane, Ernest Miller. He said he heard a lot of shouting and sounds of a scuffle coming from the Wallace place. Northeast Division sent out a patrol car, but the wife told them the kids had been watching TV too loud, so I headed over there to check things out myself."

Brooks must have known where this was heading if the look on his face was any indication. "Damn, Max. Please tell me you didn't do something stupid."

Max wished he didn't have to tell Brooks anything of the sort. The Pack's biggest werewolf had always been a friend and mentor to him, and Max felt like he was letting him down.

"Yeah, I pulled a stupid," Max admitted. "I heard

one of the Wallace girls scream, so I busted into the house. I hoped I could catch that bastard in the act of beating one of his kids, but the moment I saw the boy was standing there trying to protect his mother, blood seeping through the bandages on his hand, I lost it. I ended up pinning Wallace to the wall and almost choking him out."

Brooks shook his head, and the disappointment Max saw on his face was almost enough to crush Max's soul. "Why would you do something like that?"

Max shrugged. "Because it's not in me to let that woman and her kids stay in a house with a man who beats them."

Brooks looked at him like he was a complete idiot. "I know why you did it, you moron. I'm asking why you didn't think to tell me or anyone else in the Pack. Cooper, Becker, Zane—hell, any of us would have gone with you and helped make sure we got this piece of crap. What, did you forget you're part of a pack?"

Max cursed silently. If Brooks had wanted to say the one thing that would make Max feel like crap, he'd done it.

"I screwed up," Max said quietly.

"No shit." Brooks's mouth tightened. "What the hell has gotten into you? It's like you've gone completely off the rails."

"I don't know," he admitted. "It seems like my head is spinning lately. I can barely keep my shift under control at the best of times, and even when I do, I see myself doing stupid stuff without being able to stop it."

Brooks regarded him silently, then sighed. "I guess I should probably cut you some slack. A werewolf can't be held responsible for his actions while he's an emotional train wreck. It's happened with everyone else who found their *One*, so why not you?"

Max stared at his pack mate, surprised Brooks was letting up on him. "You think IA will be as understanding with my screw-ups as you are if I tell them my relationship status is complicated?"

Brooks let out a snort. "I don't see that helping you out very much. But this time, trust Gage and Xander to watch out for you, huh?"

Max nodded. "You sticking around for a while?"

"Nah. I'm meeting up with Diego and Zane at a sports bar for the Thursday night NFL game."

Max snorted. "Zane? He doesn't even understand the game of football."

That wasn't an exaggeration. Their British teammate was all about soccer.

Brooks chuckled. "I know. I've made it my mission to teach him. Listen, text me later and let me know what happens with IA, huh?"

Max told him he would, then headed for the main admin building and Gage's office. The moment he opened the door, a trio of unfamiliar scents hit him. He found two women and a teenage boy sitting at one of the desks in the bullpen, eating barbecued pork, beans, and corn bread while they watched a home makeover show on the TV mounted on the wall on the other side of the room.

As Cooper got up from his desk and walked over to meet him, Max took a sniff. The two women were beta werewolves. One was in her thirties, while the other was a little older, midforties he guessed. The boy definitely wasn't a werewolf, though his scent was similar to the younger of the two women, so he was probably her son. The women gave him a curious look, then went back to eating. Something told him they hadn't seen food this good in a long time.

Max glanced at Gage's office, and his heart sank. Even though the door was closed, he could pick up Vince Coletti's scent. Of all the detectives from internal affairs, why did it have to be Coletti? The man had a hard-on for the SWAT team, for sure. He'd even forced Cooper to attend anger management sessions with a shrink. And Cooper was the most laid-back, in-control werewolf in the Pack.

Max was screwed.

Cooper motioned with his head, indicating Max should follow him outside.

"So, you went back and punched out that child-beating piece of shit Wallace, huh?" Cooper said, then added, "I overheard Coletti talking to Gage and Xander." He grinned. "Good for you."

"Yeah," Max muttered. "Well, now I have to deal with the fallout."

Cooper shrugged. "Put on your best I'm-horribly-sorry-and-promise-never-to-do-it-again face, and you'll be out of here in time for dinner with that new babe of yours."

Max wasn't nearly as sure of the outcome with Coletti as Cooper seemed to be, but arguing with Cooper about anything was like chasing a greased pig. You ended up looking foolish and feeling all dirty.

"What's with the two betas in there?" he asked instead. "They on the run from the hunters, too?"

"Yeah," Cooper said. "Grace; her kid, Rudy; and

her friend Kari have been moving around the country with an omega who'd been watching out for them. Four weeks ago, a group of hunters caught up with them outside of Norman. The omega sacrificed himself so they could get away, and they've been ducking and hiding ever since. They heard about our pack and headed this way. They rolled in here about an hour ago, and haven't stopped eating since."

Cooper may have dropped all that on him casually, but there was so much crazy in that story it was tough to figure out where to start. The fact that there were hunter packs operating so close to Dallas had to make Gage and the other senior pack members a little worried. Until now, hunters had been this vague threat that hovered far enough away for people to be lulled into the belief they'd never come here at all. But Norman, Oklahoma, was barely a hundred miles north of the Texas line. That was damn close.

Then there was the weird part about the omega protecting two betas. From what they knew about werewolves, a protective omega was an oxymoron. When Max pointed that out, Cooper shrugged.

"I had a hard time believing it, too, but Kari said the omega showed up out of the blue and started taking care of them. He seemed as shocked by his own behavior as they were. I'm trying to imagine an omega sacrificing himself for anyone, and I just can't see it. But I think the rules are changing now that the hunter threat is growing."

Max shook his head. The SWAT Pack still had no idea how word had trickled out that Dallas was a safe haven. All they knew was that scared werewolves had been showing up at the compound in ones and twos every few days since mid-August. Most of the new werewolves were betas, but there were also a surprising number of omegas and even a few alphas. They'd stop by to check in and make sure it was okay for them to be in the Pack's territory. Gage would welcome them in and make sure they had a place to stay along with work and enough to eat. Gage was doing his best to keep a head count, but staying on top of the incoming was getting harder by the day. There had to be at least forty new werewolves in Dallas at the moment. That was insane.

Inside the admin building, Max heard Gage's office door open. He sighed. *Might as well go in and get this over with.*

Cooper must have heard, too, because he smiled. "Remember. Look really apologetic. And no matter what, refrain from telling Coletti you'll probably end up doing the same thing all over again next week. People like him frown on that kind of honesty."

Max lifted a brow. "So in other words, lie to him?"

Cooper opened the door and shoved him inside. "Like your frigging life depends on it, because it does."

When they walked in, they found Gage, Xander, and Coletti talking to the two betas and the kid.

"Xander will take you upstairs and show you around," Gage said. "We have some cots up there you can use until we find you a place to stay. There's a small kitchen stocked with food, if you're still hungry."

As Xander led the small pack upstairs, Max couldn't help noticing Coletti's shrewd, gray gaze following them.

"I've heard you've been putting people up here," the dark-haired IA detective said. "You know the department frowns on that kind of stuff."

Gage didn't so much as blink. How the hell did his commander stay so cool, Max wondered. Coletti was such a rule-following d-bag it was all Max could do not to pick him up and throw him off the compound.

"They're people in trouble who need some help," Gage said. "I'm making sure that no department resources are being used."

Max expected Coletti to be a dick about it, but he merely watched the two women and the kid as they disappeared up the stairs, then nodded. "Keep it low key. If Chief Curtis finds out, he'll pull a hamstring running over here to can your ass."

With that settled, both Gage and Coletti turned their attention to Max. While Gage's jaw tightened, he was calmer than Max expected.

"I'll leave you two alone to talk," Gage said, going back into his office and closing the door.

O-kay. Max hadn't seen that coming. He fully expected Gage to be present for the ass-chewing Max was sure was coming his way. Instead of focusing on Max, however, Coletti was eyeing Cooper. His pack mate returned the IA detective's look with an expression that suggested Coletti wouldn't be making it onto Cooper's Christmas card list anytime soon.

"Cooper," Coletti said with a little lift of his chin that guys did when they wanted to acknowledge the other person existed but didn't want to shake their hands. "How are your anger management classes going?"

"Not bad." Cooper smirked. "I can look at you right

now without giving in to the overwhelming urge to kick your ass, so I guess they must be working."

With that, Cooper dropped the mic and headed upstairs to join Xander and the small beta pack.

Coletti grunted, then looked at Max. "Can we go somewhere we can talk in private?"

"Not sure what we have to talk about," Max replied. Regardless of what Cooper said, he wasn't going to play the game. That wasn't his thing. "You're here to suspend me, right?"

"That depends on you," Coletti said quietly. "Nick Wallace called a lawyer right after you left, saying you broke into his house and assaulted him. Given the number of domestic violence calls the DPD has made to that address, I don't see this making it into court, but IA views this as a valid complaint, so if you decide you don't want to talk to me, you'll be suspended until the investigation is complete."

Max came damn close to saying the hell with it and let the suspension stand, but that would piss off Gage and everyone else in the Pack. So he swallowed his frigging pride and nodded.

"We can go next door to the training building," he told Coletti.

Max led the way, expecting Coletti to lay into him the moment they grabbed some seats in one of the classrooms, but instead, the IA detective merely regarded him in silence, his face unreadable.

"I know what happened with your family," Coletti said suddenly.

Max clenched his jaw. He wasn't thrilled the IA detective had poked around in his background, digging up dirt, but he wasn't surprised by it, either. And he sure as hell wasn't about to let this dickweed have the satisfaction of knowing how much it bothered him.

"And?" he said flatly, almost expecting it when he felt the sharp edges of his fangs grazing his tongue. He was losing control every five minutes these days; why not now?

"And I understand why you reacted the way you did." Coletti leaned back in his chair. "Given the circumstances, I probably would have done the same thing. Hell, in these circumstances, I *have* done the same thing."

Max frowned. "What the hell are you saying? That you're okay with what I did?"

Coletti shook his head. "Definitely not. You screwed up and let your emotions get the best of you. You took a bad situation and made it worse. Not only did you not get anything the DA's office can use to stop that bastard Wallace, but you also gave his lawyers a possible wedge they can use against the DPD if we're ever lucky enough to get him into a court. If that's not bad enough, you embarrassed Wallace in front of his kids. More than likely, he's going to take that out on them."

Max cursed silently. Like he needed the reminder. The idea that those kids might get a beating because he'd screwed up tore at him like a serrated knife blade.

"So what the hell am I supposed to do?" he demanded, not caring that his voice came out as a low growl.

Coletti didn't seem to notice. He leaned forward and locked eyes with him. "You have to stop being an idiot. Put some distance between yourself and the situation and accept that you can't save people from themselves. You have to simply be there to offer a hand and hope the mother or that boy takes the first step and reaches out to take that hand."

The IA detective made it sound so simple. "I'm not sure I can stand by and wait for something to happen."

"Then let me see if I can help you," Coletti said. "As far as IA and the DPD are concerned, there's a restraining order out on you. You get within a hundred yards of the Wallace residence, you'll be suspended and your career will pretty much be over."

Max snorted. "That's being helpful?"

"Yeah, it is." Coletti sighed. "Take it from me. Something like this can eat you up from the inside if you let it. You start thinking you're the only person who can fix this situation, and before long, you'll find it consuming you until, at some point, you wake up and find yourself standing in the middle of an out-of-control situation with your gun out, wondering how the hell you ever let it get this far."

Max stared at Coletti. Who the hell was this guy, and what had happened to him? Because it was obvious the man was speaking from experience.

They talked for a little while longer, with Coletti giving Max a lot of suggestions that actually made sense, then promising he'd get family services out there to talk to Wallace's wife and maybe make something good happen.

By the time Coletti left, Max was beginning to think the situation with the Wallace family might end with something resembling a happily ever after.

He was still sitting there when Gage stuck his head in the door fifteen minutes later. "How'd it go with Coletti?"

"Not as bad as I thought it would," Max admitted.

"I haven't been suspended at least. But he wants me to stay away from the Wallace family long enough to let the system work."

Gage sat down at the table opposite him. "You going to be able to do that, given the type of situation we're dealing with?"

"Do I have a choice?"

Gage shook his head. "Not really. But that fact has rarely kept some of the idiots in this pack from trying anyway."

Max couldn't help chuckling at that, knowing exactly what Gage was talking about. A few of his pack mates had done some really stupid stuff lately.

"Okay, I'm going to finish up some paperwork so I can get out here," Gage said as he got to his feet. "Stay away from the Wallace place."

"I will." Max stood and fell into step beside him. "Sarge, how well do you know Coletti? I'm starting to think maybe he isn't the asshole I thought he was."

Gage snorted. "I've known Vince for a long time, and actually, he really is the asshole you thought he was. At least he can be. But he's also a damn good cop."

"He said some stuff that made me think he knows a little something about letting things get personal on the job. You have any idea what that's about?"

Gage opened the door, leading the way outside and across the compound to the admin building. "Coletti didn't always work in IA. He was a detective in the Assault Unit long before that. For all the right reasons, he ended up pulling a lot of the sexual assault cases. He was good at his job, but that's some tough work, and he had to deal with more than his fair share of crappy situations. He ended up getting into trouble by putting himself in the middle of one of them. It went bad, and politics in the DPD being what they are, he got transferred to IA. It was either that or leave the force."

Max opened his mouth to ask for more details, but Gage shook his head.

"If you want to know more, you'll have to ask Coletti. Go home and give Lana a call. Better yet, go spend some time with her and clear your head."

Max didn't say anything. He wasn't sure if he was suitable company for anybody, especially Lana, after the day he'd had. But the idea of spending the rest of the night on his own definitely didn't appeal to him.

He was halfway to his Camaro when he caught sight of Coletti leaning against the driver's side door of the old jalopy with the rust spots, talking to Kari. Max stopped, sure Coletti was harassing her about being there. No doubt he was asking her all kinds of questions about why Gage was letting her and her friends stay at the SWAT compound.

Max started toward them when he heard Kari laugh. He hesitated. Maybe he should listen in on their conversation for a little bit before he went over there and made a fool of himself.

"I'm serious," Coletti was saying. "If you need anything—like help fixing this car of yours, for example—give me a call. My cell number is on the back of the card I gave you."

Kari pushed her long, blond hair behind her ear, a smile tugging at her lips. "And what if I just want to call you for something other than car repair? Is the offer still good?"

Now it was Coletti's turn to laugh. "I said anything you need, and I meant it."

Max turned and headed for his car. If he listened to any more, he was going to have to shove his claws in his ears. Coletti and a beta werewolf? Seriously?

Chapter 6

"WHAT HAPPENED TO YOUR WRIST?" MAX ASKED AS LANA shrugged out of her coat.

She'd hoped Max wouldn't notice the red, irritated spot on the inside of her lower forearm where Mr. Creepy Guy had sprayed her with his perfume, but that had probably been asking too much. Max was a cop. He was paid to be observant. Besides, the rash on her arm kind of stood out.

Lana shook her head, not wanting to worry Max. "Mom and I were at the Galleria today and someone spritzed me with perfume. It stunk to high heaven and made my skin burn until I washed it off. It's starting to fade already."

Ignoring her attempt to downplay what had happened, Max carefully took her arm and urged her from his apartment's small entryway into the living room to get a better look. Lana quickly forgot about the rash on her arm as she enjoyed the feel of his warm hands on her body. It was crazy the way a simple touch from him had her getting all tingly.

"This almost looks like a chemical burn," he said with a frown. "Are you allergic to alcohol?"

"I never have been," she said. "In fact, I've never been allergic to anything. Whatever was in this stuff burned the moment it hit my skin."

Max's frown deepened. "I hope you talked to

someone at the store you were in and made sure they stopped using the crap."

Lana nodded, not looking at him as she did. Of course she hadn't talked to anyone. What would she say? *A police officer from central division spritzed me with perfume he bought from your store and it burned me?* She didn't even know which store the guy had bought it from.

"Enough about my weird reaction to some perfume," she said, giving him a smile as she tossed her purse on the couch. "You going to tell me about this crappy day you had?"

One of the big reasons she'd come over to his place was because Max had sounded so wrung out when he'd called her earlier. She'd hoped they might get together tonight, but when eight o'clock had come and gone, she'd thought he'd gotten hung up at work and that she'd have to wait until tomorrow to see him. But when he'd called after nine and told her his day had been a train wreck and that he'd really like to see her, she hadn't complained. While the day out with her mother had helped, Lana was eager to hang out with Max. She'd also been excited to see what his apartment looked like. Max was a unique man, and when she found herself trying to imagine his place, she simply couldn't picture it. So she'd turned down his offer to come over and pick her up, figuring her dad would only make a complete butt of himself given the chance, and jumped in her car.

Max gave her a sheepish look, which was an entirely adorable expression on a man his size. "We can get into the details later, but to make a long story short, I kind of pulled a stupid today."

She had a hard time picturing Max doing anything stupid. It didn't seem possible. "What'd you do?"

"Yesterday, I went out on a domestic violence call along with a few other members of SWAT. We were there to provide backup support in case things turned violent, and when we went inside and I saw the kids, it was obvious that they'd been abused and it really pissed me off."

Lana felt a slow burn in her stomach. When it came to people she just plain hated, child abusers topped the list. "Did you arrest the guy?"

Max shook his head. "Unfortunately, no. Even though it was obvious what happened, neither the wife nor the kids would say anything, so another report was filed and we had no choice but to leave. I knew the guy would end up smacking his family around again, so when I got a call from the neighbor saying he'd heard shouting coming from inside the house, I went over there on my own."

She didn't like where this was going. "You didn't go in without probable cause, did you?"

"I had cause—I heard screams," he said. "And when I got inside, it was as bad as I'd thought it would be. But unfortunately, this guy has his family so conditioned, they won't say a word. Worse, I kind of went a little crazy and got too physical with the guy."

Lana groaned. "Did you get suspended?"

Now she was even happier Max hadn't come by to pick her up at her parents' place. If her father had gotten wind of this, he would have lost his mind at the idea of her seeing Max again.

Max shook his head. "No, I got lucky. I'm basically

on probation of sorts. I have to stay completely away from the family or I will be suspended."

She was relieved to hear that. "Why would you do something so crazy?"

He sighed. "That's the complex part of the story, so maybe it should wait until later. How about I give you the fifty-cent tour of the place first?"

She would rather have heard the details of his day but resisted the urge to push. They had plenty of time to get into it later.

"I'd love a tour." She grinned. "I've been wanting to see what your place looks like."

He flashed her one of those charming smiles. "Well, now you'll get your chance. But try to contain yourself. You're already looking at about sixty percent of my apartment from where you're standing."

Lana waved a hand. "I've been living in a college apartment for the past five years. This place is the Taj Mahal in comparison."

Max laughed and offered his arm to escort her. "If your standards are really that low, this might just work out after all."

Lana linked her arm with his and let him lead her into the small eat-in kitchen that was connected to the living room. Painted the same off-white color, it made the transition seamless and the apartment seem bigger than it was.

"As you can see, this is the kitchen," Max said as they walked around the peninsula separating the two rooms. "Better known as the place where all the microwavable magic happens."

Lana laughed. "You're kidding, right? You might

have forgotten, but I've been close enough to those abs of yours to know you don't eat junk food all the time."

He gave her a heated look. "Oh, I haven't forgotten how close you've been to my abs. But in this case, I'm being completely honest."

Before Lana could call him on the obvious lie, he walked over and opened a couple of the upper cabinet doors, revealing an endless collection of chips, pretzels, cookies, boxed dinners, and canned food—of the non-fruit and -veggie variety. But on the bright side, he was obviously getting his protein, since it looked like he had enough peanut butter to feed an army. It appeared to be his favorite food.

"Not a big fan of fruits and veggies, huh?"

He looked hurt. "I looked it up, and corn can be considered either a fruit or a vegetable, depending on who you ask. So, as you can see, I have bags and bags of fruits and veggies."

Lana raised up on her toes to get a better look. "Those are Fritos."

"Which are made of corn," he said smugly. "So I'm covered."

"I stand corrected," she agreed, since he obviously already had this all thought out. "At least you don't have pizza boxes stacked up to the ceiling."

Max grinned and opened the fridge, displaying four Pizza Hut boxes stuffed in there so tightly Lana wasn't sure if they'd ever come out.

"I prefer my pizza cold," he said.

She threw up her arms in surrender. "Of course you do."

"While we're talking about food, have you eaten

yet?" he asked. "I'm sure I can find something to your
vegetarian tastes, even in my limited pantry."

His offer reminded her that she hadn't eaten since
lunch and definitely could, even if it meant breaking into
one of his cardboard-box dinners.

"I wouldn't mind eating, but after you've finished
showing me around," she told him.

"That should only take another five minutes."

With that, Max led her out of the kitchen and back
into the living room. They slowed long enough for her
to take in the monster-sized TV and video game station,
which in her experience was mandatory for all single
guys. But he also seemed to have what looked to be a
pretty good selection of DVD and Blu-ray movies in a
bookcase off to the side.

From there, they walked down a short hallway with
a bathroom on the right, a larger-than-average bedroom
on the left, and a nice walk-in closet in the middle. Max
might have a bachelor TV and game station out in the
living room, but his bedroom was surprisingly nicely
decorated, painted in subdued tones of olive green and
earthy brown. Even the blankets on the bed had a warm
tan hue that went perfectly with everything else. Along
with the casual furniture, the colors made for a relaxing
ambience. She couldn't help noticing that his bed, with
its thick comforter and plump, fluffy pillows, was big
enough to wrestle on—at least the kind of wrestling she
had in mind.

Lana quickly forced her thoughts in a different direction. If she didn't, it was possible they might not make
it out of this room for a while.

As they turned to head back into the living room, a

framed photo on the tall dresser caught her attention. In it, a teenage boy who looked a lot like Max had his arm around the shoulders of a younger girl with the same dark hair and charming smile.

"Is that you in this picture or your brother?" she asked, sure it had to be Max even though the boy in the photo was so much smaller than he was.

Max grinned. "That's me. And I know what you're thinking, but I was only seventeen in that picture and just starting my growth spurt."

"Is the girl your sister?" she asked softly, remembering what he'd said the other night about his family not getting out of the crappy place where they used to live.

The smile disappeared, his face turning serious. "Yeah, that's Sarah. She's thirteen in this picture. It's the last photo I have of her. She died a little while after her fourteenth birthday."

"I'm sorry," she said. "What happened?"

The question was out of her mouth before she could stop it, but the moment she saw the pain in his eyes, she realized she should never have gone there.

She put a gentle hand on his shoulder. "Hey, I'm not pushing or anything."

"I know." His mouth curved into a sad smile. "It's just that I've gone out of my way to avoid talking about the subject for so long, hoping the memories would go away, that it's hard to open up about it. But after the day I've had, maybe it's better if I finally do. And if I'm going to tell anyone the details about what happened to my sister—to my family—I want it to be you."

Lana had a sudden, unsettling thought about the connection between his sister's death and the bad day he'd had. She quickly pushed it aside for the moment though and focused on the feeling that came over her at his words. Here was a guy she'd recently started seeing telling her he felt comfortable enough with her to share something this incredibly private and personal. It was a powerful admission—and a little overwhelming. Once again, she was awestruck by how lucky she was to have stumbled across Max. Men this amazing didn't come around very often. Tears stung her eyes and she quickly blinked them away before he could see.

"I'm glad you feel that way. How about we talk over dinner?" She smiled up at him. "Assuming we can find something out there to eat."

Max laughed and took her hand. "I'm sure we can. Come on."

That *something* turned out to be peanut butter and jelly sandwiches, and truthfully, she was thrilled. Lana hadn't eaten a PB&J since she was a kid, and as she and Max stood side-by-side at his kitchen counter spreading spoonfuls of creamy goodness over toasted wheat bread, she had the feeling maybe she'd been missing out.

Max drowned several of his sandwiches in grape jelly before holding the plastic bottle out to her with a questioning look. She reached out and took it, figuring she'd better do it herself or risk overdosing on sugar from too much jelly.

While she did that, Max poured two big glasses of milk; then they carried everything over to the small table. She looked down at her two sandwiches, then at the big stack on Max's plate. There was no way he could possibly eat like this all the time, not with the way he looked. Then again, maybe he had the same fast metabolism she did.

"My dad was always a mean SOB," Max said without prompting after he'd washed down a big bite of his first sandwich. "He worked for a bookmaker off the main strip, intimidating people who were late paying off their gambling debts, breaking fingers and kneecaps when it was necessary."

His words confirmed what she'd been thinking back in his bedroom, and Lana set her sandwich down, unable to eat. "Did he abuse you and your sister?"

Max took another bite of his sandwich, then another, seeming to take refuge in the repeated motion. "Yeah," he said after a little while. "He abused Mom, too. I'd like to think he didn't treat her like that from the beginning, but from as early as I can remember, he was always taking his problems out on us."

"Didn't anyone ever call the police?" she asked. "Or try to stop him?"

Max shrugged. "Mom would never say anything, and my sister and I assumed getting smacked around was the way it was supposed to be, so we never said anything, either. I doubt anything would have changed if we had."

"What finally happened?"

Max took a big gulp of milk before continuing. "I had just graduated from high school and came home from my job at the convenience store to find Dad in one of his moods. Things went the way they normally did, and he ended up punching me. Sarah tried to get involved, and that only made him madder. I don't know what came over me, but I couldn't let him hit her again, so I fought back. In all the time he'd beaten us, I'd never fought back. Never."

Max looked past her, staring blankly at something behind her, lost in old memories. "I beat him up pretty good and embarrassed him in front of my mom and sister, something he didn't take very well. While I was checking to see how badly Sarah was hurt, Dad went into his bedroom and came back with his gun. He didn't say a word. He just started shooting."

Lana had known the story didn't have a happily ever after, but this was worse than she'd imagined. "He shot your sister?"

Max looked at her, his eyes filled with pain. "Yeah. And me, too. He hit me twice before I lunged at him. I knew I was done the moment the first round hit me in the stomach, but I kept fighting, hoping to get the weapon away from him before he got around to shooting my sister, too. But he kept pulling the trigger. Sarah was hit in the head and died immediately. As my old man and I struggled for the weapon, it went off, killing him, too."

Max said the words quickly, barely any inflection in his voice, and she could tell it had taken a monumental effort for him to say them.

She blinked back tears. "What about your mom? Was she okay?"

Max shook his head. "I was hurt pretty bad, and the doctors told her I probably wouldn't make it. My dad and my sister were already dead, and I guess that was too much for her to bear. She took a handful of sleeping pills from the bottle she had in her purse, then went into a bathroom, dozed off, and never woke up."

Finished with his story, Max turned his attention to

his sandwiches again, slowly eating the rest of them. Even though she didn't feel like it, Lana ate, too.

"Thank you for telling me all that," she said when she was done. "I know it wasn't easy, but I think I understand now why you did what you did today."

He snorted. "For all the good it did. I only ended up making it worse for those kids the same way I made it worse for Sarah."

"None of this is your fault." She reached across the table to take his hand. "Back then, you were a kid taking on an adult with a gun. Now, you're a cop following the law the best way you can. You couldn't have done anything different in either case. You know that, right?"

He shrugged. "In my head, I know that. But sometimes, late at night, when I think about my sister, I wonder if things would have turned out differently if I hadn't fought back, hadn't punched my dad. What if I had turned and shielded my sister's body with mine instead of trying to get the gun away from him? Even today, I wonder if things would have turned out better if I'd slowed down long enough to think about bringing some backup, or maybe looked in a window before shoving open that door. Maybe I would have seen enough to get the man arrested."

She squeezed his hand. "Max, trust me when I tell you this. You can replay these situations in your head a hundred times, thinking about all the things you could have done differently. But all that's going to do is twist your insides into knots and make you doubt every decision you've ever made. It won't help anything, and it certainly won't change the past."

Max regarded her thoughtfully. "Something tells me you're speaking from personal experience."

"Yeah, I guess I am," she admitted. "Like you, it's not something I talk about very much."

"I get that." He nodded. "I'm not pushing, but if you want to talk about it, I'm all ears."

For the first time in her life, she actually *did* feel like talking to someone about it. Maybe because something told her that Max would be able to understand more than most other people.

"You know, I think I would," she said. "If you can tell me your deepest, darkest secrets, there's no reason I can't do the same."

He glanced down at their empty plates. "You want to get a refill on our drinks and move this conversation into the living room?"

They cleared the table, then grabbed two diet Cokes and took a seat on the couch. She kicked off her shoes and tucked her feet under her, sipping her soda slowly as she considered where to start her story. She hadn't talked to a soul about this stuff since she was a teenager, and even then, most of the conversations had been with a therapist who'd been helping her put everything behind her.

Finally, she took a cue from Max and decided the best way to do this was to jump in headfirst.

"When I was sixteen, I was in a bad car wreck with two of my best friends from high school, Shari and Viola," she said quietly. "They didn't make it, and I barely survived. For years, I blamed myself for their deaths."

"I'm sorry about your friends," Max said. "But how could you blame yourself for what happened? You weren't driving, were you?"

She shook her head. "No, I wasn't driving. Shari was. I blamed myself for the accident because it was my fault we were out on the road that night."

"What do you mean?" he asked, lifting his arm to rest it on the back of the couch.

Lana scooted closer, resting her head on his chest as she remembered how that night had changed her life.

"It was rainy and foggy, which made it hard to see," she explained. "We were at the movies and only realized how bad the weather had gotten when we came out. We should have headed straight home, but we'd planned to get something to eat after the movie and were too young and stubborn to change our minds. We passed half a dozen places we could have stopped at to grab a quick bite, but I really wanted to go to this particular drive-in because they had the best tater tots in the world. I should have realized Shari wasn't comfortable driving in bad weather, but I was so busy daydreaming about those stupid tater tots that I didn't slow down to think about how stupid we were being."

"What happened?" Max asked softly.

Tears welled in her as she thought about those last seconds before the wreck. The music playing on the radio, Shari and Viola singing along in the front seat, her laughing like crazy in the back. Then suddenly, headlights were coming right at them, and Viola was screaming.

She hadn't thought about the accident itself in a long time, and reliving the moment had her heart racing. Strangely, it also made her gums and fingertips tingle like they had today during her encounter with the cop from Central.

She pushed those thoughts aside and instead forced

herself to get the words out that needed to be said—before she chickened out completely.

"We were on Highway 12 when another car veered into our lane." She closed her eyes and listened to Max's steady heartbeat under her ear. "I found out much later that the guy driving had been drinking, but in that moment, everything was a blur. One second, we were all laughing, and the next, all I could hear were the sounds of crushing metal and breaking glass."

She took a deep breath and fought down the tears. "We all survived to make it to the hospital, but Shari and Viola didn't live through the night. I was in a coma and no one expected me to make it, either. Mom and Dad said the doctors were amazing, never giving up on me through one procedure after another. But while they thought I might live, none of them expected I'd regain full use of my body or my mental capacity."

"How long were you in a coma?" Max asked.

"Over a week," she said. "The doctors had intended to leave me under for longer, but I came out of it on my own."

"How long did you stay in the hospital after that?" Max asked.

"Only another day or two. Mom and Dad arranged for my doctor to take care of me at home. It probably cost a ton of money, but they'd been so freaked seeing me in the hospital that they got me out of there the first chance they could. I think even the doctors were stunned by how quickly I recovered. Some of them called it a miracle, but I think it was a matter of the right procedures at the right time."

"Is that why you went into the pharmacology side

of organic chemistry?" he asked. "Because of what the doctors were able to do for you?"

She nodded against his chest. "Uh-huh. They were working on the fly, giving me different drugs to help my body recover from the severe trauma I'd sustained. I wouldn't be alive if it hadn't been for that. But they didn't have anything that could help Shari and Viola. That's why I went the direction I did in college, in the hope that maybe someday I could help create medicines that would allow patients like Shari and Viola to survive until their bodies can heal some of the damage, like mine did."

Max slipped his arm off the back of the couch, curving it around her. "You said you spent years blaming yourself for Shari and Viola's deaths. What helped you get past it?"

"Therapy mostly," she said. "I was a complete mess for months after my parents brought me home. I didn't even leave the house. Like you, I spent a lot of time wondering how things would have turned out if I'd done things differently—if I'd suggested we sit in the parking lot of the movie theater until the storm passed or told Shari to stop at the first restaurant we saw instead of insisting we go somewhere else. But after a lot of sessions with a really good psychologist, the raw edges finally dulled somewhat, and I was able to understand that playing what-if games would never change what happened. It would just keep me locked in the past."

"Sounds like that psychologist really helped you," Max observed.

"She did," Lana agreed. "Maybe you should consider spending some time talking to one yourself. I'm sure the DPD has some on call that could help you."

Max chuckled. "I know this sounds incredibly guy-like, but I can't see myself sitting down and talking about my feelings with a complete stranger. I'd rather talk to you."

She smiled as she leaned there against his powerful chest. "Anytime you want to talk, I'm here to listen."

"Might be a bit tough to have deep, meaningful conversations if you end up taking a job in France," he pointed out.

She absently ran a finger up and down T-shirt-covered abs. "I think I'm going to be sticking much closer to home than I originally thought."

"Oh really? What changed your mind?"

Lana laughed softly as she pushed away from Max's chest to look at him. "I think you already know."

Max dipped his head to give her a quick, teasing kiss. "I guess I do. In fact, I've felt this thing building between us from the moment we met. I just wasn't sure you felt the same thing."

Lana traced a finger along his jawline, loving the scruff there. "Of course I've felt it. Are you that oblivious?"

He shrugged. "Well, yeah, I'm a guy. Being oblivious is what we do best."

She laughed. "Well, Mr. Oblivious, I'll spell it out for you. Yes, I realize there's something special happening between us. We've just met and I already find myself trusting you more than anyone I've ever known."

He regarded her thoughtfully. "Kind of crazy, isn't it? How fast this is happening, I mean."

"Maybe," she agreed. "But when it's right, it's right. Mom was telling me today that she and Dad fell for each other fast, too, so maybe it runs in my family or something. Whatever the reason, I find myself wanting to spend every waking hour with you, losing myself in your arms and kissing you. I'm smart enough to recognize that feelings like this don't come around very often, and I'd be crazy to walk away from them just for a job. I can work anywhere."

Max tugged her closer, dragging her up until she was straddling his lap. Having her knees on either side of his hips, the crotch of her jeans pressing down on that most wonderful part of his body, seemed like the perfect place to be.

"Losing yourself in my arms?" he asked in a husky voice. "I like the sound of that."

Leaning in, he kissed her again, more slowly this time, his tongue slipping between her lips to tease hers. She wiggled a little higher on his hips, sighing against his mouth as she felt his cock slowly harden in his jeans. She rocked back and forth on his hard-on, loving both the way it felt and the fact that she could get him so aroused so quickly. When she finally pulled her mouth away, gasping for breath and almost dizzy from his intoxicating taste, his cock was hard as a rock, straining to get out.

"I guess you're not the only one who likes the sound of that," she murmured. "Someone else down there seems to like it, too."

Max chuckled. "Yeah, he's thrilled. I'm pretty happy myself—not just at how good it feels to have you sitting on my lap like this, either. Your offer to be there when I need someone to talk to means a lot."

"I'm glad. And I'm serious about that. I'm good at listening, and after spending so much time on my therapist's couch, I picked up all the best lines."

His hands slipped down to her butt, resting there as she continued to gently move on his lap. "And what kinds of lines are you thinking about using on me?"

She smiled as the bulge in his jeans found the absolutely perfect position, making heat pool between her legs.

"Well, there's my personal favorite," she said as she gave him an extra grind. "How does that make you feel?"

His hands squeezed her ass tighter, pulling her down even harder on his cock and making her clit tingle. "I think that's obvious."

"Maybe," she agreed. "But then there's the big follow-up to that standard question: Where do you think that feeling is coming from?"

He lifted a brow. "Your crotch grinding on my hard-on?"

She shrugged. "Possibly. But I think you might be holding back on me. I think you should tell me how you really feel."

"I want to rip your clothes off and eat you up like a Snickers because I know you'll be oh so satisfying?"

"Hmm." She had to work hard to keep a smile off her face as she placed one finger on her chin and gave him a serious look. "I think we might be onto something here. Let's focus on the emotion you're feeling right this second. Where do you see this all going?"

"My bedroom?" he responded immediately, his hands moving up to the bottom of her tank top and sliding underneath to tease the sensitive skin of her sides with his fingers.

"That certainly seems like a reasonable direction to go at this point," she said, her body starting to tremble as his hands worked higher, shoving her shirt up. "But I think you might be staying too close to your comfort zone. Where else might you take this if you wanted to really stretch yourself?"

"The kitchen table sounds good about now," Max said.

A low, rumbling sound almost like a growl coming from his throat, he yanked her shirt up and over her head. Lana had no choice but to lift her arms and let him, or he probably would have ripped her top off just like he'd suggested earlier. The sexy sound he'd made combined with the alpha-male way he pulled her shirt off and tossed it across the room was a serious turn-on. She couldn't help but wonder where this was heading.

Max leaned forward to kiss and nibble her bare neck and shoulder, and she shivered even more when she felt his sharp teeth nick her. She'd never been that kind of naughty before.

"Oh yes, I think we've had a breakthrough. We should definitely keep moving down this path," Lana murmured breathlessly.

"That was kind of what I had in mind," he muttered against her neck, not slowing down for a moment.

Lana was so lost in the sensations of his lips and hands moving across her body she missed Max slipping her bra off until his warm mouth fastened on one of her nipples, making her moan out loud. Mmm, that felt so good. He went back and forth between each sensitive peak, cupping and squeezing her breasts in his big hands. She could let him do this to her all night.

She hadn't been with a lot of guys, but she'd been with enough to realize Max was getting her hotter than she'd ever been. She wasn't even naked yet and her clit was tingling so much she thought she might orgasm from grinding on his lap. It had never been like that for her before, and she got the feeling it was only getting started.

When Max pulled his mouth away from her nipples, stood up with her in his arms, and headed for the bedroom, Lana didn't complain. She did, however, remember one very important detail.

"Please tell me you have condoms," she begged as she wrapped her arms and legs around him and held on tightly.

He gave her a look but kept walking down the hall. "I'm hoping that isn't something your psychologist said to you at some point?"

She laughed. "No, that never came up in conversation. But it is a serious question. You do have protection, right? Not that there isn't other stuff we could do, but…"

"While I'm extremely interested in all that *other stuff* you mentioned, that's not going to be necessary. I have protection," he said softly, placing her gently on the bed. "But before we get to any of that, we need to get you naked."

Lana was more than ready to race Max to see who could get their clothes off first, but he didn't give her a chance. One second, she was sitting on the edge of his bed; the next, her feet were in the air when he grabbed the bottom of her jeans and yanked. She quickly undid her belt and the top few buttons at her waist so he didn't lift her right off the bed. The whole thing was so seriously sexy she swore a little growl escaped her throat. Max had her so hot she wasn't even acting like herself. At this rate, who knew how wild she'd get?

She watched as her jeans sailed across the room to smack against a wall, leaving her lying on his bed in nothing but her panties. She would have reached down to wiggle them off, but a single look from him froze her. Something told her he wanted to take care of that little scrap of clothing himself. She lay back on her elbows, locking eyes with him as he moved toward her. He looked like a jungle predator, all muscular grace and barely contained hunger.

She expected him to take his clothes off, too. It would only be fair. But as he caught her ankle in his hand and kissed his way along her leg, she realized he wasn't worried about being fair right now. He seemed more interested in eating her up—like a Snickers.

Yay for Snickers!

Max's warm mouth moved lower and lower, kissing and licking every inch of the way. In between the gentle, teasing kisses, he slipped in a little nip here and there. Why did she like that so much?

When he reached her inner thighs, he slowed even more, nearly driving her insane as his mouth inched closer to her panty-covered pussy. She was so excited she was throbbing down there. She knew she was wet and wondered if the moisture was soaking all the way through the material. If so, Max would certainly be able to see it, since he was only inches away.

He pushed her thighs wide, giving himself room to work. She was waiting for him to pull her underwear aside when she heard a tearing sound. She looked down just in time to see the remnants of her panties flying through the air. In the quick glimpse she had of them, it looked like they'd gone through a shredder.

She was about to point out that little piece of material was more expensive than it looked. But she never got the words out because right then, Max's mouth came down on her pussy.

There wasn't a whole lot of teasing buildup. He put his mouth on her and made quick, little circles with his tongue. The sensation was out of this world.

She buried her fingers in his spiky hair, not because she wanted to hold him in position—it was obvious he wasn't going anywhere—but so she'd have something to hold on to and wouldn't float off into space.

Her orgasm started as a featherlight tingle, but it came on fast after that, charging at her like a bull. She didn't bother trying to get out of the way, but simply threw back her head and screamed.

She'd had good orgasms before, but this one was different. It wasn't just focused in that familiar area between her legs nor did it simply flutter outward and make her heart beat faster. This one enveloped her completely, lightning and tingles rippling out to make her whole body throb in time with the pulsing between her legs. Even her teeth felt like they were on fire, and when she clamped down on her lip in an attempt to silence the worst of her screams, she was sure she bit the crap out of herself.

When Max pulled his mouth away, she murmured a complaint, but it was a halfhearted one since the spasms were still tearing through her body, even though he was no longer touching her. Now that was the sign of a great orgasm—it kept going even after the sex was over.

But the sex wasn't over—something Lana figured out when Max flipped her over on her hands and knees like she was some kind of rag-doll sex toy.

Actually, being a rag-doll sex toy sounded pretty damn good.

Lana snuck a few fingers down to help keep the orgasm tremors going as she looked over her shoulder and caught sight of Max's clothes flying off him. Superman in a phone booth was a snail compared to him. He tore his shirt off so fast he ripped it in two.

Oh yeah, he was as hunky as her earlier manual explorations had suggested. Strong shoulders, a chest and arms that showed why he'd been able to carry her effortlessly, ripped abs with those *V*-shaped hip flexors that disappeared into his jeans in a blatant invitation to look down and see what else he had to offer.

She was just admiring the wolf head tattoo with the word *SWAT* above it on his pec when he stripped off his jeans, displaying legs so muscular and tasty looking she had a scary strong desire to roll off the bed and sink her teeth into them. When had she gotten so oral? She'd always been a fan of it, but not the biting part. Max was bringing out a side of her she'd never had a chance to explore.

Then Lana got a good look at the hard shaft jutting emphatically from between his legs, and oral sex took on a whole new meaning. She needed him. In her mouth. Now.

But as she was about to leap at him, Max pulled a condom from a box in the nightstand and turned back for the bed. He let out a low growl when he saw she'd moved from the position he'd left her and very quickly demonstrated he had no problem spinning her right back around.

Head down, butt up. Go, caveman!

She had no idea how he was able to get the condom on while at the same time putting her exactly where he wanted. But thankfully, he had this particular style of multitasking down pat, and it couldn't have been more than a second or two before he was lining himself up with her very ready opening and sliding his thick cock inside her.

Lana moaned, burying her face into those soft, earth-toned blankets and giving herself over to the sensation of being filled up. His big hands came down and got a firm hold on her hips, and then the real pleasure started as he pulled almost all the way out and immediately slid back in.

"Yes!" she breathed, only slightly surprised when the sound came out more growl than moan. Max was definitely bringing out the animal in her.

She tried to look over her shoulder, wanting to watch Max as he took her this way, wanting to see his gorgeous face and know she was making him feel just as good as he was making her feel. But turning around to watch became impossible as Max gripped her hips hard and began to pound into her. The feel of his hard cock burying itself deep inside her over and over, his hips slapping against her ass rhythmically with every thrust, his hands taking control of her waist and moving her at an urgent, mind-blowing pace was all too much for her. She had no control over her body—certainly not enough to be able to look back at him. It was all she could do to not turn into a puddle of Jell-O right there on the bed.

Instead, she buried her face and fingernails into the blanket and held on for dear life as Max made her feel things she'd only dreamed of. She knew she was making a lot of noise, but she couldn't stop herself. It felt too amazing.

At some point, she bit down on the blanket. Of course

she was. It was all part of her new biting obsession apparently. But even as good as it felt to sink her teeth deep into the soft material, almost slicing right through it, Lana instinctively knew she would have preferred to have something else in her mouth.

The image of sinking her teeth into Max's strong shoulder muscles hit her at the same moment he slammed into her so deep stars exploded in her head.

She came.

It wasn't one of those tame, playful orgasms she'd experienced dozens of times before. It wasn't even one of those rare, powerful moments of pleasure she'd been lucky enough to have when everything — man, position, speed, size, ambience — had all come together just right. No, this was something completely different. An orgasm so overwhelming Lana was sure she'd fly apart into a million pieces. It started deep inside her, right where Max was thrusting, then spread out until it consumed her.

She screamed, moaned, growled, and clawed at the bed like a crazy animal.

In a way that didn't make a lot of sense, she knew when Max came. She just felt it inside her. Not quite in the same place where her orgasm had started, but close. He wasn't coming inside her because he was wearing a condom, but he was coming with her and that felt equally amazing.

When the waves of pleasure receded, Lana found herself lying on her stomach, Max's heavy weight smooshing her comfortably into the bed. His face was in the crook of her neck and shoulder, his teeth gently grazing her skin. It was even possible he may have bitten her, but she couldn't find it in her to care. She was too busy thinking about the way he was still wedged firmly inside her, making her spasm and clench in the most delightful way possible. Okay, that was frigging awesome.

Max must have thought he was putting too much weight on her, because his mouth came away from her neck and she felt him start to lift up. She reached back and got her fingers in his hair, tugging him back.

"Don't you dare move," she whispered. "I want you right there for the rest of the night."

"I'm not too heavy for you?" Max asked, his breath in her ear as he settled back down on top of her.

"Never," she said.

She was serious. She was more than ready to stay like this the rest of the night. This was perfect. In the very core of her being, she knew that. This man, in this moment? It was exactly where she was supposed to be.

But then a thought struck her, making her turn her head a little and look at him. "Do you mind if I stay? I know you have to get up early for work tomorrow."

He chuckled. "Of course I want you to stay. Tomorrow will take care of itself. Right now, all I want to think about is you, here, lost in my arms."

"Nice answer," she murmured.

But as good as it felt to have Max on her this way, at some point he had to hop off to clean up. The absence of his body heat left her feeling cold and she climbed under the blankets as he disappeared into the bathroom.

"You sure you don't mind me spending the night?" she called out. "I'm worried you won't be able to get any rest if I'm here."

Max flipped off the light in the hallway, standing

in the bedroom doorway looking gloriously yummy and hard.

"Who the heck said anything about getting any rest tonight?" he whispered as he turned off the light in the bedroom, then stopped at the night table for another condom. "The only way either one of us will be getting any sleep tonight is if we pass out from exhaustion."

She laughed and pulled back the blanket, making room for him. "Well, I'm not worried about that myself. Like I told you, I can stay awake for days if I really need to cram."

"I guess we'll see about that," Max said as he pulled her on top of him.

She shivered as his hard-on brushed her leg. She couldn't believe she was ready to go again, but she was. Now this was the kind of all-nighter she could enjoy.

Max's eyes caught the glow of the street lamp coming in through the window, reflecting it back with a yellow flash in the coolest way ever. Seemed like he was stoked at the idea of an all-nighter, too.

Chapter 7

"DAMN, MAX. WHERE THE HELL IS YOUR HEAD RIGHT NOW?" Xander growled at him. "Something tells me you completely missed the point of this particular exercise."

Max knelt in the sand-filled pit at the SWAT compound, breathing hard as sweat mixed with the dirt and paintball splats along his bare chest to create little trails of messy color down his body. While he certainly hadn't been the first one to cross the finish line, he'd hadn't been that far back in the crowd—definitely not enough to gain him this kind of ire from his squad leader.

This morning's physical training exercise was called Rescue, and it was simple. The goal was for select members of the Pack to race through the compound's obstacle course and retrieve their "rescue victim" from one of the training buildings at the far end of the course. Next, they were supposed to get their victims back through the obstacles and deliver them safe and sound at the finish line marked by the sandpit. The body dummies being used as the victims were heavy, but for the most part, it was a piece of cake.

Of course, since Cooper had come up with this exercise, there was one small detail that made it harder. Xander and the other squad leader, Mike Taylor, were positioned along the course with paintball guns. If you got hit with a paintball, it wasn't a big deal, but if your victim took a round instead, that meant you had to go back to the start of the course and do it again. Oh, and there was also the thing that said each werewolf could do anything within the rules to ensure that no one finished in front of them. Of course, there weren't any rules.

He'd seen several pack mates take a tumble off the course as their teammates tripped them or threw things at them. He'd even caught sight of Brooks nailing Becker in the back of his head with his body dummy and pitching the other werewolf off a twenty-foot-high tower.

Max had to admit he'd been somewhat distracted while running the course. He'd spent the night making love to his soul mate, after all. But he'd still been the fourth werewolf across the finish line, behind Brooks, Cooper, and Khaki. Becker would probably have won since he was too fast to catch in most games, which was why Brooks had beaned him with the dummy. They might have to get an official ruling on the legality of throwing your own victim. Cooper said there weren't any rules, but it didn't make sense to use the people you were trying to rescue as a weapon.

Regardless, Max had done well, considering the rest of their teammates were out on the course, and he was sure his victim had never gotten hit with a paintball.

"What are you talking about?" he asked Xander.

Xander pointed at the body dummy Max had used. "That's what I'm talking about."

Max looked down, wondering if maybe he'd missed a paint splat on some part of the dummy he hadn't noticed when he saw that the dummy's head was missing. Huh. How had that happened?

"You didn't notice your victim's head getting caught in the lines on the rope bridge?" Xander demanded.

"Or feel that slight bit of resistance as the head got ripped off?"

All Max could do was shrug. "I guess I'm a bit distracted."

Xander shook his head. "I don't have to ask what that distraction might be since we can smell your new soul mate all over you. Congratulations."

Max tried to look properly chagrined but failed. "Do you want me to run through the course again?"

"With a headless dummy? Why bother?" Xander quipped. "Hit the benches with Khaki, Cooper, and Brooks."

Max left his headless dummy where it was, hoping Gage didn't make him pay for it, and followed his teammates over to the benches by the volleyball course to watch the rest of the PT session. Kari and Grace were sitting there, watching as the SWAT alphas ran around with their shirts off getting all sweaty and dirty. The two betas didn't seem to mind the sweat—or the dirt.

"Where's your son?" Khaki asked Grace as she sat beside the woman.

The younger of the two beta werewolves smiled. "On his way to school. He's not thrilled about going, but I think it's important for him to get some structure now that we're settled. Of course, that means I now have nothing to do all morning but sit out here and watch muscular men run around and glisten."

Khaki laughed. "You guys want to take part in the PT session? I'm sure Mike and Xander would happily show you how to shoot a paintball gun."

The two women exchanged looks.

"You don't think your alphas would mind getting shot at by two betas?" Kari asked, clearly tempted.

"Nah," Cooper said. "But if you're worried about it, you could always promise to wipe off any paint splats you manage to land."

The two women looked at each other again.

"I'm in!" they both said at the same time, hopping off the benches.

"Maybe the guy with the British accent will let me help him clean up even if I don't hit him," Grace said as they headed for the SWAT squad leaders. "I'm sure I can get to all those hard-to-reach places for him."

Kari laughed, even though Max didn't think the younger beta was kidding.

While Cooper, Khaki, and Brooks watched the rest of the PT session, Max leaned back and zoned out, lost in thought about Lana and the Wallace kids.

He'd driven past the house on Park Lane this morning, even though he knew he was supposed to stay away. But that was hard to do. Fortunately, he hadn't heard anything coming from inside that made him think there was a problem, but then again, it had only been five thirty in the morning. He'd take a victory where he could get it, he guessed.

He yawned. He was tired, but it was a good tired—the kind that comes from a long night of awesome sex. It had been better than amazing, and if he had any lingering doubts that Lana was *The One* for him, they were gone now. He was sure Lana felt the same way. After everything they'd talked about and the way she'd responded last night, Max couldn't deny the obvious. Lana wasn't simply hiding her nature. She really didn't know she was a werewolf.

Max hadn't had the chance to talk to Gage about it yet, but since only a traumatic event could flip the gene that turned a person into a werewolf, he was sure the car wreck Lana had been in was the event that had both changed her and stunted her development as a werewolf at the same time. He'd never heard of a werewolf going into a coma for as long as she had, and his mind whirled at the possibilities. Did she only partially turn because she'd been sixteen years old at the time, or had the drugs they'd given her after the accident somehow inhibited her initial transformation, allowing her to survive the wreck that had killed her friends but preventing her from healing herself as fast as other werewolves did?

"I'm heading in to shower before everyone else finishes," Khaki announced, interrupting his daydreams as she stood and headed for the admin building.

"I think she did that so you could talk freely," Cooper said, glancing at Max. "Khaki's nice that way."

He must have missed a vital part of the conversation. "Talk freely about what?"

Cooper and Brooks looked at him like he was a moron.

"Lana, of course," Cooper said. "It's obvious she has your head spinning. Even if you hadn't ripped that dummy's head off, Xander would probably have put you on the bench just to keep you from walking yourself off the top of one of the bigger obstacles out there on the course."

Max opened his mouth to complain, but Brooks interrupted him. "And we know it's not only Lana that has you tied up in knots. That stuff with the Wallace kids is messing you up, too. Look me in the face and tell me you haven't driven by there at least once or twice in the past twenty-four hours."

Max didn't bother to deny either accusation. "Okay, so yeah, both those things are on my mind right now. It doesn't mean I can't do my job."

"We never said differently." Brooks frowned. "It's just that you're distracted. It's understandable. Finding *The One* for you is reason enough to be more than a little preoccupied."

Cooper snorted. "When I met Everly, it was like my head turned to mush. I can't even count the number of bad decisions I made. So if being with Lana has you spinning right now, don't feel bad. You're in good company."

"Lana and I are doing great," Max admitted. "I mean, there's hardly any stress at all. Sure, there's the thing with her not knowing she's a werewolf, but that's not too bad. And then there's my control issues."

"What control issues?" Brooks asked. "You talking about something beyond occasionally flashing your fangs and claws?"

Max looked around, hoping the rest of the Pack was too intent on their game to hear any of this. "To tell the truth, my control has gotten worse since getting involved with Lana—and this domestic violence case. First, I just about choked Wallace to death. Then, I almost shifted in front of Lana last night when we were making love."

"Choking Wallace I get," Cooper said. "What do you mean, you almost shifted in front of Lana?"

Max shrugged. "Just that. I went full-on fangs and claws as we were getting busy. We had to do it doggy style just so she wouldn't see—not that doggy style with Lana isn't spectacular, but still."

Cooper made a face. "Okay, that's a bit of visual imagery I could definitely have done without."

Brooks chuckled. "Where do you think this sudden lack of control is coming from? Is it simply the fact that Lana is *The One* for you or because she's a werewolf, too, and that's ramping up the pheromones? Then again, maybe it's related to your own history with domestic violence. Could all this stuff with the Wallace kids have brought some deep-seated issues bubbling back to the surface?"

Max didn't have a clue, and he wasn't keen on digging too deeply into some of those areas to figure it out. "I don't know. It could be all of the above—or none of them. All I can say for sure is that I almost frigging bit Lana last night. I can't keep doing that."

Brooks regarded him thoughtfully. "Have you ever considered talking to a professional about this, maybe the psychologist the DPD sent Cooper to—Hadley Delacroix?"

Max gaped. "Are you serious? What am I going to tell her, that I grow fangs and claws every time I start to make out with my girlfriend? Somehow I don't see that working out."

Brooks shrugged. "She seems to have helped Cooper a lot. He's not nearly as psycho as he used to be."

Max didn't know about that. Cooper still seemed pretty psychotic to him most of the time.

"Brooks might be onto something," Cooper said. "I still stop in to see her now and then when I need to talk. I could probably get her to see you, too, just to let you try it out. Hell, if we can get enough of the Pack to go with us, she might give us a bulk discount."

Fortunately, Max didn't have to reply because Gage came out of the admin building.

"We got a call, Sarge?" Max asked, hopping up from the bench.

"Sort of." Gage grimaced. "Brooks, take Max and head out to that industrial loft in Deep Ellum we set up for our visiting werewolves. I think we might have a problem brewing out there."

Brooks grunted and got to his feet. "This has the potential to be interesting."

Interesting. That probably wasn't the term Max would have used.

—◦—

Lana rang the doorbell, hoping Brandy and Miriam were home. She sagged with relief when it opened. A pajama-clad Brandy stood in the doorway regarding her sleepily, a pair of pink fuzzy slippers on her feet.

"I feel like crap, but you look like crap," Brandy said, motioning her in. "Bad night?"

"Actually, the best night ever," Lana said, keeping her voice down in case Miriam was still sleeping.

Brandy must have caught on because she shook her head. "Miriam went in early. One of the other nurses got sick and she's covering for her in the ER."

Lana headed straight for Brandy's coffeemaker, thrilled to find the pot full and steaming away merrily. She grabbed two mugs out of the cabinet and fixed them both a strong cup of liquid sunshine.

"I stayed at Max's place last night," she said casually as she added just enough milk to keep the coffee from melting the inside of the mug. She never used to drink much coffee. The caffeine didn't do a damn thing for her, but the act of holding a steaming cup of coffee always relaxed her. Plus, she simply liked the flavor, so she'd gotten into the habit.

She turned to see Brandy sitting at the kitchen table, a big smile on her face. "Were you two getting to know each other in the friendly manner or the biblical one?"

Lana handed Brandy one of the mugs, then sat across from her friend. She was having a hard time keeping the smile off her face as she remembered everything she'd done with Max last night. "Oh, definitely the biblical one."

"And?" Brandy asked, leaning forward eagerly. "How was it on a scale of one to oh-my-God-stop-melting-my-panties?"

"Well, I'm not sure where it places on your scale, but I'll probably just stop wearing panties altogether when I'm in Max's presence. They'll just end up in tatters anyway."

"That good, huh?"

"Better," Lana said. "It was simply incredible, and I don't just mean the sex. This is going to sound positively insane, but I'm falling for this guy so fast it's scary. It's thrilling, too. It's the most alive I've ever felt."

"Well, all righty then. Sounds like you hit the romantic lottery with this guy." Brandy sipped her coffee. "In which case, why are you sitting in my kitchen looking somewhat less than thrilled?"

"Because my dad was waiting for me when I went back to my parents' house early this morning. To say he was pissed is an understatement."

Brandy blinked. "You're kidding, right? Your gun-toting daddy does realize his daughter isn't a teenager anymore, right?"

"I'm not so sure of that."

As she sipped her coffee, Lana explained how her

father had ambushed her the moment she'd walked in the door.

"He's never yelled at me in my life," Lana added. "And it's all because he thinks Max is wrong for me."

Brandy lifted a brow. "What did you say to that?"

Lana shrugged. "I told him that who I see is none of his business. As you can imagine, the argument went downhill from there."

The situation probably wouldn't have been quite so bad this morning if she hadn't been so tense to begin with. But for some stupid reason, the moment she'd walked into her parents' house, her teeth and fingertips had started tingling again. She couldn't explain what was causing the sensations, but they'd gotten so bad the hair on the back of her neck had actually stood on end, which really put her in a weird mood. When her father confronted her, she naturally counterattacked. Not that her dad didn't deserve it. He was being a butthead. Still, Lana was sorry things had gotten out of hand.

"When I said I wasn't going to stop seeing Max simply because he said so, he told me to get out," Lana said.

Brandy looked about as shocked as Lana had felt hearing those words. "What? You're not serious, are you?"

Lana could only nod, remembering how stunned she'd been. She'd never seen her father so angry. You'd think she was dating a drug dealer, not one of her dad's best SWAT officers.

"Your mom isn't going along with any of this, is she?" Brandy asked.

Lana shrugged. "Mom was already at the restaurant, but when she finds out, I imagine she's going to be pissed at Dad. But what's done is done. I told him that if he's going to try to play that silly game of my house my rules, then I'm out of there."

"What are you going to do?" Brandy asked.

"I guess that depends on you," Lana said. "If it's okay with you and Miriam, I'd like to crash on your couch for a while. If not, my backup plan is to get a room at an extended-stay hotel."

Brandy's brow furrowed. "What about staying at Max's place? You just admitted you're already head over heels for the guy."

Lana had thought about it—a lot.

"I'm sure Max would say yes," she told Brandy. "But even though there's something serious going on between us, I don't want to take the risk of screwing things up by moving too fast. I mean, we've only known each other for a few days. The things I'm feeling for him are insane, but moving in would be even crazier."

Brandy looked at her over the rim of her mug. "You just told me you spent last night at his place. Something tells me that even if you have a space on our couch, you'll still be over there most of the time anyway."

Lana smiled. "Yeah, probably. But sleeping over and moving in are two completely different things."

Her friend sighed. "You really spend too much time reading *Cosmo*, you know that? But it doesn't matter. If you need a place to crash, then of course you can stay here. Miriam and I are hardly ever here anyway. We both work too much. But if we come in some night and find you and Max going at it, don't get mad if I start taking pics."

Lana laughed. At least she had a plan for the short term. Now she had to figure out what to do next.

On the other side of the table, Brandy yawned behind her hand.

Lana grimaced. "Sorry for waking you up so early. Did they have you working late at the hospital again?"

Brandy shook her head. "Not really. I didn't sleep very well last night."

Lana hadn't slept much last night either, but she'd never needed as much sleep as her friends. Besides, missing sleep due to sex was completely different from lying in bed tossing and turning.

"What kept you up?" Lana asked. "Something you're dealing with at work?"

"No, nothing that simple. I couldn't sleep because every time I closed my eyes, I kept thinking about Chris."

Lana searched her memory for the name. "The guy you met at that party at the SWAT compound? The one you said you weren't interested in?"

Brandy rolled her eyes and sighed. "That's the one. I was all prepared to forget about him, but then he called and left a message. I was dumb enough to listen to it and now I can't get his voice out of my head."

Lana waited for her friend to elaborate, but Brandy didn't say anything else. Instead, her friend sat there staring morosely into her coffee mug.

"Wow," Lana said. "That must have been one heck of a message. What did he say?"

Brandy ran her finger around and around the rim of her mug. "That he had a good time and hopes we can get together again sometime soon."

Once again, Lana waited for the rest of the story, only to realize there wasn't any more forthcoming. "And that's why you couldn't sleep?"

Her friend shook her head. "I know it doesn't make any sense. I've never gotten this crazy for a guy. I have no plans to call him back, but I'm so gaga over his voice I can't even get myself to erase the message. I must have listened to it twenty times before bed, then tossed and turned the whole night thinking about him." She gave Lana a stricken look. "What the hell is wrong with me?"

Lana laughed. "Maybe you just like him. You should call him back and go out with him. Who knows? It could be the beginning of a beautiful relationship."

Brandy crossed her index fingers in the universal symbol of protection. "Get back, beast! I don't do relationships, and you know it."

Lana ignored her friend's theatrics. "Maybe you should start."

"Like that's going to happen." Brandy scoffed. "I'm going to take a nap. When I wake up, I'll delete his message and forget I ever heard it."

"Sure you will," Lana said. "But before you take that nap, how about helping me drag some stuff in from my car?"

Brandy thought about it a moment. "Can I wear my slippers and pajamas?"

"Sure. No one will notice."

———

"What the hell just happened in there?" Max asked Brooks as they walked down the steps of the industrial-warehouse-style loft Gage had set up for some of the recently arrived werewolves.

Brooks didn't answer right away—mostly because he was too busy trying to piece together parts of his

shredded tactical vest. Luckily, his skin hadn't been
shredded along with it.

"If I had to guess," the big alpha said, shaking his
head and giving up on his vest, "I'd say we just wit-
nessed the start of some new werewolf adaptation, an
evolution of how the different werewolf breeds behave
in response to the hunter threat."

Max thought about that and realized it made sense.
An hour ago, he and Brooks had gotten there expecting
to find the omegas causing trouble for the small pack of
betas who lived there, and instead finding two omegas
aligning with the betas as part of their pack and squar-
ing off against two other omegas who felt they would
do a better job leading the pack and protecting the kids
who lived there from any hunters who might show up.
Although it had turned into a big ass brawl, the omegas
were still behaving a lot more rationally than Max was
used to.

Even more bizarre, the betas living in the building
were acting much more aggressively than Max had
ever seen them. One of them had jumped into the fight
between the omegas. That wasn't the way beta werewolves normally reacted.

Betas acting like omegas, and omegas acting alphas?
If Max hadn't seen it with his own eyes, he'd call BS
on the idea.

"You think it's a good idea to leave them all together
up there?" he asked.

Brooks snorted as they reached their response vehicle
parked on the street. "What choice do we have? They
agreed to work together to protect their pack. We can't
ask much more than that. Besides, I think that beta up

there, Allen, has the situation pretty well in hand. If I
didn't know better, I'd say he's undergoing a beta-to-
alpha transformation."

Max climbed into the passenger seat. He had noticed
Allen's fangs and claws seemed longer than they were
before. It looked like the guy had put on a couple pounds
of muscle, too.

Brooks was just pulling away from the Deep Ellum
apartment building when Max's phone rang. His heart did
this seriously unmanly backflip thing when he thought
it might be Lana calling. He'd left her lying naked and
beautiful in his bed this morning, and if he was lucky,
that was where he'd find her tonight after work.

Unfortunately, it wasn't Lana. It was Detective
Peterson from Austin homicide, and though Max's
stomach was doing that backflip thing again, it was for
a completely different reason.

"Lowry," he said when he put the phone to his ear.

"Max, it's Detective Peterson, Austin PD. I'm not
sure what this means, but I thought you should know.
We found another murder victim with an MO similar
to Denise Sullivan's. Signs of torture and the guy had a
large-caliber bullet through his forehead."

"Who is he?" Max asked, a sickening feeling growing
in the pit of his stomach. Two people shot through the
forehead? It couldn't be a coincidence, not when hunters
preferred putting down werewolves exactly that way.

"We're still trying to ID him, but getting prints is
tough because the guy's fingertips are a mess," Peterson
said. "This guy was a big bruiser type, with a nose that
had been broken a couple times, lots of scars like the
ones you'd get fighting, and a collection of prison ink.

Bottom line, he's the kind of man more likely to do the torturing than to get tortured. The ME is saying he was probably killed at least two days before Denise, maybe three. We're trying to ID him from his prison ink, but that's probably going to take a while."

No kidding.

"Any way to connect this guy to Denise?" Max asked.

A big guy with prison tats didn't sound like someone Denise would hang out with, but maybe Lana hadn't known her roomie as well as she'd thought. Max knew better than most that everyone kept secrets.

"Actually, there is," the detective said. "But probably not the way you're thinking."

"What do you mean?"

"Before you and Ms. Mason came down, we'd been digging through old police reports, parking citations, and traffic cam footage for the area around their apartment complex. It's standard practice when we don't have any other leads. Sometimes you get lucky, you know? So we ended up finding a complaint filed by one of Denise's neighbors almost a week before the murders. He reported seeing a man lurking around Denise's apartment building a couple times, watching the place. He thought the guy was casing the apartments for a robbery, but when dispatch sent a patrol out, they didn't find anything. They talked to the other neighbors and increased patrols in the area, but no one saw the guy again, so the report was left open and pending."

"You think this guy the neighbor saw is the one who killed Denise and your unnamed male victim?" Max asked, trying to figure out where this was all going. The hunter angle wasn't lining up.

"No," Peterson said. "This guy the neighbor saw *is* the unnamed vic. We showed a photo of him to the witness who had called in the report and he confirmed our John Doe is the one who'd been watching Denise's apartment."

Max tried to wrap his head around this nugget of information—and failed. Was this new victim a werewolf or a hunter taken out by his own people? None of this stuff was making any sense.

"Can you send me a picture of your John Doe and anything else you have on him? I'll see if Lana recognizes him."

Max wanted to get a look at the guy, too.

"I'm already working on it," Peterson said. "The paperwork to release the file and photos to you is on my captain's desk, but I don't think he's going to cause me any grief on this one. Let me know what Ms. Mason says."

Max promised he would and was about to hang up when Peterson stopped him.

"One more thing. I'm not sure how to say this without freaking you out, so I'm just going to put it out there."

That didn't sound good. "Okay."

"It goes without saying that I have no idea who killed Denise Sullivan and this John Doe or what their motives might be. All I can say for sure is that the person who did it is vicious, probably unhinged, and somehow connected to that apartment building your girlfriend used to live in. I probably don't need to say it, but I'd keep a close eye on her, just in case."

Max appreciated the warning, even if it wasn't necessary. "I will."

Peterson was about to hang up, but this time it was Max who stopped him. His gut was telling him it was time to trust the other cop. "This is going to sound really weird, but can you have your ME run a tox screen for animal tranquilizer in both Denise and the John Doe you found?"

There was silence on the other end of the line. "Do you know something about this case you should be telling me?"

"Just call it a crazy hunch," Max said. "But if I'm right, your case might be tied to a string of murders that have been happening all across the country. I ran into a similar case in New Orleans a while back. The gunshot to the head is similar."

"And you're just mentioning it now?" Peterson demanded, sounding a little pissed.

"Because nothing else seems to fit," Max told him. "The extensive torture prior to the head shot isn't anything like the previous MO, so I'm just grasping at straws here."

Max could tell the other cop wanted to ask a lot more questions, but he refrained, saying he'd get the ME on the screening. "I'll keep it quiet for now, but if this comes back positive for animal tranquilizer, I'm going to be asking a lot more questions."

"I understand," Max said. "But if this comes back positive, you won't be the only one with questions."

Brooks had obviously overheard everything Peterson said because the moment Max hung up, he looked at him in concern. "Are you worried there are hunters after Lana?"

Max shoved his phone in his pocket. "I want to say

no. Because how could the hunters know she's a wolf if
she doesn't even know?"

"Then why bring up the animal tranquilizer thing at
all?" Brooks asked.

"Because my gut is screaming that there's something
wrong here, and I have to know if Lana is in danger,"
Max said.

He and Brooks spent the rest of the drive to the compound talking about Lana and how incredibly unusual
she was. They'd just pulled into the parking lot when
Max's cell rang again.

"You're a popular guy today," Brooks remarked as
Max reached for his phone.

Max hoped it was Lana this time, just so he could
hear her voice, and was disappointed when he didn't see
her name on the screen. He was even more disappointed
when he heard Detective Coletti's distinctive voice on
the other end of the line.

"I don't know what Wallace told you, but I haven't
been anywhere near that house," Max stated firmly
before the other cop had a chance to say anything.

"Yeah right." Coletti snorted. "Like I frigging believe
that. But it doesn't matter. That's not why I called. I
figure you'd want to know the Department of Family
and Protective Services gave me a call. According to the
DFPS, Mrs. Wallace finally decided she's had enough.
She took the kids and left her husband a few hours ago.
They're at the Safe Campus in Bluffview."

Max couldn't believe how amazing those few simple
words made him feel. It wasn't until that moment that he
realized he'd been holding his breath, expecting Coletti
to tell him that Wallace had killed his family.

"You think I could stop by and check on them, see if they need anything?" Max asked, not really sure why he was even asking Coletti.

"The department wanted you to stay away from Wallace and his residence," Coletti said. "I don't see any reason you can't go see those kids now that they're out of the house."

Max didn't say anything for long time, fighting some emotions he wasn't sure what to do with. "Thanks, Coletti. I didn't think it was going to work out, but I guess it did."

"Sometimes it does," the detective said. "Those are the ones we hope for."

Max hung up to see Brooks regarding him with a smile on his face.

Max grinned. "I think Mrs. Wallace and her kids are going to be okay."

"So I heard," Brooks said. "Better not mention to Cooper how cool Coletti is being. It might ruin his opinion of the man."

Chapter 8

"I DON'T HAVE A SKULL...OR BONES," MAX SAID, SPROUTING yet another one of his favorite movie lines, and making the Wallace kids laugh like crazy. Lana couldn't blame them. He was making her laugh, too.

Lana, Max, Terence, Nina, and Natasha were sitting at a picnic table outside one of the dorm-style buildings of the Safe Campus emergency shelter, talking about animated movies while they worked their way through a ridiculous pile of cheeseburgers, fish sandwiches, onion rings, and fries. It hurt to see Terence eating his burger with one hand heavily wrapped in gauze, especially after knowing how the injury had happened. Even so, she couldn't help smiling at the way the boy's face lit up when Max talked to him. The connection between the two of them was obvious. It was like Terence had found an older brother to idolize.

Even the two girls were looking at Max like he was the best thing since sliced bread. The fact that Max had brought them both french fries and onion rings because he'd been worried they might not like one or the other probably had something to do with it. Or maybe it was because Max knew all the best lines from the movie *Frozen*, as well as the words to the songs, too. That probably didn't hurt, either. Lana was definitely going to grill him on that surprising bit of knowledge later. Right now, she was having too much fun being around this family that was, maybe for the first time in years, happy.

Lana had been thrilled when Max called and told her that Mrs. Wallace and her children had gotten away from her abusive husband and moved into a safe place. She'd been even more overjoyed when Max asked her to go with him to visit them.

They had to sign in to get past security at the gate of the Safe Campus shelter on Preston Park. The guard there had gone so far as to check the bags of food they'd brought with them, even after Max had flashed his badge. But that was a good thing. No one wanted the wrong people sneaking onto the shelter's property.

She and Max had talked to Mrs. Wallace briefly, while she'd been filling out paperwork to get assistance with longer-term housing arrangements. Lana had cried a little when the woman had tearfully hugged Max and said it was his words that had given her the strength to leave her husband.

"I always believed he would wake up one day and see what he was doing to us," the woman told them. "But he got drunk last night and woke up this morning in a rage. When he came at Natasha with a kitchen knife because she'd woken him up with her laughter, I knew he was never going to change. It was like you said, that this would keep happening until one of my children ended up dead. Unless I stood up to him. So that's what I did. I put my children first and walked out of there."

Max's eyes had gotten a little misty at that as well. He wasn't the only one. Half the staff in the building had tears in their eyes. It was one hell of a moment.

Lana kept Nina and Natasha entertained, spelling

words with all the french fries they had on the wax paper from the sandwiches, while Max and Terence went over to the nearby swings to talk for a while. The girls seemed to understand that their brother needed some time alone with Max, and didn't complain about his absence.

"Are you two going to get married?" Natasha asked suddenly, a ketchup-covered onion ring halfway to her mouth.

To say the question caught Lana off guard was an understatement. The two blond-haired sisters regarded her expectantly, their expressions adorable.

"Um…" she finally said. "Well, we only met a few days ago, so we're just dating now."

Natasha considered that as she took a bite of her onion ring. "Don't you like him?"

Lana glanced at Max, glad he couldn't hear any of this all the way over by the swings. "Sure I like him. He's great."

"Then you should marry him," Natasha said seriously before eating the rest of her onion ring. "If I had a boyfriend who brought me both french fries and onion rings, I'd marry him. Not that I'm old enough to get married yet. I can't do that for another year or two."

Lana nodded at that well-thought-out opinion. There was a certain logic to basing your marriage decision on a willingness to buy alternative side dishes. She'd certainly seen women get married for lesser reasons.

As she and the girls discussed the various menu options for her wedding to Max—just in case—Lana caught snatches of Max's conversation with Terence on the breeze. What she heard made her want to cry.

"I should have protected my sisters better," Terence said. "That's what older brothers are supposed to do."

"You protected them as well as you could," Max insisted. "In fact, I'm willing to bet you put yourself in between your dad and your sisters a lot."

"Yeah, but it was never enough," Terence said. "I couldn't stop him."

"No, you couldn't," Max agreed. "Because the only person who could stop your dad from doing that stuff is your dad."

Lana glanced over to see Terence sitting on the swing, staring at the ground. "I hate my father."

"I know," Max said softly. "And that's pretty normal, I guess. But if you can, try not to dwell on that too much. If the only thing you ever let yourself feel is hate, pretty soon, that's the only thing you'll be able to feel. Instead, think about how much you love your mom and your sisters, and what kind of life you're going to have with them now."

That was good advice, Lana thought.

Max and Terence came back over to the table a little while after that, and they all sat there, eating the rest of the fries and talking about any silly subject the kids brought up. Lana couldn't help but notice how patient and thoughtful Max was. He made sure each of the kids memorized his cell number, telling them they could call him day or night, even if they simply needed to talk. Or wanted french fries.

She was thinking about the fact that Max was going to make an awesome dad someday when another thought popped into her head. He wouldn't merely make a great dad to a bunch of kids. He'd make a great dad to her kids.

Whoa. Where the heck had that come from?

She'd known Max for a grand total of three days and had spent the night with him once. Even if you counted multiple orgasms as separate sexual events, she still hadn't been with him long enough to be thinking about having a family with him.

This was insane. No, this was about four miles past the turnoff to insane. But at the same time, she realized she couldn't convince herself it was wrong. In some ways, it all made complete sense. Her head might have been trying to tell her she was moving too fast, but her heart—and those funny flutters in her belly—were saying this was exactly what she wanted.

She glanced at Max to see him regarding her with a smile that made her pulse go crazy. "You want some more fries?" he asked. "Or onion rings?"

Returning his smile, Lana reached over and took a handful of each.

Maybe Natasha was onto something here. How many guys would offer you fries…and onion rings?

Max opened the door of his apartment, holding on to Lana's small overnight bag as she walked in ahead of him. He certainly hadn't minded that Lana wanted to stay at his place tonight, but he'd been shocked when she asked him to stop at her friends' place near Medical City Hospital first so she could pick up her toothbrush and some other essentials.

"Isn't that stuff at your parents' house?" he'd asked in confusion.

That's when Lana mentioned she'd moved in with Brandy and Miriam after getting into a fight with her father that morning. He hadn't pushed for details at the time, but now that they were back at his place, he figured it was about time she told him the rest of the story.

"So, does this thing with your dad have anything to do with me?" he asked, setting her bag on the floor by the couch and tugging her into his arms.

She shrugged, as if trying to make it seem like it wasn't a big deal. But Max could tell she was upset. He could feel the tension in her body.

"Yeah," she said. "He told me that if I wanted to keep seeing you, I wasn't welcome in his house."

Max had feared it was something like that, but he was still stunned to hear it put so bluntly. None of this made any sense. Even if the deputy chief knew Max was a werewolf, why would he be this vehemently against his daughter seeing him?

He leaned down and kissed away the line of stress between Lana's brows, hugging her close until he felt her relax.

"Do you think he'll back off in a while, once he realizes that you aren't going to give in to his threats?" he asked.

"If he wants to see me again, he's going to have to," she said. "You and I are going to be together—that's as plain to me as the nose on my face. Dad is just going to have to get used to the idea."

Max wasn't sure the deputy chief would give in that easily and had no doubt that this would come back to haunt them at some point, but he had to admit, he was stoked to hear Lana talking like that. She might not have realized she was a werewolf or have a clue what it meant to find *The One*, but she could obviously feel the strong connection between them. At the moment, that was good enough for him.

He slipped a hand under her chin and tilted her face up to capture her lips with his. He'd only intended to give her a light kiss, but the moment he tasted her, he couldn't help groaning as a familiar tingling sensation raced through his body. Damn, one little kiss and he was already getting hard.

Lana didn't seem to mind. Reaching up, she wrapped a hand around the back of his neck and kissed him even harder, her tongue slipping into his mouth to tease the hell out of him.

Max wasn't sure how it happened, but at some point, they ended up on the couch, Lana straddling his hips as she ground against him in the most arousing way ever. He'd been wondering if she wanted to watch a movie on Netflix or play some video games, but he decided this was a lot more fun.

When his cell dinged, he was seriously tempted to ignore it. But he was a cop and didn't have the privilege of blowing off his phone whenever he felt like it. Lana behaved while Max dug his phone out of back pocket. She'd been raised in a cop family. She knew how this worked.

It was an email from Peterson. Max opened the message quickly. There were several photos and a pdf document, along with a note from the detective, letting Max know he was still working the animal-tranquilizer angle and reminding him to email back ASAP if Lana recognized their John Doe.

Max opened the photos first and frowned. One look at the John Doe's injuries and Max knew he had to be a werewolf. Not only had he clearly put up one hell of a struggle, but he'd also sustained a lot more damage than Denise. A beating like this would have killed a normal human.

He skimmed the case file next, looking at injury diagrams and statements on where the body had been found and who'd found it. There wasn't a whole lot to go on, certainly nothing that connected directly to Denise—or Lana.

Up until now, Lana had been waiting patiently on his lap, but she finally reached out and pulled the phone down a little to give him a curious look. "Everything okay?"

He sighed. "Yeah. I hate to do this, especially in the middle of kissing you, but Peterson sent me some photos of a John Doe they found murdered, who they think might be related to Denise's death. They'd like you to take a look and see if you recognize him. The ME cleaned him up, but I have to warn you, it's still pretty bad."

"Like Denise?" she asked hesitantly.

Max nodded, wishing there were some other way to do this.

She climbed off his lap and sat next to him, then took a deep breath. "Okay."

He pulled up a photo that cropped out just about everything but the man's head and shoulders, although that was still pretty bad.

Lana studied the photo carefully, then shook her head. "I don't recognize him."

Max breathed a sigh of relief. He hadn't expected Lana to know the guy, but until they got the toxicology report back confirming there were no animal tranquilizers involved and that the murders had nothing to do with werewolves or hunters, Max was going to be on edge.

After he shot a quick text to Peterson, he filled Lana in on what little they knew about this newest victim; then they headed into the kitchen for a couple slices of cold pizza. Mostly because neither of them felt like immediately picking up where they'd left off before he'd gotten Peterson's text, but also because the burgers and fries they had with the Wallace kids earlier simply hadn't been enough to eat. Lana tried to play it off like she wasn't hungry, but she took a small slice out of the box he tossed on the kitchen table anyway.

As they ate, they talked about the Wallace family. Max had been thrilled to get a chance to see Terence and his sisters, and he especially liked watching Lana interact with Natasha and Nina. Those girls adored Lana, and overhearing them talk about boyfriends and getting married had been downright hilarious. It had been tough keeping the grin off his face when he and Terence had joined them at the picnic table.

"You were pretty good with those kids," Lana said as she nibbled on her pizza. "Terence really looks up to you."

He took a swig of diet soda. "He's so much like me when I was his age that it's tough looking at him without thinking about the way things were for me."

Lana smiled at him. "Well, things are going to be different for his family than it was for yours. And that's all because of you."

"All I did was give some advice," he insisted. "It was their mom who made the hard call by walking away."

"You're not giving yourself enough credit," Lana said, slyly reaching over to grab another slice of pizza, as if he wouldn't notice. "But that's cool. Those kids know what you've done for them, and that's all that matters."

They chatted about the kids for a while longer before Lana finally picked up the half-eaten box of pizza and shoved it back in the fridge.

"If I don't, you'll eat the whole thing," she pointed out.

Max chuckled. "Yeah…me…all by myself, right?"

"Of course you," she said, coming back over to the table. "I ate more than enough at the shelter. I just had a slice with you so you wouldn't have to eat alone."

"Mm-hmm. Sure, whatever works for you." He stood, taking her in his arms. "You feel like putting on a movie and snuggling up on the couch for a while? Or should we go out and get some exercise, so you don't have to feel guilty about eating that pizza?"

Lana hooked her arms around his neck, giving him a sexy grin. "We can move to the couch, but why don't we skip the movie and go straight to the exercising? I'm sure we can come up with some way to burn off a few calories."

Max felt himself get hard again just from the way she was looking at him. Not that he was complaining. If Lana was interested in a little physical exertion, he could definitely help with that.

"I'm game, but shouldn't we wait for at least an hour after eating before doing anything strenuous?" he teased.

Lana laughed. "You're thinking about swimming, but don't worry. We'll start slow and work up to the strenuous part later."

"Slow works for me," Max said, scooping her into his arms and heading for the couch.

Chapter 9

"WHAT DID PETERSON SAY?" LANA ASKED.

Max didn't say anything as they walked toward the big dance club on the corner of Pearl and Main. Lana thought maybe Max hadn't heard the question, but that was impossible. There were a lot of people out and about tonight, but it wasn't that noisy. He'd heard her. He was simply too worried to answer. That scared her.

Lana had spent last night at Max's place; then today, they'd gone to visit the Wallace kids and their mom at the shelter again. They'd brought Mrs. Wallace some clothes, toiletries, and food for her and the kids, as well as coloring books for Natasha and Nina and games for Terence. After that, they'd gone back to Max's place and hung out, watching TV, playing video games, and, of course, making out a lot. It was the best day she'd ever had in her life, and she couldn't wait to do it again tomorrow. Except tomorrow, maybe she'd spend the whole day naked, just so she could drive Max crazy. She enjoyed the fact that he couldn't see her naked without wanting her.

They'd just gotten out of Max's Camaro and were heading toward the club when Peterson had called. She'd only heard Max's side of the conversation, and while he hadn't said much, he'd definitely been in cop mode.

"Max?" she prompted when he still didn't reply.

He slowed his steps, pulling her over to the side. When

he looked at her, his expression was serious. "Peterson doesn't have an ID on the John Doe yet, but they think the same person who murdered him killed Denise."

After seeing the photo of the guy, Lana had suspected as much. "Do they have any leads on the killer?"

"No. But they both had the same drug in their system, administered at some point prior to their deaths."

"What?" Lana frowned. "Denise didn't take drugs, I know that for a fact. They must have made a mistake."

Max shook his head. "This isn't a drug she took on her own. It's a heavy-duty animal tranquilizer the killer injected into both of them with a dart gun of some type. The ME found the puncture marks once he knew what to look for. He said Denise had so much of the stuff in her system she barely felt the pain during the torture—for what that's worth. The drug was what killed her. The gunshot to the head came afterward."

Lana's knees went weak and she reached out to grab Max's arm to steady herself. "Why would the killer give animal tranquilizers to Denise? Who does that?"

Max didn't answer.

A couple walked past them, laughing about something. Lana didn't even look at them.

"If Peterson said something else, something that explains all of this, please tell me," she begged. "Because I'm getting really scared now."

"You should be scared," he said. "Unfortunately, this isn't the first time I've seen these people's handiwork. My teammates and I first heard about one of their victims in New Orleans back in September. While that murder happened over two years ago, we've since learned there have been a lot more of them all across the

United States. There could be some in other countries, too, but we can't confirm that yet."

Lana's head spun. What was Max saying? That these people were globe-trotting serial killers?

"What's the deal with the animal tranquilizer?" she asked, not sure now whether she really wanted to know.

Max waited while a group of women strolled past before answering. When he finally spoke, his voice was tense.

"Before I tell you about that, there's something else I need you to know, something I hope will help you understand how serious this all is."

Lana tightened her grip on her purse as her teeth, gums, and fingertips began to tingle. She barely noticed. The strange sensations were starting to feel almost normal to her now.

"Peterson told me that Denise's parents got in from Alaska today," Max continued. "They went through the apartment and noticed that whoever killed Denise went through her address book."

Lana remembered the book Max was talking about. She used to tease Denise all the time about keeping a physical address book when everyone else on the planet stored all that stuff in their phone. But what the heck did that book have to do with any of this?

"How do her parents know that?"

"Because they tore out some pages in the middle— including all the contacts listed under the letter M." He took a deep breath. "Lana, they have your parents' address. They know where you're staying while you're here in Dallas—or at least where you were staying."

She frowned. She didn't understand any of this and

the confusion was frustrating the heck out of her. Her heart was thumping like mad and every noise around her was beginning to sound way louder than it should. "Why would they care where I'm staying?"

Max grabbed hand, squeezing it tight. "Lana, I think the people who killed Denise did it because they thought she was you. Once they realized she wasn't, they tortured her to figure out where you were. With all the tranquilizers in her system, I doubt she told them very much, but now that they have those pages from her address book, it doesn't matter. They know where to find you."

She shook her head. "That's crazy, Max. Why would anyone come after me? I'm a recent college graduate with fifty thousand dollars in student loans. And what does any of this have to do with animal tranquilizers?"

For a moment, Max looked like he was at a complete loss for words, which only made her worry more. What could be so bad he couldn't even say it?

"I never wanted it to come out like this." He sighed. "Once I realized you had no clue how special you are, I was going to wait until later, when I could bring it up in a way that wouldn't freak you out."

If Max thought he was helping her understand what was going on, he was wrong. She appreciated that he thought she was special, but right then she wasn't interested in romantic terms of endearment.

She fixed him with a look. "Max, if there's something you've been hiding from me, now is the time to say it."

He opened his mouth, then closed it again, looking around helplessly. Still holding on to her hand, he led her down the street and into an alley.

"Max, please tell me what's happening," she pleaded.

He looked around again, as if he was worried some-one might overhear. "Lana, what I'm about to tell you is going to sound insane, but you have to believe me. You're special, and the people who killed Denise are willing to kill you because of it."

She cupped his face in her hand. "I love that you think I'm so special, but there's absolutely no reason for anyone to come after me. I'm not a witness to some kind of major crime and I'm not hiding some deep, dark secret worth millions of dollars. I'm just a recent college graduate with a cop for a dad…and a cop for a boyfriend."

Max's mouth curved slightly at that, but then he turned serious again. "This isn't about something you've seen or a secret worth a lot of money. This is about *what* you are. It's something these people—these hunters— are willing to kill you for."

Lana didn't say anything. She was too tired to keep chasing after the secret Max seemed to be working toward.

He must have figured that out, because he took a deep breath and looked her straight in the eye. "Lana, you're a werewolf."

She blinked, waiting for the punch line that had to be coming. When it didn't, she realized Max was serious. Or he thought he was.

"You're kidding, right?" she said. "That's—"

"Insane," Max interrupted. "Remember, I told you it was going to sound insane. But that doesn't mean it's not true. You're a werewolf, Lana. I know that because I'm one, too."

Lana felt her anger flare. Denise was dead, murdered in the most horrible way possible. Some other guy she'd never met was dead, too, and Max was playing games talking about stupid werewolves. She never would have thought he'd do something so juvenile and thoughtless.

"I need to show you something, and I don't want you to be scared." He tugged her a little farther down the alley, away from the street. "I won't hurt you. I'd never hurt you. But you have to see this so you'll believe what I'm telling you."

She snorted as he released her hand, about to ask him what the hell he was planning to do—grow fangs and a snout. But before she could get the words out, Max changed right in front of her eyes. His jaw broadened and filled full of teeth, long canines descending over his lower lip, even as his eyes went feral, seemingly lit from within by a yellow glow.

Lana wasn't the kind of woman who normally freaked out. Heck, bugs, rats, and snakes didn't even bother her. But at that moment, she freaked—and screamed.

Max took a step toward her, lifting his hands as if trying to calm her down. That's when she saw the long claws extending from his fingertips.

Long, sharp claws, a mouth full of teeth, and glowing eyes.

Her boyfriend *was* a frigging werewolf.

She screamed again. Why the hell was she doing that?

Then her Max was back, standing in front of her looking as gorgeous as he'd ever been. No fangs, no claws, no glow-in-the-dark eyes. But no matter how normal he looked now, Lana couldn't forget what she'd just seen.

She didn't realize she was backing away from him until she saw the pain in his eyes. But she couldn't stop herself. There was something wrong here. Something wrong with *him*.

"Lana, calm down," Max said gently. Thankfully, he didn't come any closer. "I promised I wouldn't hurt you, and I meant it. But you needed to see that, so you'd understand what I am...what you are. The people who killed Denise are werewolf hunters. They travel the country killing any of our kind they can find. That's where the animal tranquilizer comes in. It's tough for a person to take out a werewolf, but the heavy-duty drugs slow us down long enough to allow them to do it. These people know you're one of us, and they're coming for you."

Lana refused to listen. She had no idea how Max was able to do what he'd just done. She was too smart to believe in monsters—especially werewolves. She knew one thing for sure—she was nothing like him.

"Stop it!" she yelled. "I can't explain what I just saw, but I'm not like you."

She ignored the devastated look on his face, telling herself she'd deal with it later, once she had time to process all of this. Right now she needed to get away from this situation—from Max—for a while. She started to edge past him, hoping he wouldn't try to stop her.

He stepped in front of her. "Lana, you can't leave. Not like this."

"She can leave if she fucking wants to," a deep voice said from behind Lana.

She spun around and found two guys standing there looking pissed. They were both big and brawny, one blond, the other dark haired. They must have heard her screams and come to help. She supposed chivalry wasn't dead. She didn't need their help, though. It wasn't like she was scared of Max.

Okay, maybe she was scared of him a little bit. The mere thought of his fangs and claws made her shudder.

"You okay, lady?" the blond guy asked, looking back and forth between her and Max. "This dude messing with you?"

Lana had no desire to get Max in trouble—or a fight. But she needed to get out of the alley, and these two men were as good a distraction as any.

"No, there's no problem," she murmured. "I was just leaving."

She moved to sidestep Max, but he blocked her path again. "Lana, seriously. It's too dangerous for you out there."

Lana opened her mouth to tell him that she needed some space to think and wrap her head around everything she'd seen, but she didn't get the chance because the beefy, dark-haired guy took a swing and blindsided Max with a punch straight to the temple.

She screamed, sure the savage blow had killed him, but Max barely rocked on his feet. Jaw tight, he glared at the guy who'd sucker-punched him, his eyes glowing yellow-gold again, a low rumbling growl emanating from his throat.

The sound slipped under Lana's skin, vibrating there and making her whole body tingle in response. Her teeth were aching so badly she thought they might tear right out of her gums.

In a blur, Max backhanded his attacker across the alley, bouncing the man off the redbrick wall of the far building. Lana was almost certain she heard something crunch and did everything she could to convince herself it had been the brick breaking. A part of her almost swore she could hear the dark-haired man's heartbeat from where he lay unmoving on the ground. But that was impossible. She couldn't hear something as subtle as a heartbeat.

Another blur caught her eye, and she turned to catch sight of her other would-be protector launch himself at Max, a wicked-looking knife in his hand.

She opened her mouth to shout a warning, but it was too late. Her throat constricted in terror as the blond man plunged the blade deep into Max's chest.

Lana hurried over to him only to slide to a halt as Max batted the guy across the alley. He hit the building with a thud and a crunch before dropping noiselessly to the ground. He was still alive—Lana knew because she could hear his heart beating—but he'd definitely need medical attention.

Max turned to look at Lana, his eyes glowing like the high beams of a car, his fangs extended so far she wasn't sure how they could possibly have been hidden in his jaws, the blade still sticking out from his chest. She took a hesitant step toward him, but then stopped as he casually reached down and pulled the knife out of his chest, dropping it to the ground with an irritated flick of his hand.

The glow in his eyes didn't dim as he regarded her, and she swore time ceased. In the near quiet, she heard his heart pounding loud and fast.

Then the smell hit her nose—metallic, harsh, overpowering.

She had no idea how she knew what the scent was

or how she could possibly smell it, but she knew with a
certainty it was Max's blood.

This couldn't be happening—the sights, the sounds,
the smells, the way her body was responding to all of
them was too much.

She was running out of the alley before she realized
her feet were moving.

"Lana, wait!"

Behind her, she heard Max following. That only fed
into the complete panic trampling rampantly through her
body, and she ran faster. Soon enough, the sound of his
footsteps died away, like he'd given up chasing her. The
sobs coming from her throat made breathing difficult,
but she kept going anyway. She didn't know where she
was running to, but she couldn't stop.

Max cursed as he got out of his Camaro and made his
way up the walkway to the Masons' house. He wasn't
sure if he was relieved Lana had sought shelter in her
parents' home or not. Something told him the deputy
chief and his wife wouldn't be very happy to see him.
But if he wanted to talk to Lana, he had no choice but to
walk up there and ring that doorbell.

Shit, this would have been so much easier if she'd
simply gone to Brandy and Miriam's place. He snorted.
Like anything about this was easy.

It had been nearly two hours since the fiasco in the
heart of the downtown club area, and Max was hoping
Lana had calmed down enough to talk to him. That
might have been wishful thinking, considering how
scared she'd been earlier.

She hadn't answered her cell when he'd called—not that he'd expected her to—so he'd stopped by Brandy and Miriam's apartment, assuming Lana had gone there. But she hadn't. All he'd accomplished was freaking out the other two women when he'd mentioned that he and Lana had gotten into an argument and she'd run off. They weren't too thrilled to help him find her after that, but he'd finally been able to convince them he was simply worried about her and only wanted to talk.

Brandy had finally called Lana's cell. Lana's mother had answered, saying she was there. When Mrs. Mason had asked Brandy if she knew what was going on, Lana's friend had shot him a look of pure malice when she'd said she had no idea either and that she planned on finding out.

Brandy and Miriam had refused to let him leave, grilling him for ten minutes about what he'd done to their best friend to make her run off in the first place. Max had gotten away only after telling them he loved Lana and had scared her by getting too real, too fast. It was the best he could come up with on the fly, and it wasn't exactly a lie.

It wasn't the truth, either. In reality, his attempt to convince Lana that she was a werewolf had been a complete train wreck. Why hadn't he waited until he could sit down with Gage or Cooper or Khaki—or anyone else in the Pack? Hell, since Lana was a beta, it probably would have been better to have another beta explain it to her. Maybe they could have done that bonding thing betas did, and everything would have been fine.

Instead, he'd shifted right in front of her, completely blowing her mind in the middle of downtown Dallas. What was he, stupid?

You're not stupid, a little voice in his head whispered. *You're scared*.

That call from Peterson had rattled him. The moment the homicide detective had confirmed both their John Doe and Denise had been dosed with animal tranquilizer, he'd known hunters were involved. After that, the pieces had started to fall into place so fast Max had almost hyperventilated. The John Doe had probably been hanging around Lana's apartment building because he'd most likely been obeying the same pack-building instincts the omegas in Dallas had been feeling. The hunters had gotten the omega and somehow figured out there was a female werewolf living in Austin. They'd busted into Lana's apartment and darted Denise, only realizing after the tranquilizers had rendered the girl nearly unconscious that she wasn't a werewolf. But they'd tortured her anyway simply because they were vicious bastards.

And thanks to Denise's address book, they knew Lana was in Dallas and had come here to kill her. The idea they'd do the same thing to her that they'd done to Denise twisted his guts into knots.

He'd scared Lana so badly in that alley that she'd almost gone into a shift herself. He could smell it when he'd been fighting with those two idiots. Her scent had completely changed from that half-werewolf, half-human mix into a true beta scent. Not only had her heart been racing, but her eyes had also started to glow. He was pretty sure he'd caught sight of the cutest set of little fangs poking out of her mouth, too.

Then she'd run like a terrified animal. He'd only made it worse by chasing after her. He was glad she'd calmed down enough to stop running and go somewhere familiar and safe. If she hadn't, who knew how far she might have run?

Max stepped onto the front porch just as the door opened. Deputy Chief Mason stepped outside, closing it behind him. Lana's scent—back to the half-and-half mix he was used to—hit him in the face like a physical blow, and he nearly shifted right there in front of the deputy chief. Every instinct in Max's body screamed at him to kick down the door and run inside to take Lana in his arms and protect her, but he stopped himself. Going in there like that would only frighten her again.

Not that it looked like Mason had any intention of letting Max get anywhere near the door. Lana's father was planted on the porch, one hand shoved in the side pocket of the jacket he wore. Max didn't need to have X-ray vision to know the man had a gun in there.

"You're not welcome here," the deputy chief said coldly. "Lana doesn't want to see you…ever again."

Max frowned. When he'd realized Lana had no idea she was a werewolf, he'd also bought into the idea that her parents didn't know, either. That had gotten harder to believe when she'd told him about her parents paying a buttload of money to get her out of the hospital after that car wreck and take care of her at home. That sure as hell sounded like someone trying to hide that their daughter was a werewolf. Even then, he'd been ready to give the man the benefit of the doubt. Lana was unique. Anything was possible with her.

Now, Max couldn't shake the feeling that this was way more than a father being overprotective. Mason wasn't trying to chase him off because he wasn't good enough for his little girl. This man was too practical and rational to take that line with his daughter. This was something more, something deeply personal.

"You've known all along what your daughter is— what we are—haven't you?" Max asked.

Mason's mouth tightened. "I have no idea what you're talking about, Officer Lowry. I want you off my porch right now, or you'll be a civilian by morning."

Max stood there, fighting the urge to shift. Mason was lying, Max was sure of it. But he got a grip on himself. Losing control right then wasn't going to help anything. There was something more important going on here than Mason knowing about werewolves.

"Chief, your daughter is in danger. There are people out there who will hurt her simply because of what she is."

"The only one who's a danger to Lana is you," Mason ground out. "If you hadn't forced your way into her life, she wouldn't be in there crying right now."

Max opened his mouth to argue, but Mason turned and walked into the house, slamming the door behind him.

Max was so torn about leaving he almost shifted again. Shit, he had to get himself together and think. What the hell was he going to do? The hunters could be coming for Lana at any moment.

He could stay and sit in his car, keep an eye on the place. But if he did that, how long before the deputy chief called a patrol car out here to chase him off?

Max cursed. This wasn't something he could deal with on his own. He was the member of a pack, and right now, he needed them more than ever. He also needed the advice of someone he trusted like Gage and Xander and

Mike. Hell, he'd even listen to Cooper at the moment if it would help him figure out what to do next.

The hunters didn't pose an immediate threat to Lana, not here in the home of the deputy chief of police. The hunters were vicious, but they weren't reckless. They'd never come at anyone like a cop, not in the middle of a fully populated residential neighborhood. Lana would be safe for the moment—until he could come up with a better plan.

With that in mind, Max jogged back out to his Camaro and cranked the engine. Pulling a U-turn, he headed back the way he'd come.

Gage and Mac's home was a frequent hangout for a lot of the werewolves in Dallas—Pack and otherwise—so when he pulled up in front of the two-story house thirty minutes later, Max wasn't surprised to see Xander's pickup truck alongside Mike's Sierra in the driveway. There were two other vehicles Max didn't recognize.

Gage's wife, Mackenzie, answered the door. Tall with long, dark hair and blue eyes, she was a journalist at the *Dallas Daily Star*. She didn't have to be a reporter to pick up on the fact that something was up with him.

"Is everything okay?" she asked the moment he stepped inside.

Since she'd married the SWAT team commander, Mac had turned into the Pack matriarch—even if she refused to consider herself old enough to play that part. Regardless, she'd jumped into the role of helping the rapidly growing Pack deal with day-to-day issues.

Max gave her a rueful look. "Not really. I sort of pulled a stupid, and need to tell Sarge about it."

"Gage mentioned you'd found your *One*," she said,

her lips curving. "I wondered how long it would be before you showed up here—or ended up in jail."

Max smiled wryly. "Good to see you have so much faith in me."

"It's not that we don't have faith in you," she said as she led him toward the back of the house and the kitchen. "It's just that we know how finding *The One* can make a werewolf behave. Gage will be thrilled you decided to come and tell him up front instead of calling him after the crap hit the fan."

Max grunted. He wasn't so sure the boss would be as thrilled when he found out the deputy chief had been ready to pull a weapon on him.

Gage, Xander, and Mike were sitting at the kitchen table along with Khaki, while Florian and Armand Danu, the oldest members of the family Cooper had married into, were leaning back against the granite counter of the island. The two men had become ingrained in the Pack's effort to form a safe haven for werewolves here in Dallas. With their knowledge of werewolf hunters, their presence at gatherings was as important as anyone's.

"No handcuffs," Xander observed dryly. "I'm going to say that's a good thing even before I hear the details."

Gage didn't seem as amused. "What happened?"

Max took the empty seat next to Mike and told them everything that had happened that night, starting with the call he'd gotten from Peterson and finishing with his decision to reveal to Lana that he was a werewolf. He might have downplayed the part where he'd beat up on the two Good Samaritans in the alley. For all the good it did him. One look at Gage, Xander, and Mike convinced him they knew he was keeping something from them.

"Well, that's one way to let Lana know she's a were-wolf," Mike said. A big guy with light-brown skin, dark eyes, and close-cropped, black hair, he had been an undercover narcotics cop before he became a werewolf and joined SWAT. "Probably not the way I would have done it, but I give you an A for intentions. How did she handle it?"

"Not well," Max admitted. "She flipped out and almost shifted. I don't think she realized what was happening to her, though. Before I knew it, she took off running and didn't stop until she reached her parents' house."

Gage grimaced. "And you decided to go over and try to talk to her, right?"

Max shrugged. "I had to try to make sure she was okay. She still doesn't believe what she is or how much danger she's in."

"Try?" Xander prompted. "You didn't talk to her?"

Mac shook his head. "No. The deputy chief was wait-ing for me at the door with a gun. He wasn't going to let me within ten feet of Lana. I could hear her crying upstairs, though. I really scared her."

On the other side of him, Khaki put a comforting hand on his arm. "When she realizes what the two of you have, she'll come back to you."

Max snorted. "You sure of that? You didn't see her face. She was terrified when she saw me fang out."

"If she's *The One* for you, it will happen," Armand said, his French accent slight but still discernible. "Everly was horrified when Cooper showed her he was a werewolf."

"You mean after you stabbed him and forced him to partially shift, don't you?" Xander pointed out.

Armand shrugged. "Maybe. But the important thing is that even though my sister ran away, she was unable to resist the tug pulling her back to her soul mate. She was bound to him so strongly that being away from him made her physically ill." He looked at Max. "If you're meant to be together, it will be the same with you and Lana. You can't force her to accept something she's not ready for. Just give her a little space."

Max hoped that was true. If Lana felt like he did right now, he didn't understand how she could stay away from him. It felt like he had a hole in his chest where his heart should be. "What about the hunters? What if they come looking for her while I'm not around to protect her?"

The mere thought made his gut clench.

"There's not a lot we can do about that right now," Gage said. "I think she'll be safe with her father watching out for her."

Max opened his mouth to complain, but Gage cut him off. "Even so, I'll work up a duty roster and have the Pack do drive-by patrols every couple hours. We'll keep an eye on her."

"I'll take the first two rotations," Max said eagerly.

"No, you won't." Gage scowled at him. "In fact, you'll take none of the rotations. The deputy chief will suspend you if he catches sight of you anywhere near his home. If he doesn't shoot you. Let the rest of the Pack handle this. You figure out what the hell you're going to say to Lana if Armand is right and she comes back to you. And please try to come up with a more intelligent approach than showing off your fangs and claws, would you?"

Max was about to point out that the whole tell-her-the-truth thing had been Cooper's idea but decided to keep that to himself. Admitting to Sarge he'd taken anything Cooper had to say seriously probably wouldn't make him look any better in his alpha's eyes.

He only hoped the hunters wouldn't show up before Lana came back to him.

Chapter 10

LANA KNEW BRANDY AND MIRIAM WERE TRYING TO CHEER her up, but dragging her out to a dance club had been a horrible idea. There was a good crowd for a Sunday night, mostly college-age types who didn't seem to need sleep or care about crashing at their desks tomorrow. But it was the same club she'd been planning to go to with Max last night, and that made going there hard to handle. Right then, all she wanted to do was go back to her friends' place and curl up on the couch with Netflix and a cheese and spinach pizza.

Since running away from Max last night, Lana had felt like complete crap. She normally wasn't a moody person, but as Sunday morning stretched into afternoon and then evening, the ache in her middle had gotten worse. She couldn't help wondering if this was what people meant when they talked about being lovesick. If so, it sucked.

Lana had only stayed at her parent's house for a couple hours the night before. Just long enough to get through the initial rush of emotions that had inundated her after what happened with Max in the alley. The instinct to run home to her parents had been understandable, but it had also been stupid. It was bad enough that her mother had badgered her, wanting to know what Max had done, but her father had been a complete pain in the butt, swearing a blue streak about firing Max first thing in the morning. Unable to take it, she'd left and headed back to the refuge of Brandy and Miriam's couch. Both women had been out, leaving her with the silence necessary to figure out what the hell had happened.

The truth was that Lana still no idea what she'd seen in the alley, but as the hours wore on, she was becoming increasingly sure it hadn't been what she'd thought. Max might have acted odd, but there was no way she could have seen claws and fangs. That was just stupid. And all the crap he'd said about her being in danger had to be some kind of hero complex gone to the extreme. Max had simply been playing off her grief for Denise, wanting to be her knight in shining armor. She'd read about that kind of stuff happening. The thing was, he didn't have to do anything to make her like him even more than she did. She'd already fallen for him like a ton of bricks. She'd been thinking about having kids with the guy, for heaven's sake. Now, it looked like her father had been right all along. Max wasn't the right man for her.

While that sounded logical, it did little to help her get over the ache in her chest. Clearly, her heart had already made up its mind about who it wanted her to be with.

Lana blinked back a rush of tears and forced herself to move away from the bar. As she wandered around the club, she kept an occasional eye on her friends, nursing a drink she really didn't want and trying to make it look like she was having a good time. She wished she could find a spot in the club that wasn't so loud. Between the music and everyone talking, it felt like her eardrums were about to burst.

She'd finally settled on a location between two giant

speakers a few feet away from the dance floor when a shiver ran through her body. At first she thought she'd been hit with a blast from the air conditioner, but then her skin began to tingle so badly she felt like she needed to scratch all over. It was like she'd just walked into a spiderweb.

Following an instinct she didn't fully understand, Lana began to move around the club again, trying to figure out what was making her feel so freaky. Her steps took her into one of the larger side rooms decorated in a Goth style with plenty of black lights and heavy drapery covering the walls and ceiling. There were fewer people in here than in the main room, and it wasn't as noisy. Catching a flash of movement out of the corner of her eye, she turned to see a man on the far side of the room, partially hidden by a thick velvet curtain. She moved a little to the left, trying to get a glimpse of his face and was surprised to realize it was the police officer from Central who'd spritzed her with perfume at the mall. The moment she set eyes on him, her gums and fingertips tingled. Crap, that was getting old.

She tried to duck out of the room before he saw her, but just then he looked her way. She cursed as he made eye contact. Maybe she could pretend she didn't recognize him.

Suddenly, her whole body tingled all over like she was holding on to an electric fence. What the hell was making her feel this way?

She was still trying to figure that out when the cop from Central gave her a smile so creepy she thought her skin might slide off and run screaming out of the club. Kids who pulled the wings off of flies would look at this guy and head the other way.

And that's exactly what she did, too.

Lana had almost reached the arched doorway that led into the main part of the club when two stocky men wearing leather jackets and jeans came into the room, blocking her path. She froze midstep as she realized one of them was the guy who'd been with the cop from Central at the mall the other day. That couldn't be a coincidence.

She didn't hesitate to follow her body's instincts this time either, turning away from the two men and heading in yet a third direction. She had no idea where she was going, but she hurried past a group of women and ducked into the nearest curtain-covered doorway she saw, praying it would lead somewhere good.

She found herself in a dimly lit hallway with a red, illuminated sign at the end, declaring *Emergency Exit. Alarm Will Sound.* The easing of the tension in her stomach told her this was the way to go, and she immediately took off running down the corridor. She had to zig and zag around some chairs and tables stacked up against the walls, but then she was slamming through the emergency exit, tripping the fire alarm.

Lana hoped that would dissuade the men from following her, but just in case, she raced down the alley behind the club, heading for the main road out front. Once there, she'd be able to get lost in the shuffle of people hurrying out the front entrance by now.

But when she reached the street, two motorcycles slid to a stop in front of her, cutting her off. She initially thought they'd hit their brakes because of the people running out of the club, but then one of the men reached inside his jacket and came out with a pistol.

Crap.

"Boyd, this is Seth," the man with the gun said, obviously talking to someone on a mic. "The girl just came out of the alley to the north of the club."

Lana stared, shocked she could hear him through the full-face helmet he wore. But right then, she could hear every tiny sound around her. The noise was deafening.

"Good," a familiar voice answered in Seth's earpiece—the cop from the mall who probably wasn't a cop at all. "Herd her back into the alley. We'll take her out in here."

Lana's heart hammered. Safety was only a few hundred feet away on the other side of those two bikers, but she'd never get through them. Turning, she ran down the sidewalk away from the club as fast as she could, sure she was going to feel a bullet slamming into her back at any moment. She couldn't think about that, though. All she could do was pray.

She heard the roar of the bikes behind her, but as fast as they were, she stayed ahead of them. She was moving so fast that everything around her was little more than a blur.

As if following some instinct she didn't know she had, Lana turned into another alley, almost running right out of her strappy shoes. She dashed down the narrow space cluttered with dumpsters and trash cans, dodging some, leaping over others. She heard the bikes stop and knew they'd been forced to turn back because of all the rubble in their way.

She darted out of the alley and turned right, sprinting down the sidewalk for a few blocks before sprinting down another side street. Even though she should have easily outdistanced the men chasing her, she soon heard the sounds of pursuit. First the motorcycles, then three sets of heavy, pounding footsteps behind her. She knew it shouldn't have been possible for her to discern three particular sets of footsteps out of all the noise around her, but she could.

She sniffed the air as she ran, not sure why, but her instincts were telling her she should be able smell the men behind her. More insanity, she knew. Those instincts had gotten her out of that club alive though, so she wasn't ready to ignore them, even when the scents that should have been there never showed up. It was like a void where a scent should be. Even more insanity, but something inside her was terrified by this strange lack of odor.

While she was blazing, speed alone wasn't enough to get her away from the three people chasing her and the other two on motorcycles. Every time she put some distance between her and her pursuers, the bikes seemed to get ahead of her and cut her off, constantly turning her back toward the three runners fanning out behind her. No matter what she did, the guys on the bikes kept finding her, herding her where they wanted her to go. It was like they knew how these new instincts of hers worked better than she did.

She considered digging her cell phone out of her cross-body bag and calling someone. But who would she call, and how would it help? She wasn't even sure she could convince the police she was being chased, and even if she could, the men would almost certainly be able to catch her while she stood around playing with her phone. Even the idea of calling Max, as tempting as that might have been, didn't come with any assurances.

She might be dead long before he could get to this part of town.

She had no choice but to follow her instincts, the ones screaming at her to run in a certain direction even if that direction made no sense. The GPS in her head led her farther and farther from the more populated parts of downtown, along dingy backstreets she never would have ventured in, over industrial dividing walls she shouldn't have been able to climb, and through deserted construction lots so dark she shouldn't have been able to see her hands in front of her face. But for reasons that probably would have freaked her out if she'd had time to think about them, she could see just fine.

Lana didn't know how far she'd run, but it was a long way. Oddly enough, she wasn't out of breath. Finally, she ran into an old building that looked slated for demolition. All the windows were broken out or boarded up, with graffiti everywhere. As she flew past the homeless people squatting in the lower rooms, she wondered if she should ask them for help, but her instincts told her she'd do better on her own. Plus, she didn't want to get anyone else hurt. If she were lucky, Boyd and his crew would keep going down the street.

She was almost to the far side of the building when she realized that she'd made a big mistake. Her pursuers hadn't kept going. All five of them had followed her in, and they had her cornered.

Before she could slip out one of the rear windows, the wall beside her exploded in a shower of concrete fragments, throwing chips and dust everywhere. Crap, they were shooting at her with silenced weapons. Who the hell were these people?

She stopped thinking and simply ran for her life as one bullet after another smacked into the wall, pulverizing the sheetrock and the concrete blocks underneath. The acrid odor of smokeless powder filled the air, stinging her nose. She'd gone shooting with her dad enough times for the smell to be unforgettable, only now it was way more pungent.

But when a bullet smacked into the wall only a few feet away from her face, she picked up another scent. It wasn't nearly as familiar as the stench of gunpowder, but she recognized it all the same. It was the damn perfume Boyd had spritzed on her. It even burned her nose as she breathed it in.

She tried escaping out a back exit, the door long ago ripped off the hinges and cast aside. But the moment she turned in that direction, two men stepped through the doorway and started shooting at her with silenced automatic weapons. It was surreal to run screaming from a hail of gunfire she could barely hear. If it wasn't for the impact of the bullets hitting the wall, she'd have thought this was all some kind of game.

Lana had no choice now but to run up the sagging metal stairs, toward the upper floors, even as every horror movie she'd ever watched screamed at her that she was making a big mistake. Footsteps echoed behind her, heavy boots on steel reverberating in the concrete stairwell. They were right behind her.

Gunshots pushed her higher and higher, past the second- and third-floor landings. Not that there was anywhere to run on those levels, because most of the flooring had either fallen through or been ripped out. Only a monkey could have escaped across the remaining grid work of metal beams and rotten wood slats.

She raced up the last flight of stairs, praying there'd be a fire escape or some other way off the roof. But when she reached the top level and saw the heavy chain running through the space in the door where the knob used to be, then snaking back through a hole that had been drilled through the brick and metal of the doorframe, she knew her luck had run out. There was no way she was going to get through that chain and the big padlock holding it in place.

But whatever instincts had kept her alive this long refused to give up. Refused to let her mind consider how devastated her parents would be—how devastated Max would be—if they found her beaten and tortured like Denise.

Letting loose a growl, she ran across the last few steps between her and the door, lifting her leg to kick the door with her foot as hard as she could. The chain going through the door held, but the rusted hinges on the left didn't. They snapped with a shriek of metal and the door tumbled out of its frame.

Lana braced herself for the pain of broken bones to come screaming up her leg, but she got lucky. Either that or she was so high on adrenaline she couldn't feel anything. Either way, nothing hurt as she climbed over the remnants of the door and sprinted across the roof.

She heard the loud thump of boots nearing the top of the stairs just as she reached the far side of the roof and discovered there wasn't a fire escape. She gaped at the ten-foot chasm between the roof she was on and the one on the building next to it. But it wasn't the gap that scared the crap out of her. It was the fact that the far roof was at least two floors lower. If she tried to jump over there, she'd have to throw herself hard enough to cross the gap and pray she'd survive the landing. She'd have to be insane to try it.

She turned and hurried toward the left side of the building, hoping for better luck over there. But she barely made it halfway there before the sound of boots announced she'd run out of time. Boyd stood in the doorway of the stairwell. He was holding a small automatic rifle in his hands, a sick, demented smile slowly spreading across his face. The other men chasing her would join him soon enough, but for that moment, it was just the two of them.

She glanced in the direction she'd been running, calculating the possibility that there might be a fire escape on that side of the roof. But with Boyd there, it was a chance she couldn't take. If she ran over there and found nothing to help her, she was going to die up here.

Lana spun and went back the way she'd come. The gravel and tar of the rooftop exploded around her at the same moment she heard the *Pop! Pop! Pop!* as Boyd shot at her with his silenced weapon. She ignored the near misses, running faster as she approached the far edge of the roof.

She didn't slow and she didn't think. She simply held her breath and jumped as hard as she could.

Bullets zipped past her as she sailed across the open gap between the buildings. How she continued to be so lucky was a mystery to her, but she'd easily cleared the chasm dividing the two rooftops. She had no time to marvel at the feat because the far rooftop was quickly rushing up to meet her. She braced herself for impact but envisioned so many things breaking she couldn't imagine walking away from this. But when her feet hit the gravel, the impact wasn't nearly as bad as she'd thought it would be. Those amazing instincts she was coming to trust with her life tucked her into a ball and rolled her twice across the roof before propelling her right back to her feet.

She almost let out a whoop of excitement as she regained her balance and raced for the far side of the building she'd landed on. Bullets continued to slap into the roof around her, but she ran even faster now as she realized she could really get away from the men chasing her.

Lana threw herself off the roof of the two-story building, far less concerned about how she'd handle the landing this time. The hail of bullets disappeared before she even landed, replaced by the sound of angry cursing. She almost laughed as she landed in the tall grass of a long-abandoned building and took off running again. It would take the men a little while to get down from the roof, and she wasn't going to be around by the time that happened.

She ran at full speed toward the more populated part of town, where the stores and clubs were. When she got there, she slowed to a fast walk, not wanting to attract attention. As she passed a darkened storefront, she caught her reflection in the glass, and the image stopped her cold.

Lana stepped closer, her instincts telling her the threat from her pursuers had passed. Stunned by what she saw in the glass, she lifted her hand to touch her face simply to convince herself it wasn't some kind of trick.

But it wasn't a trick. She was really seeing her reflection in the glass—except in this particular reflection, she had half-inch long canines protruding from her upper jaw. The canines on the bottom were longer than normal, too. And her eyes were glowing green. She touched one of her fangs and was shocked not only to realize it was sharp as hell, but also that the tip of her finger was now graced with a slightly curved claw half an inch long. A quick glance down confirmed that all her fingernails were similarly equipped.

Crap.

She had claws and fangs and glowing eyes.

She gasped for breath, barely able to stand. Max had been telling the truth all along. She really was in danger, there really were people after her, and she really was a werewolf.

A werewolf like Max.

The fact that Boyd and his crew had been trying to kill her didn't seem important right now. The only thing that mattered was getting to Max and telling him she was sorry. There'd been something special between them, and she'd walked away in a heartbeat rather than trust him. She had to fix that horrible mistake.

The instincts that had saved her life were screaming at her again, except this time, they weren't telling her to run *away* from something. They were begging her to run *toward* something—Max. At that second, the need to find him and tell him exactly how she felt about him was so overwhelming she couldn't have resisted it if she'd wanted to.

She gazed at her reflection in fascination as her fangs and claws slowly receded. It felt so normal she couldn't imagine why she'd been so hung up about seeing those same weapons on Max.

One more thing to apologize for.

Lana pulled her phone out of her purse as she walked toward the nearest intersection. There were several text messages from Brandy and Miriam, asking where the hell she'd gone off to. She thumbed back a quick reply, saying the music had gotten too loud and she'd grabbed a cab.

You going back to the apartment? Brandy immediately texted back.

Lana didn't bother to lie. No, I'm heading over to see Max. We need to talk.

There was no response for several long seconds, but when it came, it was slightly different than she expected.

> Good. That's what you should have been doing
> instead of coming out to the club with us.

Lana threw back a thumbs-up emoji, then flagged down a cab. Giving Max's address to the driver, she settled into the backseat, trying to figure out exactly what the hell she was going to say to him.

She still had no answer to that question when the cab pulled up in front of his apartment building fifteen minutes later. By the time she paid the driver and walked upstairs to his place, she decided less talk and more action was called for in this case.

Max jerked open the door before she could ring the bell. He was wearing a pair of black athletic shorts, his hair was sticking up, and he looked like he hadn't slept in days, but he'd never looked more handsome. Why the hell had she ever walked away from him?

"Are you okay?" he asked.

She knew she probably looked more than a little rumpled after her mad dash through downtown and that tumble along the gravel-covered rooftop, but she didn't care. She didn't want to get into any of that at the moment. There was more important stuff to cover first.

Holding his gaze, she held up her right hand and let her claws extend. She'd discreetly practiced the move in the backseat of the cab on the way over and had been shocked at how easy it was to make her claws extend and retract by doing little more than tensing her fingers.

"I know everything." She stepped inside and wrapped her arms around him, hugging him tightly. "I'm sorry I ran away from you."

She felt him take a deep breath, as if he was about to say something in reply, but she hadn't come here to talk. They could do that later. When they talked about all kinds of stuff—like how she'd become a werewolf. Right now, she needed to be with the man she loved like he was the air within her lungs.

Reaching up, she tangled her hand in his rumpled hair, jerking his mouth down to hers. Then she kissed the hell out of him, trying to say with a single touch of her lips something that would likely take a thousand words.

Her body immediately began to tingle all over, and Lana felt her claws and fangs slide out. She simply couldn't help it, and besides, it felt so right. Even so, she pulled back, worried about cutting Max's tongue. Then she saw his fangs were out, too, and his eyes were glowing so bright they lit up the dim entryway.

He reached out and kicked the door closed behind

her, then his mouth was on her neck, nibbling and kissing her there, driving her crazy. She heard a deep growl coming from his throat before she realized she was raking his back with her nails. She started to apologize but stopped as he slid his hands under her shirt and pushed it up. Things got a little wild after that, as clothes flew everywhere and claws gently raked across naked skin.

Then her back was pressed up against the door and Max's cock was sliding deep inside of her. The pleasure was so intense she feared her growls would force the neighbors to call the police—or animal control.

Biting her fist in an attempt to hold in the noise wasn't going to be enough, but she had to do something. So she once again followed her instincts, sinking her fangs into the muscles of his shoulder.

Growling, Max slammed into her so hard she thought the door behind her might shatter. But any concerns about that disappeared when she felt her orgasm approaching like a speeding train. Lana wrapped her legs around his powerful body and held on tight.

She was home. Where she was supposed to be.

"So I'm a werewolf," Lana murmured as she sat astride his hips and grazed her extended nails across his chest, watching with fascination as her claws left light welts on his skin that faded almost immediately.

It took a minute for Max to reply. He was too busy catching his breath. They'd made love for nearly three hours straight, and this was the first time they'd slowed down enough to talk.

Talking was so frigging overrated.

Lana wiggled back and forth on his hips as she waited for his answer. Even after making love like two overly caffeinated Tasmanian devils, one little sexy move of that ass was all it took to get him going again. He couldn't believe he was ready for more. But the night was still young, so anything was possible.

He was pleasantly tired, his body completely wrung out. He had bite marks on his neck and shoulder, not to mention claw marks on his chest and back. Most were shallow, but he felt a few on his back that might take a day or so to heal up completely.

The urge to mark Lana the same way she'd marked him had been intense, but she was a beta and wouldn't heal as fast as he did. Still, he'd left a few reminders on her skin she was going to notice for a while. He couldn't be sure without coming straight out and asking her, but he had the feeling she kind of liked the way those marks looked on her perfect skin. Possession was nine-tenths of the law after all, and it definitely felt like Lana was his now, the same way he belonged to her.

"Yup," he said in answer to her question, feeling himself getting harder under her rocking hips. "An extremely sexy werewolf."

Lana smiled but didn't say anything. Instead, she lifted her hands and stared at her fingers, her claws extending and retracting over and over. Damn, her claws were so cute. Shorter and daintier than an alpha's or omega's, but still long enough to do some damage if she wanted to. His back was a stark testament to that fact.

Suddenly, Lana jumped off him, moving so fast she almost damaged the part of his anatomy that had been trying to get her attention. She stood beside the bed and stared at her feet, her brow furrowing slightly.

"Why won't my toenails extend like my fingernails?" she asked, her face screwing up in effort as she looked down at her bare feet.

"They will." He chuckled. "You're kind of new to this, so it will take some time to learn. The claws on our feet are naturally inhibited in most cases unless we really push it. Probably a genetic adaptation to modern footwear, I guess. Wouldn't want to shred your shoes every time your claws came out."

Lana nodded, not taking her eyes off her feet. "That makes sense."

She pursed her lips as if she was trying to push her toenails to extend regardless of what he'd said. Sighing, she climbed back on the bed and straddled him again, leaning forward so that the tips of her beautiful breasts were pressed against his pecs, her face close to his.

She opened her mouth and tried to look down her nose so she could see her canines as they extended. Then she reached up and pushed down on his chin, opening his mouth.

"Show me yours," she said, never taking her eyes off his teeth.

He chuckled, making her frown at him with the sexiest look of fanged disapproval he'd ever seen. But he behaved, letting his fangs slip out.

"Whoa." She tipped his chin this way and that so she could see. "Yours are so much bigger than mine. And before you even go there, I'm not talking about some kind of fang envy here or anything. It's just that my fangs aren't even half as long as yours, and you seem to have a lot more of them than I do. Where the heck do they all go when they slide back in? They seem too long to fit."

He would have laughed at the pure, simple curiosity of her question if it wasn't for the fact that having her breasts teasing him like this was seriously distracting.

"They slide into curved pockets along the upper and lower jaws. The longer the fangs, the more horizontal those pockets are. That's why your upper canines are longer than the lower ones—more room to hide them. I'm a slightly different kind of werewolf than you are, so I have more fangs, and they're bigger. If I need to get even more of them out, my entire jawline can widen to make room. Yours won't do that. You're not that kind of werewolf."

Lana seemed to consider that for a second, and he wondered if he was going to have to explain the whole alpha versus beta thing. He hoped not. Science and medical stuff weren't his strong suit.

"Okay," she said, apparently happy with his explanation. "That makes sense. In that whole this-shouldn't-be-possible kind of way. But why didn't my dentist see these pockets when he was taking X-rays?"

"When was the last time you went to the dentist?" he asked with amusement, already having a good idea what the answer might be.

She frowned, seeming to put a lot of thought into that question. "Oh wow! I just realized that I haven't been to the dentist since the accident. After I started going to college, I never thought about it."

He nodded. "Now that you're a werewolf, you won't ever go back to a dentist. Werewolves don't get cavities."

Her eyes widened. "Seriously?"

He laughed. "Seriously. And you won't get colds or the flu or any of the other common illnesses that affect most people. You'll heal faster from cuts and fractures than a regular person, too. And by the way, you won't gain weight or get drunk, either, not without a tremendous amount of effort."

Her eyes widened more with every werewolf advantage he listed. But then her face became intensely serious. "I can still have kids, right? Being a werewolf didn't change that, did it?"

Max felt something inside his chest expand, making him want to grab Lana and squeeze her until she squeaked like a werewolf chew toy. He settled for reaching up to curl her hair gently around his index finger. He loved her so much it made him dizzy thinking about it. He was wondering if he should say the words, just to make it official, but she repeated her earlier question, reminding him he hadn't answered it yet.

"You planning on having kids sometime soon?" he asked, a smile creeping across his face.

Lana blushed, which only made her cuter in Max's opinion. "Yeah, I guess so. I've never really given it any thought, until I saw you with Terence and the girls. That's when I started thinking that you'd make a great dad—when the time is right."

He tugged her down for a long, soulful kiss where he attempted to convey exactly how much he cared about her—and her idea of future parenthood. Like Lana, he hadn't really thought about kids very much. In fact, given his screwed-up background, he'd always assumed it would be best if he never did. Too much chance of passing on some abusive gene that no one understood yet. But with Lana, the idea of kids didn't seem so scary. With her, he thought having children might be the most amazing thing in the world.

Max was still kissing her, his cock taking that as a sure sign they were getting ready for round two—or was it round five?—when Lana quickly pulled back. He was just recovering from the bout of sensual whiplash when he realized Lana was looking at him with those wide eyes of hers again.

"Will our kids be werewolves, too?" she asked, clearly thrilled at the thought.

"Whoa, slow down a little," he said trying hard not to laugh. "Figuring out who's going to become a werewolf is kind of complicated. I've been one since I was eighteen and part of the Pack now for nearly two years, and I still don't understand everything about how it all works. All I know is that there's a gene all werewolves have that switches on and turns them when something traumatic happens. Like the accident you had when you were in high school."

She frowned a little. "That's what turned me into a werewolf? I thought I must have gotten bitten or something."

"Nah. That's all folklore," he said. "You should probably talk to Gage or Brooks or any of the older werewolves. They could help answer your questions. Of course, if you're looking for the scientific details, I'd suggest Triana, Lacey, or Dr. Saunders. Triana is Remy's mate and works in the medical examiner's office, Lacey is Alex's mate and is a veterinarian, and Saunders is the Pack's doctor. He probably knows more about werewolves than anyone. Except maybe for

Gemma. She's Triana's mother and has been around werewolves for over twenty years. Her knowledge is a little skewed toward the mystical side of things, though, since she practices voodoo."

Max was about to say more, but then he realized Lana was lying on top of him with a completely dumbfounded expression on her face.

"What's wrong?" he asked, trying to remember what he'd said that could have confused her. It had seemed straightforward to him.

"All of those people you mentioned are werewolves?"

The question came out slow and careful, like she thought it was something she shouldn't ask. He replayed the conversation in his head again to see if he'd said something strange. If he had, he couldn't figure out what it had been.

So he simply shook his head. "Not all of them. Triana and Lacey are soul mates of two members of the Pack, and Saunders is a doctor Gage has known for years. He's helped us out a couple times. Gemma isn't a werewolf, either, though she was married to one."

"Gage, Brooks, Remy, and Alex are all werewolves?" she asked. "They're all in your pack?"

That's when Max finally figured out what Lana was getting at. She wanted to know how many other werewolves like her were out there. Now that he thought about it, it was a question he probably should have seen coming. The fact that he hadn't likely had to do with the multiple orgasms. It was a well-known fact that orgasms made men stupid—or at least dulled their wits for a period of time. Years in some cases.

"Yes, they're all werewolves." He ran his fingers down

her back to rest his hands comfortably on the upper curve of her butt. He liked her butt—it was a nice butt. "Just like all the other members of the Dallas SWAT team—all seventeen of us. We're one large pack, extended to include the women each of us have bonded with."

"Like me?"

He smiled. "Yes, like you. You have a pack now, a group of werewolves who will always be there for you, no matter what you need."

Lana must have liked the sound of that, because she smiled like crazy. "I can't believe there are so many werewolves in Dallas and I never knew. I can't wait to meet all of them. I have so many questions."

"And they'll be thrilled to meet you too. But as long as we're talking about the subject of werewolves in Dallas, I guess I should mention there is more than just our pack. One of the guys in the SWAT Pack bonded with another werewolf who already had her own pack, so they're here, too, with all their various mates. Then there are all the smaller packs and the loners who started showing up when the hunter threat started to get worse. There are maybe fifty werewolves in the metro area these days who have shown up hoping to get protection by being close to a large pack."

"Hunters? You used that word before in the alley when you changed in front of me. I guess that's who chased me earlier tonight," she said casually, almost curiously. "Go ahead and say it now—you were right about them, too."

Max started to nod, but then the words sunk in. "Wait a minute." He sat up so fast he almost dumped Lana off his lap. He quickly adjusted her so she was sitting back on his thighs, any thought of another round of fun and games completely gone now. "You were chased by someone tonight, and you didn't think to mention it to me?"

She looked at him in confusion. "I didn't mention it when I walked through your front door? I'm sure I did."

"I think I would have remembered you saying something like that," he said. "It's kind of important. You walked in, showed off your claws, then jumped on me."

Her lips curved. "Oh yeah. I guess that's how it happened. But in my defense, the concern that you might not want me in your life after the way I'd treated you outweighed any worries I had about being shot at by a bunch of crazy men in downtown Dallas."

They'd shot at her, too? Max cursed. "I need you to go into excruciating detail about everything that happened. Leave nothing out."

Max sat there with Lana resting on his thighs, listening in stunned silence as she explained what had happened at the club and how the same guy who'd spritzed her with that nasty perfume at the mall had chased her, along with some of his buddies. By the time she was done, he didn't know if he was furious with her for not telling him about it right away or impressed as hell that she'd gotten away from five heavily armed and well-trained hunters.

Regardless, he picked Lana up and deposited her beside him on the bed, then grabbed his phone from the bedside table to call Gage. He hadn't even thumbed in his passcode before the thing rang in his hand, almost making him drop it. At the sight of Gage's name on the screen, he thumbed the green button. Good freaking timing, he guessed.

"Max, is Lana with you?" Gage said before Max could even get a word out. But Sarge's tone said it all. Something was wrong.

"She's here," Max said. "What's wrong?"

"Get her to Medical City Dallas Hospital, ASAP. Paramedics just brought in her father. Someone broke into their house and attacked him."

Max wished she hadn't, but it was obvious Lana had heard everything Gage said, even though it wasn't on speaker.

He heard her heart kick into high gear as she leaned forward and thumbed the speakerphone button. "How bad it is? Was my mom there, too?"

"Your mother wasn't there. She was handling some kind of crisis at the restaurant. She's on the way to the hospital now."

"How badly is my father hurt?" Lana asked again.

Gage hesitated. "It's bad. They broke in and beat the hell out of him, no doubt trying to get him to tell them where to find you. Then they shot him and left him for dead. He's hanging on, but he's in critical condition."

Chapter 11

Brandy and Miriam met Lana and Max the moment they walked into the Medical City ER, hurrying them down the hall as fast as they could.

"Your dad is heading in for surgery, but he's asking for you," Brandy said. "He's refusing the surgery until he sees you and Max. Talk to him fast, then convince him to let us take him into the OR. Every second we waste is making it harder to save his life."

Lana started to hyperventilate, her gums and fingernails tingling like mad. She probably would have shifted right there if it wasn't for Max holding her hand. He was like a rock, a steady presence she latched on to as emotional waves threatened to drown her.

There were a dozen cops in the hallway outside the ER, some of whom were Max's SWAT teammates—his pack mates. Well, hers now, too, she guessed. All of them looked as worried as she felt.

Brandy and Miriam quickly hustled her and Max into a curtained-off triage area, then left. Lana's mother was already there, unshed tears in her eyes, but surprisingly, so was Gage. Lana choked back a sob at the sight of her father lying in a hospital bed, his face cut and bruised. He had an oxygen mask on and multiple IV lines in both arms. His forehead, both hands, and chest were swathed in heavy bandages, blood already soaking through several places. He was conscious, but he didn't look good.

All the terrible things she'd said to him the other day when they fought echoed in her head, bringing a fresh rush of tears to her eyes.

"Okay, your daughter is here," a doctor Lana hadn't noticed standing by the bed said to her father. "Can we please take you into surgery now?"

Her father reached up and pushed the oxygen mask aside. The doctor quickly moved to put it back, but her dad gave the woman his patented deputy-chief glare, stopping the woman cold. "I need to talk to my daughter and her boyfriend alone."

Her father's voice sounded stronger than Lana thought it'd be, which was a relief. The doctor didn't look happy, but she nodded.

"Two minutes," she said, then left, pulling the curtain closed behind her.

Lana hurried over to the bed, leaning close to kiss him gently on the brow. "Dad, you need to let them do the surgery."

He waved her concern aside. "I will, but first I need to talk to you. Before it's too late." His voice seemed weaker now that the doctor had left, like he'd been putting on an act for the woman.

"Don't talk like that," Lana insisted, refusing to even let him think such a thing. "You're going to be fine."

He took her hand, gazing up at her fondly. "Lana, I love you dearly, but you're a terrible liar. There are things I need to say, things I should have told you long ago."

"Things we both should have told her long ago," her mother added.

He shook his head, his gaze going to her mother. "I

convinced you to go along with my plan. You're the one who wanted to tell her from the beginning."

Dammit. There wasn't time for this. Lana glanced at the heart monitor on the cart near the head of the bed. She wasn't a doctor, but she had a general idea about what she should be seeing, and her father's rhythms didn't look very steady to her.

"Dad, you can tell me everything later, after you come out of surgery," she said. "We can sit together and talk as long as you want."

Her father ignored her, looking at Gage, then Max. "The people who did this weren't after me. They were after Lana. I don't know how they found out, but they know she's different and they're planning to kill her. I need the SWAT team to protect her. She's special like you and the other people on your team. I know you can keep her safe."

Gage nodded. "We will."

That must have been good enough for her father because he turned back to Lana. "I know this is all happening so fast, and you don't understand any of it, but you're special. You have been for a long time. I should have told you everything a long time ago, but I was scared you'd be mistreated. You're different, and our world doesn't treat people who are different very nicely. But it's time you know everything."

Lana had had enough. Her father was getting weaker by the second and the patterns on the heart monitor looked even more erratic. They needed to hurry this along and get him into the operating room.

"I already know what I am," she said softly. "I'm a werewolf. I figured it out earlier tonight, though I've been getting an idea that something was different ever since I met Max. He's the one who helped me figure it all out."

"A werewolf." Her father gazed at her, awe in his eyes. "Yes, I guess that makes sense."

She smiled even though she was on the verge of tears. "It doesn't make sense at all, but it's true anyway. Now that we have that out of the way, it's time to get you into surgery."

He shook his head. "Not yet. There are so many things I need to tell you—how it happened, why we hid it from you, what those men look like."

Lana opened her mouth to tell him they could talk about all that later, but then an alarm sounded from the heart monitor. There was also a red light blinking on the side of the main console. She didn't know what it meant, but it couldn't be good.

Beside her, Max whipped the curtain back and called for help. Brandy, Miriam, and the doctor hurried in. Lana quickly got out of their way. Seconds later, they were wheeling her father away, leaving Lana with Max, her mother, and Gage.

Her mother wrapped a comforting arm around her shoulders. "I have a few things I need to tell you. Then maybe you can help me understand a few things as well."

—⁓—

"We knew there was something unusual happening within forty-eight hours of the accident," Nora said.

They were sitting in a quiet corner of the cafeteria, drinking bad coffee, Max on one side of the table with Lana, her mother and Gage opposite them. At this time of night, the place was deserted except for the guy cleaning the food-prep area behind the counter. He was wearing a set of earbuds and was completely lost in his music.

They'd come in about thirty minutes ago, after Lana had finished giving statements to the detectives investigating her father's assault. She told them about the men who'd chased her from the club the previous night and about the run-in with the same men at the Galleria. She'd given good descriptions, so Max knew the detectives were out there right now gathering video footage from both the mall and the downtown street cameras, hoping to get a look at the men and find out where they might have gone after that. Max couldn't help but wonder what they'd think when they saw video of the blur Lana probably made as she ran away from the hunters. But she and his pack would worry about that after the hunters were off the streets.

Max had told the detectives about the case Austin PD was working on, hoping they'd share anything they learned in Dallas. The lead detective hadn't said anything one way or the other, but Max hoped he'd be willing to work with Peterson.

"The doctors said that with all the injuries you'd sustained, you'd never make it through the night. A zero percent chance…that's what they said," Nora said quietly. She wrapped her hands around her coffee cup as if trying to gain comfort from the warmth inside as she remembered the events surrounding the accident that had turned her daughter into a werewolf. "But the next morning, you were still hanging on. You still had a lot of internal injuries, so even though the doctors were worried you wouldn't survive another surgery, they had to do it to save your life. But when they took you in for another CAT scan beforehand, they couldn't find the damage that had been there on the earlier scan. The doctors thought your scan had gotten confused with someone else's."

"But that wasn't it, was it, Nora?" Gage asked softly. "The injury healed itself, didn't it?"

She nodded. "Some of the fractures Lana had sustained weren't as bad, either. The doctors couldn't explain it and didn't try. They took her in for exploratory surgery, only to come out a little while later and tell Hal and me that all Lana's injuries were healed."

"Is that when you and the deputy chief took her out of the hospital and arranged for private care at home?" Max prompted, remembering what Lana had told him a couple days ago.

Nora glanced at him, her blue eyes tired. "Yes. Some of the doctors started talking about doing tests and taking samples, so they could figure out how she recovered from injuries that severe so quickly. Hal and I didn't want that, so we refused to okay the tests and took her out of the hospital as soon as possible."

"How did you hide all this from Lana?" Max asked. "The fangs, the claws, the eyes—everything? Typically, a new werewolf has trouble controlling all those things."

Nora gave Lana a small smile. "We didn't know she was a werewolf. As far as we knew, she was simply unique. We had no way of knowing there were others like her. The only times we ever saw any of those things you described was after she experienced a horrible nightmare in the month or two following the accident. She'd wake up screaming in fear, her teeth and fangs out, her eyes glowing bright green. But once she got into therapy with Dr. Delacroix and stopped having the dreams, the fangs and claws disappeared, so Hal and I didn't think about them. I never dreamed that we were living in a town with a whole SWAT team just like her."

Max exchanged looks with Gage at the mention of Delacroix's name. What were the chances that the psychologist who'd worked with Cooper was also the same woman who'd worked with young Lana Mason? What was Delacroix, a werewolf whisperer?

Gage merely shrugged and turned his attention back to Nora. Max had no choice but to do the same, wondering if maybe therapy was the reason Lana's inner werewolf had stayed hidden until recently. He was about to ask Gage if he thought that was a possibility when Nora spoke again.

"Have the fangs and claws come back?" she asked, looking at her daughter.

Lana glanced over to make sure the guy with the headphones wasn't looking their way, then put her right hand on the table and extended her claws.

"Well, I guess they have." Nora eyed Lana's claws with an expression of wonder on her face before glancing at Max. "And Hal is right. You're like Lana...a werewolf?"

Max smiled at the way she whispered the word. In answer, he placed his hand on top of Lana's and extended his much longer claws.

"You don't seem very alarmed by all of this," Gage

pointed out. "Which makes me wonder why Hal went to such great lengths to try to keep Lana and Max apart. If you knew what my team and I are, why didn't you want Lana to know there were other people like her in the world?"

Nora sighed. "That was Hal's idea. I thought he was simply being an overprotective father, but now I realize he must have figured out you and your team are like Lana and was worried that being with Max would undo years of therapy and that the nightmares would come back along with the claws and fangs."

Max would have liked to say he disapproved of what the deputy chief had done, but he probably would have done the same thing if he thought it would protect the person he loved.

On the other side of the table, Nora looked at Gage. "These men who assaulted Hal, the ones looking for Lana—they kill people simply because they're werewolves even if they've never harmed anyone?"

Gage nodded, his jaw tight. "These hunters have killed dozens of werewolves. They've murdered others, like Lana's roommate in Austin, simply because they've made a mistake or were looking for information. They're vicious and cold-blooded serial killers."

Nora frowned, her gaze going to Max. "But you'll protect Lana and keep her safe?"

Max entwined his fingers with Lana's. "I swear that I'll never let anything or anyone hurt your daughter."

"Good." Nora looked at Gage. "And you'll find the men who did this to Hal and make sure they never do it to anyone else again?"

"We'll find them," Gage promised.

Chapter 12

"I REALLY DON'T THINK I NEED THIS MUCH PROTECTION," Lana complained as Max, Zane, Brooks, and Trey followed her into her parents' house.

She would rather not have come at all, but her mother needed a prescription she took daily as well as a few other personal items. Lana figured she could use some stuff, too, since now the plan was for her to stay at the SWAT compound until the hunters could be caught. She hadn't packed very much when she'd left in a huff the other day, and Max said there weren't a whole lot of creature comforts there. Brooks had volunteered to pick up what she and her mom needed, but Lana didn't really feel like having the big SWAT guy going through her panty drawer. Besides, it wasn't likely the hunters would come back here, especially in broad daylight.

"We're not going to let anything happen to the newest member of our Pack," Zane said in that charming British accent of his. "So you might as well get used to it."

"Just think of us as the four big brothers you never had," Brooks added.

"Well, three brothers and a boyfriend," Trey clarified, his blue eyes serious. "Otherwise, the analogy is a little creepy."

Lana couldn't help but laugh. Maybe it was the whole Pack thing, but it felt like these guys were already her brothers. Really tall, really muscular brothers. Having

Max around made her feel safe, but having these other guys wasn't bad for backup.

Her sense of humor faded as soon as she stepped through the front door of her parents' place and saw the crime scene tape and broken furniture. Max quickly hustled her upstairs, but it was too late. The signs of violence—and the smell of her father's blood—were impossible to miss. Her fangs and claws strained to come out, though she had no idea what she would do with the weapons if they did. It wasn't like the hunters were around for her to slice to ribbons.

"Why do my claws and fangs tingle every time I get upset, angry, excited, or scared?" she asked Max as they headed upstairs to her old bedroom. Brooks and the other guys stayed downstairs to keep an eye out for Boyd and the other hunters.

"It's an instinct thing," Max said, following her into the room that didn't look very different than it had when she'd left for college.

Her mom had insisted on keeping it the way Lana liked for those occasions when she came home from school. Lana hadn't done it that often, something she regretted now.

"Think of it as a fight-or-flight response," Max added. "Any of the strong emotions you mentioned flood your body with chemicals. Your inner werewolf doesn't have a clue why you're geeked up; it only knows you are. So it prepares you for both possibilities—running or fighting. Normally, a werewolf would have learned how to control that stuff early on, but in your case, you're just picking it up now."

Lana was still trying to get this whole alpha, beta,

omega thing straight—Max had spent a lot of time explaining it to her last night while her father had been in surgery. She still had a bunch of questions, but they could wait until later. Right now she wanted to pick up her stuff, drop it off at the compound, then get back to the hospital. She didn't like being away so long. Her father's surgery had gone well last night, but he was in an induced coma to help his body recover. It was scary to think about him being kept under like that, but she knew it was the best thing for him.

"So, you changed into a werewolf when your dad shot you. I changed because of the car wreck," Lana said as she packed some extra socks in a small suitcase. Max had mentioned that the floors of the compound were hard and cold. "I'm guessing werewolves don't get created from warm, fuzzy situations?"

Max shook his head. "Afraid not. As I understand it, the werewolf gene only flips on as a result of a major traumatic event, usually involving the release of large amounts of adrenaline, cortisol, and other stress hormones. I've never met a werewolf, regardless of breed, who turned because of a pleasant event."

She and Max were still talking about that as they rejoined the other SWAT officers downstairs.

"Got everything?" Brooks asked.

At her nod, Zane opened the door, leading the way outside. The moment they stepped onto the porch, Max and the others immediately tensed. She barely had time to register the black SUV pulling away from the curb across the street before all four of them closed around her like a shield, almost crushing her.

She opened her mouth to ask if it was the hunters,

but the words never got out as the front windows of her parents' home exploded around her. Then she was being pushed to the ground and covered with a solid weight as shots were fired over her head and tires squealed. Her teeth and claws extended as her nose filled with the horrible stench of the hunters' acrid perfume. They were using the same bullets they'd used downtown.

When the weight lifted off her, she looked up to see Brooks and Trey hauling ass down the street after the black SUV as it rounded the corner at the end of the block. Max was heading that way, too, but he was well behind the other guys, probably because he'd been the one on top of her, protecting her with his body.

Lana scrambled to her feet, every instinct screaming at her to chase the vehicle, too, and help catch the men so they couldn't hurt anyone ever again, but then she caught movement on the other side of the porch. She looked over to see Zane drop to his knees, one hand clutching his left bicep, blood pouring from between his fingers.

"Max!" she shouted. "Zane's been hit!"

Zane howled, and Lana could practically feel the gut-wrenching pain underlying the primal sound. It was the most soul-searing thing she'd ever heard.

She raced to his side to find him shifting, his body convulsing as his upper canines bit through his lower lip. She grabbed the hand he had clamped to his arm, trying to see how bad the wound was, but he refused to loosen his grip and she couldn't make him. He was too strong for her.

The familiar stench of the hunter's perfume hit her then. Crap, Zane had been hit by one of those bullets. If it stung as much as her skin had when Boyd spritzed it on her, it had to be painful as hell.

She was still trying to get Zane to let her take a look at the wound when Max and Trey ran onto the porch. They kneeled beside her to check on Zane, who was grinding his fangs together in an attempt to hold back another howl of pain.

"What the hell happened?" Trey asked as he tried to pry Zane's fingers away from the wound. Lana swore she heard bones breaking as Trey worked, but she doubted the other werewolf even felt it.

"They shot him," she said, helping Trey by grabbing Zane's right arm and trying to hold it down. Max got a grip on the left, and between the two of them, they finally restrained him.

Trey scowled as he tore the entire sleeve of Zane's uniform off, exposing the wound. "We get shot all the time. A bullet to the arm should be a joke."

"It's not the bullet that's the problem. It's the stuff the hunters put in the bullet," Lana told him. "Can't you smell it?"

Trey leaned forward to sniff the wound, then quickly recoiled, his eyes watering. "What the hell is it?"

"I don't know," she said, practically yelling to be heard over Zane's growl. "But when that guy sprayed it on my arm, it felt like lava. I washed it off within seconds but it still left a burn mark that lasted for two days."

The sound of footsteps on the porch made her look up. Brooks stood there, his chest rising and falling as he caught his breath, his blue-gray eyes filled with concern as Zane continued to writhe in pain.

"We have to go," he said. "Neighbors are starting to

come out to see what the hell all this noise is about. Can we move him?"

Trey and Max exchanged looks, clearly torn at the idea of moving Zane, who was going through uncontrollable shifts now.

"We have to do something," Trey said, his words coming out way calmer than Lana felt. "I need to get the bullet out and probably flush the wound to get rid of the poison."

"I'll carry him," Brooks said.

Lana immediately moved out of the way along with Max and Trey. Despite how much Zane was thrashing around, Brooks easily picked him up. Lana and Max ran ahead and lowered the backseat of the SUV so Trey would have room to work. Brooks set Zane down as carefully as he could, then stepped back to let Trey climb in.

"I'll drive," Max said, running around to the front of the SUV.

Lana moved to join him, but Trey stopped her.

"I need you back here with me," Trey said as he grabbed his medical bag. "You too, Brooks. I can't work on Zane with him thrashing around this much."

Ignoring the curious neighbors coming out of their houses, she and Brooks climbed into the back of the big SWAT vehicle and held on as Max jumped behind the wheel and squealed out of her parents' driveway.

Lana glanced back at her parents' house as they drove away, staring at the blown-out windows and bullet holes. The weekender of stuff she'd come to collect that had seemed so important a little while ago was still lying on the porch, forgotten. Zane had been shot over nothing.

"Do we take him to the compound?" Max asked.

"No," Trey shouted back. "Head for Saunders's private clinic. This is more than we can deal with in the kitchen of our barracks."

She had no idea where this private clinic was, but she hoped they could get there quickly.

"Lana, I need you to hold Zane down while I get the bullet out," Trey said. "Normally, something like this would be a piece of cake, but now, I'm not so sure."

She climbed around Brooks, which took a little doing. The guy was so big he took up the majority of the space back there. Clearly, the manufacturer had never planned to have this many alpha werewolves in the back of one of their SUVs.

Lana climbed on top of Zane's legs, holding them with her body weight, then leaning forward to latch on to his right hand in an effort to keep his flailing claws from tearing anyone apart.

"Brooks, we could really use your help here," Trey grated out as he tried to hold Zane's left arm and cut into the man's triceps at the same time.

"Hold on," Brooks said. "I'm getting Doc Saunders on the phone. I'm hoping he has a clue what the hell we should do."

When he got through to the doctor, he flipped the speaker on, then threw himself across Zane's chest. "Trey, do that paramedic shit of yours and start talking. I'll keep him still."

"Doc, Zane took a bullet to the arm that was filled with poison of some kind," Trey said. "The wound isn't serious, but it's causing him major problems."

"Describe *major problems*," a calm voice responded from the other end of the line.

Easy for him to be calm, Lana thought. He wasn't holding on to a thrashing 240-pound ball of claw-covered muscles who was bleeding and in pain.

"He's nearly unconscious, but his body is going through spasm shifts, back and forth from one form to another. I've even got some fur growth going on, and Zane has never come close to achieving full wolf form."

Lana looked at Brooks in shock, but he shook his head. "Later."

"He's been convulsing nonstop since getting hit, and his heart is racing like crazy," Trey continued. "He's sweating like hell, too."

"Have you gotten the bullet out yet?" Saunders asked.

"I'm working on it," Trey snarled through gritted teeth. "It's rather difficult at the moment."

Lana's eyes widened as Trey slashed the wound open wider with a scalpel, then shoved two fingers into it. A few seconds later, he came out with the bullet, or at least what Lana took to be the bullet. It didn't look like much more than a piece of mangled metal to her.

Trey dropped it in his medical bag. "Taking the bullet out didn't help, Doc. He's still thrashing and convulsing."

"Flush the wound with as much saline as you have," Saunders ordered. "And while you're doing that, can you describe this poison? What does it smell like?"

Trey frowned as he took a bottle out of his bag and began irrigating the bloody wound with saline. "Um... it stinks."

"Not helpful," Saunders snapped.

"It's medicinal smelling," Lana clarified, talking loudly as Zane howled. "Like sulfur mixed with a mild wild onion. It burns on contact with the skin and can cause an allergic-like reaction similar to a first-degree burn after only seconds."

"Okay, not sure who I'm speaking to now, but you sound like you know what you're talking about, so keep going," Saunders said. "Tell me everything you can about the poison."

Lana related what had happened at the mall and the other night at the club, making sure to mention that washing the stuff off her skin had helped.

"Trey, how's the wound doing now that you've cleaned it?" Saunders asked when she finished.

Trey studied the wound, pressing on the skin around it with his fingers to get some of the blood out. It was darker than it should have been and oozed more than flowed. A putrid smell suddenly filled the SUV, making Lana almost gag. It smelled like something rotting.

Zane howled louder than before. Jerking his right hand away from Lana, he grabbed Trey by the front of his uniform T-shirt. "Cut the fucking thing off," he begged. "I can't deal with this. Cut it off!"

When Trey didn't respond fast enough, Zane released him to claw at the wound, like he thought he could rip his own arm off.

With Brooks's help, Lana got a grip on the man's right wrist, yanking his hand to his side. It didn't help much. Zane was thrashing so hard it was nearly impossible to hold him down. Cursing, Brooks drew his fist back and punched Zane in the jaw so hard she heard at least one bone break. On the upside, it knocked Zane out, which meant he wasn't fighting them anymore.

"Shit," Trey muttered. "Doc, this is bad. The poison is rotting the muscles. Everything within a two-inch radius around the wound is black, and it's starting to spread. What the hell will this stuff do if it reaches his heart?"

"We're not going to find out," Saunders said firmly. "You're going to cut out the necrotic tissue to keep it from spreading."

Trey looked stricken at the thought. "How much?"

"As much as you have to. Do it quickly before you have to take even more."

It was the most horrible thing Lana had ever seen, especially since she had to help hold back the skin as Trey removed some of the muscle. When he was done, he leaned over and put his nose near the wound, sniffing it. After a moment, he sat back on his heels. He looked drained.

"I think I got the worst of it," he told Saunders. "I could try for more, but if I do that, I might as well take the whole arm. I've already damaged it beyond the point of repair—even for a werewolf."

There was silence on the other end of the line for a moment. "You did what you had to do," Saunders finally said. "We'll worry about saving his mobility after we save his life. Get him here as fast as you can. I'll have a team waiting."

"We'll be there in less than five minutes," Max called out from the front seat.

Trey leaned over again and put his ear to Zane's chest. "His heart rate is still dropping. That poison must have made it into his bloodstream. I don't know if he'll make it five more minutes."

Lana reached over and took Trey's hand, giving it a squeeze. "He's going to make it. We'll find a way to save his life. I promise."

"I hope so," Trey said. "But this was just a flesh wound. What happens the next time we tangle with the hunters and they put a poison bullet through a were-wolf's chest? He or she won't live more than a couple minutes—if that."

Lana didn't say anything. She only prayed it never came to that.

Lana found Max in the small observation deck over-looking the main operating room in Saunders's research clinic. He was standing with his arms folded across his chest and his gaze locked on Zane, who was barely vis-ible on the bed below. She wasn't surprised to find Max here. It's where he'd been going on and off for the past day and a half since his friend had gotten shot.

Right now, Zane was in an induced hypothermic coma. He was heavily drugged and wrapped in cooling blankets in an effort to slow his heart rate and limit the effects of the poison on his body. He was stable for now, but the longer those toxins were in his bloodstream, the worse it would be for him. Max and the rest of his SWAT team were worried Zane might never be able to use his left arm again, but Lana was more concerned about whether he was even going to survive.

She knew it was hard for Max to see Zane in a hospital bed, unmoving and covered in wires, tubes, and insulated wraps, but it was the only way Dr. Saunders had been able to keep him alive long enough for them to find an antidote to the poison. At least they hoped it would keep Zane alive that long. It was still a race against time, and they'd barely gotten off the starting line so far.

Max turned at the sound of her entrance. "I thought you'd be getting some sleep."

Lana smiled and walked over to wrap her arms around him, pressing her face against his strong chest and breathing in his scent. It was amazing how much different the world was now that she could smell just about everything. But even with all the scents out there, there was only one that was both calming and energizing at the same time—Max's. It was like nothing she'd ever experienced before, and she couldn't help but think that she might actually be able to live on nothing more than his scent. It had that much of an effect on her.

"There's no way I could sleep any more than you could," she said softly against his chest. "I'm not going to sleep until we figure out an antidote for this poison and bring Zane out of his coma."

She expected Max to complain, but he only squeezed her tighter. He'd stuck close to her ever since they'd brought Zane in yesterday morning, clearly worried. When he wasn't doing that or checking in on Zane, he was outside, walking the perimeter of the clinic's property. Lana tried to convince him there was little chance the hunters would find her there, but Max would only nod, then go back out to make another circuit of the area around the clinic, as if he thought the hunters were going to show up any minute.

"Have you made any headway with the antidote?" he asked, stepping back to look down at her hopefully. "Or at least gotten something back from any of your college professors that might help?"

Lana and Dr. Saunders had started working on an antidote for the poison within minutes of getting Zane into his hypothermic coma. A short time later, Lacey and Triana had joined them. As a veterinarian, the tall, willowy Lacey had a good understanding of human anatomy and physiology from her undergrad work. While the dark-haired Triana didn't have a background in medicine, as a forensic scientist, there was little in the way of lab equipment that she didn't know how to use. It wasn't the setting Lana would have chosen when it came to meeting the two women for the first time, but at the moment, it wasn't about getting to know the other members of her new pack. It was about figuring out where the hunters' poison had come from and how to get it out of Zane.

Unfortunately, identifying the chemical makeup of the drug had been much more difficult than they'd hoped. Lana and the others had worked straight through the night, trying every test they could think of to figure out the basic structure for the poison, but it was a complicated process, and finding something when you didn't know where to start looking was hard as hell.

Realizing they needed all the help they could get, Lana had sent every scrap of data they had on the samples to some of her former professors, telling them that a prospective employer had stumbled over this complex chemical formulation and needed help identifying it. She knew her former professors, and few of them could resist a puzzle. Figuring out what this poison was made out of was definitely a conundrum.

In the end, the answer hadn't come from any of her professors or even Dr. Saunders.

"Triana's mother, Gemma, put us on the right track," Lana said. "When Triana asked her if she'd ever heard of a poison that could hurt a werewolf, she mentioned an old folktale about *Aconitum lycoctonum*."

Max frowned. "What's that?"

"Wolfsbane. It comes from a very poisonous plant that has been used for millennia to kill people—and wolves. Once we knew where to focus our search, we were able to figure out that the poison in those bullets is a synthetic and highly concentrated form of the juice from one of the *lycoctonum* subspecies that grows on the high plains of Europe. We think it's been genetically engineered to make it especially deadly to werewolves, even in tiny amounts."

"So you have an antidote?" Max's face brightened. "Something you can give to Zane right away?"

Lana hated to disappoint him, especially when he was obviously so desperate for good news. But she couldn't lie to him.

"Nothing yet," she told him gently. "But we're moving in that direction and hope to have something we can try soon."

Max took a deep breath and slowly let it out, his eyes glowing bright yellow-gold, his control teetering on the edge. Lana rested her hand on his chest, standing there with him and matching her breathing to his until the glow faded from his eyes.

"How the hell did these hunters stumble on this damn poison?" he finally asked.

"Dr. Saunders doesn't think they stumbled over it," Lana said. "The poison came from an engineered species of the plant. That means they have scientists growing, testing, modifying, and retesting over and over until they get the effects they want."

Max eyes narrowed. "You mean these hunters have been testing this poison on werewolves? That they have werewolves in captivity somewhere, injecting this crap into them?"

It was horrible to think Max was right and they were dealing with people who were so demented they'd actually experiment on werewolves to figure out how to kill them more efficiently.

"There's no way we can know for sure," she said. "But Dr. Saunders thinks it's a good possibility."

Max cursed, then fell silent for a moment before tipping her chin up with gentle fingers. "I'm sorry I brought all this trouble into your life," he said quietly. "Werewolf hunters and poison bullets are a lot of baggage to ask anyone to deal with."

Lana caught his hand and held it. "This isn't your fault. If you remember, the hunters came after me, then followed me here from Austin. So if anyone should apologize, it's me. If I wasn't a werewolf, Denise would still be alive. If I hadn't led the hunters here to Dallas, we wouldn't all be looking over our shoulders. If I hadn't decided I needed to go to pick up that stuff from my parents' house because I didn't want Brooks going through my panty drawer, Zane wouldn't be in a coma down there in that bed."

His brow furrowed. "You aren't responsible for any of this, Lana. There was no way we could have known those assholes would show up at your parents' house again. And as for coming to Dallas," he added, his expression softening, "if you hadn't, we never would have met, and neither one of us would have found *The One* we're meant to be with for the rest of our lives.

Speaking of which, I should probably explain the significance of what that means, even though this isn't exactly the most ideal setting."

He was right. It wasn't. But something told her Zane would be the first to be happy for them.

Giving Max a smile, she said, "Lacey and Triana already told me about the legend of *The One*. I only wished someone—no names mentioned—would have clued me in on it earlier. It would have helped explain all this crazy whirlwind of emotions I've been dealing with since we met."

Max let out a soft chuckle. "Would you have believed me that first night we met if I'd told you we were magically connected and destined to be together?"

She considered that. "Probably not that night, but after that night you drove me down to Austin, then spent hours afterward talking with me about Denise, I think I would have been open to it, since I'd already figured out you were something special."

He pushed her hair back from her face. "I was worried I'd chase you away if I told you too much too soon."

"It took a little while, but we have each other now," she said. "And I'm not going anywhere."

He bent his head and kissed her. "Do you have any idea how much I love you?"

Lana's breath hitched, her heart doing little pirouettes. She'd been fairly certain he loved her, but hearing him say the words to make it official made her feel warm and gooey inside. "I have a pretty good idea," she whispered with a smile. "Since, if it's anything close to the way I feel about you, it's like you can't imagine being able to breathe without the other person in your life."

His mouth curved. "That puts it into words better than I ever could."

"Hearing you say you love me is what matters to me," she said, going up on tiptoes to kiss him again.

Max wrapped his arms around her, holding her close. "Then I love you, Lana Mason."

"And I love you, Max Lowry."

His mouth covered hers for another long, lingering kiss before the murmur of voices downstairs made them take a step back.

"It sounds like Gage is here. We should go down," Max said. "Hopefully, he'll have something on where to find those damn hunters."

They found the SWAT team commander outside the double doors of the OR, talking quietly with Dr. Saunders and Trey.

The doctor looked exhausted, which wasn't surprising since he'd been pushing himself nonstop since yesterday morning. Unfortunately, he didn't have the luxury of taking a break because Zane's survival rested squarely on his shoulders.

Trey didn't look as physically tired as the doctor, even if he hadn't rested any more than the other man. He'd stood outside the OR, gazing at Zane through the small square window in one of the swinging doors as if he could will his pack mate to wake up. Even though Dr. Saunders had told him multiple times that cutting the muscle out of Zane's arm had undoubtedly saved the werewolf's life, it was obvious Trey blamed himself for doing it.

Dr. Saunders was updating Gage on Zane's condition as she and Max walked up, and the man wasn't pulling any punches as he laid out how horrible the poison they were dealing with truly was.

"Even if we're able to come up with an antidote, and that's no given, it may not be in time," the doctor said. "If a miracle does occur, and he lives, there's no telling if his arm will ever be functional again."

Gage's tightly controlled emotions slipped a little, sorrow crossing his face. But he quickly recovered, nodding at the man. "Do what you can. That's all I ask."

Dr. Saunders reached out to give Gage's shoulder a comforting squeeze, then turned and headed back to the lab.

"Any word on the hunters?" Max asked.

Gage shook his head. "The DPD was able to get video stills of the big guy Lana told us about—Boyd—and the other man who was with him at the mall. Their faces are pasted all over the internet and the news. We haven't identified either of them yet, but it's only a matter of time. There's no way in hell these men don't have police records. This kind of evil doesn't just show up out of the blue."

Max cursed. "Isn't there something else we can be doing to find these assholes?"

"We are," Gage said. "Becker is hacking into every video feed in the Dallas metro region, using a bootleg copy of the Department of Homeland Security's facial recognition software to screen through thousands of hours of footage, but it's going to take a while."

Trey took his eyes off Zane long enough to glance at his commander. "What about Max and me? Can we do anything?"

"As a matter of fact, that's one of the reasons I came

over here." Gage looked from Trey to Max. "I need you two back at the compound."

Max frowned. "Sarge, I can't leave Lana here on her own. She's their target."

"I know," Gage said. "I wouldn't ask you to leave her side if I had any other choice, but I need you. With Zane out of the lineup, and everything else going on, we're spread too thin to have you two on the bench."

It was Trey's turn to frown. "What else is going on?"

"Becker and Connor are digging through video feeds, looking for the hunters. Xander has Hale, Cooper, and Alex out covering every anonymous tip coming in from people claiming they've seen the hunters. And Brooks and Carter are rounding up all the werewolves in the area living on their own or in small groups. I want them staying at the compound until this is over."

Lana hadn't yet met the majority of the Pack that Gage had mentioned, but she found herself worrying for their safety anyway.

"What about Trevor and Khaki?" Trey asked.

"They're still at the hospital guarding Mason and his wife," Gage said. "Chief Curtis figured out Zane was injured yesterday and lost his mind. The only reason he doesn't have a dozen cops outside this place right now is because I convinced him Zane would be safer if we didn't draw any attention to this clinic."

Max exchanged looks with Trey. "Then who's on standby for regular calls?" he asked Gage.

"Mike, Diego, Remy, and me," Gage said. "If we get a major incident, we're not going to be able to cover it and protect the compound, too. That's why I need the two of you back at the shop. I need you to do your jobs, even if it's the last thing you want to do right now."

Max glanced at Lana, clearly torn. "We can't leave this place unguarded, Sarge. If the hunters come here…"

Gage's mouth edged up. "I'd never think of leaving this place unguarded. You should know me better than that. But simply because a place needs to be protected doesn't mean it has to be by you or one of your teammates. The Pack has grown enough to give me some other options."

Max and Trey were still looking at their boss in confusion when Lana heard a door open at the end of the hallway. A moment later, she picked up scents she was coming to associate with werewolves. Two women and four men walked over to them, including Chris, the guy Brandy had met at the cookout. She was still focusing on the fact that her friend was crushing on a werewolf when Gage started making introductions.

"Lana, this is Jayna," he said, gesturing to a tall, slender woman with long, honey-blond hair. "And her pack—Megan, Chris, Moe, and Joseph." Then he jerked his head at a fourth man. The guy was lean with close-cropped hair and tattoos along his arms and across the top of each finger. "And this is Allen."

She offered her hand, shaking each of theirs in turn.

"I know you don't know any of them yet, but I promise they'll do whatever is necessary to protect you and everyone else in this clinic," Gage told her, then gave Max a pointed look. "We'll wait for you outside."

Catching Trey's eye, the SWAT commander jerked his head toward the exit. A moment later, the two men disappeared, leaving her and Max alone with the other werewolves.

Max lingered, clearly not thrilled with the idea of leaving her. Lana didn't like it any better than he did, but she'd be safe here. She was more worried about him out there, where the hunters could get to him, than she was about herself.

She took both his hands in hers and gave them a squeeze. "Max, I'll be fine. The hunters don't have a clue I'm here and there's no way they're going to stumble across me. Go and take care of the other werewolves at the compound. I'll be safe here."

He still hesitated for a moment, gazing at her so intently it was hard not getting lost in his beautiful, blue eyes. Then he leaned forward and kissed her. She kissed him back, wondering how it was possible that she loved him even more now than she had five minutes ago.

"Be careful," he whispered, resting his forehead against hers. "Don't go outside unless someone is with you, okay?"

"I won't," she promised, stealing another kiss before he turned to leave. "You be careful, too."

Lana watched him walk out, praying he'd be safe out there. But he was a cop, as well as a werewolf, and cops did a dangerous job. As the daughter of the deputy chief of police, she knew that better than anyone. Fortunately, she had a job of her own to do now that would keep her distracted.

Chapter 13

"GAGE WANTS TO PUT ANY GROUPS WITH KIDS ON COTS IN THE training room," Max said, stopping Remy as he led a pack of four werewolves and their children toward the exit of the building.

Max's head was spinning a hundred miles an hour as he tried to figure out where the hell they were going to put so many people. The whole place was crawling with betas and omegas, all of them trying to find a place to sleep for the night.

Remy shook his head. "Sorry to tell you this, brother, but the training room is already full. Before you ask, so is the basketball court. And a dozen new omegas just showed up. They're waiting in the admin building."

Max bit back a growl as the two little girls in the group turned big, curious eyes on him. The werewolves who'd come here for protection were already rattled by the news that not only were the hunters in town, but they had also succeeded in taking down a SWAT alpha. He didn't need to freak them out any worse by losing his cool in front of them.

"We still have the break room and the maintenance bay," Max pointed out. "And if we fill those up, we can move some equipment around in the storage areas on the second floor of the admin building and squeeze a few more in over there."

Remy considered that, then nodded. "Okay, I'll see

how many more we can fit. But some of the omegas are going to have to sleep in the rappelling tower. There isn't enough room for everyone inside."

"That'll work," Max agreed. It wasn't ideal, since it didn't have any doors or windows, but it was better than nothing. "At least the walls are thick enough to"—he almost said *stop hollow-point bullets* but glanced at the kids and caught himself—"keep them warm. Just make sure they stay away from the window openings."

Remy agreed and disappeared without another word, leading his small group back down the hallway and into the training room, finally giving Max time to slow down enough to think a little for more than five seconds.

Then again, that probably wasn't a good thing, since the first thought that popped into his head was that the hunters were still out there looking for Lana while he was here at the compound coordinating bedding accommodations like he was a frigging hotel concierge. He understood why Gage had wanted him and Trey to come back here, but damn, it was hard to think about anything but the woman he loved being in danger. If something happened to her, he couldn't imagine wanting to live.

Max felt another growl of frustration building in his chest and headed for the exit. He didn't want to be around the betas—or their kids—if he lost control and started to shift. That would be all they needed right now—one of the alphas they were depending on to protect them fanging out for no reason.

He stepped out the back door of the maintenance building and took a deep breath of the brisk November air. The sun was going down, so it was a little cooler than it'd been earlier in the day, but it was still unseasonably mild for this time of the year, so he wasn't complaining.

A few minutes later, Remy walked out, leading a big group of omegas toward the far end of the compound, where the rappelling tower was located. The omegas moved warily, keeping an eye on the perimeter fence, as if they expected hunters to start shooting at them at any moment. Considering how easily the hunters had been able to catch the SWAT team off guard, Max supposed he couldn't blame them. He only hoped they could catch the sons of bitches before they grew bold enough to hit the compound. The thought of another werewolf writhing in agony like Zane wasn't something he even wanted to consider.

He pushed that image aside and turned to head back inside. He still had a ton of work to do, and if he buried himself in it, he wouldn't worry about Lana so much. Before he could open the door, his phone rang. He yanked his cell out of his pocket, praying it was Lana, but he didn't recognize the number. He thumbed the green button and put it to his ear.

"Max?" a soft, familiar voice said before he could get a word out. "Is that you?"

Even with his keen ears, Max had a hard time hearing Terence. "What's wrong?"

"Dad showed up outside the shelter today and convinced Mom to go out and talk to him," the boy said, still whispering. "I begged her not to go, but she said he only wanted to talk. She came back in a little while ago and said she was taking us home."

Max's stomach dropped like a rock. "Terence, is your father there now? Are you and your sisters in danger?"

The words were barely out of his mouth when he heard Wallace shouting in the background.

"Max, it's bad. He's been drinking for hours and I've never seen him this mad," Terence said, barely audible over his father's shouts. Then his voice dropped down even lower. "Max, he has a gun."

Shit.

"Get out of the house now, Terence," Max ordered, interrupting whatever the boy was going to say next. "Get out of there and run to Mr. Miller's house."

"I can't leave," Terence said. "Dad has my mom and sisters in the living room. I can't leave them. I have to take care of them."

Max opened his mouth to argue, but before he could say anything, there was a curse, then a loud crash, followed by a gunshot.

The phone went silent as the call disconnected.

Max gripped his cell so tightly he almost crushed it in his hand. His first thought was to call Terence back, quickly followed by the urge to run to his car and drive straight to the boy's rescue. He resisted calling, knowing it would only make things worse for Terence, his sisters, and their mother. But as he headed for his car, he remembered how badly things had gone the last time he'd tried to go it alone. Spinning around, he ran for the admin building, barreling through the door and freaking out half a dozen betas in the process.

He was moving so fast he slid through the open door of Gage's office, skidding to a stop in front of the boss's desk. Gage was leaning over it, scanning a map of the city with Mike, and he looked up with concern at Max's sudden appearance.

"What's wrong?"

"Terence Wallace just called," Max explained quickly. "His mother decided to move back in with her husband. The man's drunk and angry. I heard a gunshot right before the phone disconnected."

"Dammit," Gage growled. "Mike, grab Remy and Diego and get on the road. I'll alert dispatch and get a crisis and hostage negotiation team over there to meet you."

Max looked at Gage even as Mike headed for the door. "Sarge?"

He didn't expect Gage to let him go, especially considering how he'd lost control the last time he'd gone out to the Wallace house. But he had to try. He needed to be there for Terence and his sisters.

Gage regarded him thoughtfully for a moment, then surprised him with a nod. "Go. Just don't do anything stupid."

Max didn't hang around and wait for Gage to change his mind. He caught up with Mike and the other guys in the parking lot, jumping in the response vehicle before Remy closed the back door.

The drive to Northwest Dallas seemed to take a lifetime, especially since they kept getting updates over the radio telling them that the situation at the Park Lane address was deteriorating by the second. They were still a mile away when the on-scene patrol officers reported that the occupant of the house was shooting at them. And all Max could do was sit on his hands and listen while a perimeter was established and nearby residents were evacuated.

Senior Corporal Alvarez met them the moment they

arrived at the roadblock at the end of Park Lane, and he looked worried. "This is bad," he said to Mike as Diego hurried over to join the civilian negotiator a little farther down the street. "Nick Wallace has completely lost it. He's shot at us half a dozen times already and refuses to talk to our negotiator. He's shouted out the window that he's not letting us take his family away from him again, but the truth is, we can't even confirm there's anyone in there left alive."

Max's heart was pounding so hard he thought he might lose control and shift right there in front of half the DPD. But a glance from Mike calmed him down enough to keep his fangs and claws in, not to mention the fact that he knew he needed to keep it together for those kids in there. They were still alive—he had to believe that.

"Remy. Max. Work your way around to the back of the house and see if we can get some eyes on the situation in there," Mike said. "Don't go in until I give the word. I want to give Diego a chance to see if we can talk Wallace out of there."

Max and Remy had just gone around to the back of the response vehicle to grab the bags that held their surveillance gear when a familiar white Chevy Caprice sedan pulled up to the barricade with a squawk of tires and lights flashing. A moment later, Coletti jumped out and ran over to them. He didn't look too thrilled to see Max.

"DFPS called and told me what happened," he said. "Are the kids okay?"

Max shook his head, focusing on tightening the straps of his tactical vest. "We don't know. We're slipping around back to get some cameras set up so we can get an idea of what's going on in there."

"You think it's a good idea for you to be going in there, Max?" Coletti said, looking back and forth from him to Remy, then over at Mike, who'd moved over to join Diego and the other negotiator closer to the house. Beyond them, Max could see Wallace standing inside the broken front window in the living room, waving his weapon around and shouting at them to go away.

"Probably not," Max admitted. "But we're a little shorthanded right now, so I'm the one going."

The IA detective seemed ready to argue that point, but Mike's firm voice interrupted. "Max. Remy. You need to get a move on. This situation isn't going to improve with time."

Max turned to follow Remy, but Coletti grabbed him by his vest. He couldn't stop the growl that slipped from his throat or keep his fangs from sliding out far enough that he felt the tips digging into his tongue.

Seriously, the guy was doing this now?

"If you have to go in there, be careful," Coletti whispered, locking eyes with him. "Remember that this isn't a replay of your life. It's the here and now. Don't let your own demons keep you from changing the way this situation plays out."

To say those were not the words—or the tone—Max expected from an internal affairs cop like Coletti was an understatement. All Max could do was nod.

He caught up with Remy as his pack mate slipped behind the closest house; then they were jumping over fences and running across yards. Wallace was still shouting out the front window as they jumped the last fence and dropped into his backyard.

"Stay the fuck away, or I'll kill them all!"

Max hoped that everyone was still alive in there.

Farther up the street, the civilian negotiator was speaking through a megaphone, trying to calm Wallace as Diego whispered suggestions. They weren't having much luck. Wallace seemed to be getting more wound up with every passing minute.

Remy dropped to a knee to the left of the back door, pulling the surveillance bag off his shoulder and unzipping it. Max joined him, reaching in for one of the small wireless cameras and the mounting bracket that came with it. Remy grabbed another one, pointing at himself and the backdoor, then Max and the left side of the house. Max nodded and took his camera around that way. As he moved toward a window he hoped would give him a view into the living room, he strained his ears for any clue about what might be happening inside the house.

In between Wallace's drunken ranting, Max picked up sobbing. It was soft and muffled, as if whoever was crying was trying to hold it in. Natasha. Only a frightened little girl could make a sound like that, and it tore at his heart. His sister, Sarah, had cried like that after their old man had punched her. Had Wallace done the same to Natasha—or worse? The thought made his fangs slide out.

Then Max remembered what Coletti had said about not letting his own demons cloud his focus. Sarah wasn't in there. This was a completely different family, in a completely different time.

Forcing his fangs to retract, he focused on the other sounds coming from inside the house. He heard at least

four distinct heartbeats. He strained to hear a fifth heartbeat, but everyone was pressed so closely together he
couldn't do it.

"I have no view of the occupants from the rear of the
house," Remy said into his mic.

Max moved his tiny surveillance camera up, position-
ing it on the edge of a side looking into the living room.
The urge to peek was hard to resist, but he didn't do
it. If Wallace saw him, it would push the man over the
edge for sure. With that in mind, he instead flipped the
power switch on the camera, hoping it was sending a
clear signal to Mike back at the response truck.

"Camera one set," Max whispered into his mic as he
moved around to the back of the house again. "You getting a clear visual inside the house?"

"We have a visual on camera one," Mike's voice
came back softly in his earpiece. "Adult female and
three kids huddled together on the floor near the couch.
I can't tell if any of them are injured, but they all seem
to be moving. Adult male over by the front window. His
back is to the others and he has a weapon in his right
hand. It's an automatic."

Max reached the back of the house to see Remy
crouched down by the door, peeking inside. The coast
must have been clear if Remy was doing that, so Max
moved to join him.

Beside him, Remy reached up and cautiously put
pressure on the handle of the sliding glass door. Max
didn't expect it to be unlocked, but it was. Remy slid
it open an inch. Now, they could hear and smell everything better.

Unfortunately, Max didn't like what his ears and

nose had to tell him. Blood had definitely been spilled in there, and Wallace was muttering to himself about not ever letting his family go.

"Remy. Max. If you can get in the house, do it," Mike whispered in their earpieces. "Wallace just reloaded and the negotiator isn't getting through to him. The way he's waving the weapon around doesn't give me a good feeling about this."

"Roger that," Max said softly.

Remy slid the glass door open the rest of the way and noiselessly slipped inside. Max joined him, easing his Sig Sauer out of its holster as he went. He normally would have used his M4 carbine for a house entry like this, but with so many hostages in such a small space, he couldn't take the risk. He noticed that Remy was following his lead, pulling his own 10mm auto out as they both moved through the kitchen and down the hallway toward the living room.

"Baby, why are you doing this?" Eileen Wallace pleaded in a quavering voice. "We came home with you."

Max commended her for trying to talk some sense into her husband. He only prayed she'd be able to say something that would help this turn out differently than he feared it would.

"You came home?" Wallace shouted. "You never should have fucking left! Who the hell do you think you are, walking away from me, taking *my* kids with you?"

Every heartbeat in the living room kicked up a notch. It didn't take Mike coming on the radio telling them Wallace was moving toward his family with his weapon pointed straight at them to understand the situation had rapidly gone from bad to worse. Wallace was done ranting.

"Nick, please!" she begged. "We love you. Why do you keep treating us like this?"

Wallace didn't answer. A moment later, Max heard a cry of surprise, followed by a slap.

"Go now!" Mike ordered.

Max didn't hesitate. He slipped out of the hallway and into the living room, his weapon raised and his finger on the trigger. He quickly jerked it away at the sight before him.

Shit.

Nina and Natasha were on the floor, their mother shielding them with her body even as blood flowed freely from a freshly split lip. Wallace was standing in front of his wife and daughters, holding Terence close to his chest, a small-caliber automatic pressed to the boy's temple. The man's eyes were red, bloodshot, and glassy, like he'd been drinking for hours. His eyes narrowed when he saw Max.

"You!" he sneered, his eyes fixed on Max, all but ignoring Remy as the other werewolf moved off to the side and pointed a weapon straight at Max's head. "You're the one who took my family away from me!"

Max suspected Wallace would have shot him right then if he could have taken his weapon away from Terence's head long enough to do it. But even drunk, the man was smart enough to know the gun he was holding on his son was the only thing keeping Remy from killing him.

"I didn't take your family away," Max said quietly. "You did that all on your own."

Max slowly lowered his weapon, holstering his gun and taking a step toward Terence and his father. There was a risk Wallace would say the hell with it and put a bullet in Max's head. That would be fatal, even for a werewolf. But he had to do something to get Terence away from the man.

"The first time you punched your kids and your wife, you lost a little piece of them," Max continued.

He was so close now he could almost reach out and touch Terence. Behind Nick, outside the front window, Max saw Mike, Diego, Coletti, Alvarez, and half a dozen uniformed officers closing in on the house. But none of them could take a shot, not without risking an innocent.

"And every time you hit them after that, you lost a little more," Max said, remembering exactly how being the victim of an abusive father had felt. "Until you were nothing more to them than the man who beat them. That's when you really lost them."

He took another step closer. Wallace was so different than his own father, yet so similar at the same time. Even the bleary, half-defiant, half-accepting glare in those eyes was the same.

"Your wife held out longer because she loved you before you were like this," Max told him. "But how many times did you think you could hit her and her children before she started to despise you?"

Wallace threw a quick glance at his wife. Whatever he saw on her face must have hurt because his rage-filled demeanor slipped for a moment. But it came right back, and he looked angrier than ever.

"You think I give a shit what they think of me?" he shouted, pressing his weapon harder against his son's head.

Tears of pain sprang into the boy's eyes, but Terence

didn't utter so much as a whimper. Instead, he kept his gaze on Max, as if he believed Max would save him.

"Somewhere inside you, I think you do care," Max told Wallace. "Else why bother to go to all the effort of getting them back?"

As Max spoke, the cops outside the house moved closer until they were at the broken windows, their weapons pointed at Wallace from a dozen different directions. The laser sights on Mike's and Diego's M4's were little red dots on the side of Wallace's head, and it was hard to believe the man didn't see them out of the corner of his eye.

Maybe he did. Maybe that was the reason his face suddenly hardened. Or it might have been the simple fact that Max's words had finally gotten through to him and he'd realized he'd lost the only thing that should have mattered to him—his family.

Regardless, the man's heart rate spiked and his finger tightened on the trigger, slowly pulling it.

Max lunged forward, slamming into Terence and ripping him out of Wallace's arms. He twisted in midair, so his body was between the boy and the barrel of the gun. He expected to hear the report of the gun going off followed by a bullet in his back, but as he hit the ground with his arms wrapped protectively around Terence, all he heard was the mad shuffle of feet as Mike, Diego, and the rest of the police moved in, shouting for Wallace to drop his weapon.

Max drew his own weapon, his body still shielding the boy, praying it was over and that they'd disarmed Wallace already. Instead, he caught sight of the man backing away with the barrel of the auto planted firmly

under his chin, his eyes locked on his wife as he ignored
the police ordering him to put down his weapon.

Max expected Wallace to say something, to blame
everything on his wife and kids. Instead, he simply
pulled the trigger. The weapon wasn't very big, but
it was big enough to make a mess, and Max quickly
moved to shield Terence—not from injury, but from
seeing his father die like that.

He was only partially successful. Terence had still
seen enough, and his sisters had seen even more. No one
moved. Then Terence, Nina, Natasha, and their mother
were all in his arms, crying hysterically.

All Max could do was hold them and let them cry.
Thankfully, one of the uniformed cops got a sheet from
one of the beds and covered Wallace's body, but there
was only so much it could cover. No matter what was
hidden now, the memories never could be. Max knew
that all too well.

Sensing someone, Max looked up and saw Coletti
standing there. Wordlessly, the detective sat down on
the floor beside him and helped comfort the Wallace
family even as he gave Max a nod of approval.

Max nodded in return. This hadn't turned out the way
he'd hoped. A father was dead, and that was going to
take a long time for this family to get over. But Max had
saved a woman and her kids, and at the moment, that
felt like enough.

Chapter 14

"ANY PROGRESS YET?" MEGAN DORSEY ASKED AS SHE AND Lana stepped out the main doors of the clinic into the cool night air.

Lana had been hoping for a few moments alone, but the moment the petite, dark-haired werewolf spotted her heading for the exit, she fell into step beside her. Then again, Lana had promised Max she wouldn't go outside by herself. Besides Megan, she had the added protection of Jayna and the other werewolves, who were patrolling the perimeter of the property. While Lana couldn't see any of them, she could smell them moving around among the trees.

"Quite a bit, actually," Lana said. "We've been working all day on several different approaches to developing an antidote, and Dr. Saunders finally thinks we may have something that could work."

Megan stopped to look at her, excitement evident on her face. "Is the doctor giving it to Zane now?"

Lana ran her hand through her hair. She wished it were that simple. "We can't try it yet. Not until we do some additional testing to make sure there aren't any unintended side effects of the antidote that's worse than the poison itself."

Megan's brow furrowed. "Does Zane have time for that?"

"Probably not. But what choice do we have?" Lana

wrapped her arms around her middle with a sigh. "If we give him an untested drug, we're as likely to kill him as save him. Especially in his weakened state."

Megan didn't say anything to that, and they both stood there quietly, staring off into the darkness beyond the clinic. Lana used the quiet moment to take a few deep breaths, trying to get herself to relax. She didn't know why, but she'd been feeling twitchy for the past hour, and it had nothing to do with the pressure to find an antidote for Zane. She wished she could call Max and talk to him, but she didn't want to bother him. She had called her mother a few times to check on her dad, though. The doctors were still keeping her father in a coma, but he was stable. That was something at least.

"So, what will you do next?" Megan asked after a few minutes. "With Zane, I mean."

"We'll work on the chemical analyses throughout the night," Lana said, though she didn't know how they were going to compress all the normal drug-testing pro-tocols she'd learned in school into the shortest possible time. "Then we'll start running computer simulations of cellular interactions in the morning. Even with every computer in the building working on it, that could take a while. On top of that, we'll need to find a few were-wolves willing to serve as volunteers for low-dosage trials to make sure we haven't missed anything."

"I'll do it," Megan said without hesitation.

Lana blinked, a little taken aback at Megan's willing-ness to face a risk she probably didn't even understand.

"Megan, this could be dangerous," she said. "Even if it doesn't cause an immediate reaction, there could be long-term effects we don't know anything about. Even

Dr. Saunders—who's studied werewolves for a long time—can't tell us what these kinds of drugs will do a few years down the road."

Megan nodded. "I know that, but I'll still do it. And there are a lot of other werewolves who will volunteer along with me. Everyone in Dallas knows what's at stake here when it comes to finding an antidote to this poison and helping Zane. We need a way to protect ourselves from this new weapon, and we need to keep the SWAT Pack strong. They're the only thing standing between us and the hunters."

Lana couldn't argue with that. "Okay. I'll tell Dr. Saunders that we'll have no problem coming up with volunteers. Now it's just a matter of whether Zane can survive until then." She sighed. "Speaking of which, I'd better get back inside."

She turned toward the door only to jump as the sound of a roaring engine echoed in the night. Heart pounding, Lana spun around in time to see two big, gray SUVs jump the curb and speed straight at her and Megan.

Lana's werewolf instincts immediately took over and she leaped to the side to get out of the way. Megan slammed into her at the same time, sending her flying. She hit the ground hard, rolling a few times to avoid the vehicle sliding to a squealing stop on the sidewalk a few feet away.

She scrambled to her feet, her instincts screaming at her to run. But then she froze. Megan lay on the ground near the front bumper of the vehicle, unmoving. Megan had been hit when she'd shoved her out of the way.

No…

Heedless of the vehicle and the people in it, Lana

hurried over to Megan, dropping to her knees. She sagged with relief as Megan groaned. She was hurt, but she was alive.

"Come on," Lana whispered urgently, helping Megan up even as the petite werewolf started getting to her feet.

She'd barely gotten Megan to her knees before she heard the thud of heavy boots behind her. The men's scents hit her at nearly the same time, making her whole body go rigid. Fangs and claws extended, Lana straightened and spun around, shielding Megan.

She found herself face-to-face with Boyd and the other man who'd been at the Galleria Mall. Three other men were just now getting out of the second SUV, and they were all carrying the same automatic rifles as before.

"Damn," Boyd laughed, an arrogant smile spreading across his face as the man raised his weapon and pointed it at Lana. "I thought this would be a lot more difficult. But I'm not complaining, especially since it looks like I'm going to get two of you freaks for the price of one."

"She's not a werewolf," Lana lied. If they thought Megan wasn't a werewolf, there might be a small chance they wouldn't hurt her. "You can let her go."

"Isn't that sweet?" Seth sneered. Even though she hadn't seen his face last night in the alley, Lana recognized his voice. "The freak is trying to protect her friend—like we'd give a shit if she's a werewolf or not. She's with you, so that makes her as bad as you."

Lana tensed. She'd never been in a fight and didn't know the first thing about throwing punches, but she had the feeling her inner wolf would help with that. She doubted charging the men would do any good, but she wasn't going down without a fight. Hopefully she'd be able to take at least one of them with her and make it easier for Max and his pack later.

Thinking of Max made her heart seize. The knowledge of how much her death would hurt him was more painful than the idea of the hunters killing her.

She fixed an image of Max's face in her mind, then transferred her weight onto one leg, getting ready to attack. She would have liked to take out Boyd, but something told her he'd be expecting that. Instead, she'd go for the guy on the far right. He was the smallest of all the men, and if she jumped on him fast, her unexpected move might keep the other hunters from killing her too quickly. Maybe then, Megan could get away.

Boyd must have read her mind because he moved a step closer and adjusted the aim of his weapon, his face completely emotionless, like he was simply stepping on a bug.

Lana growled, about to pounce, but suddenly gunfire erupted around her. She instinctively dropped to the ground, covering Megan with her body. A split second later, one of the hunters fell to the ground, blood pooling around him. The SUVs didn't fare so well, either. Glass shattered and metal shrieked in protest as bullets hit them. One tire blew out with a loud pop, then another.

Boyd and the other hunters returned fire, facing out into the darkness. That was when Lana realized what was happening. Jayna and her pack were the ones shooting the hunters. Lana hadn't even realized Megan's friends were carrying weapons, much less automatic rifles.

The hunters were shooting in every direction at once, occasional muzzle flashes in the darkness the only thing giving away the other werewolves' locations. Lana's

first instinct was to attack Boyd, but that wouldn't gain
her much of anything—except vengeance. So instead,
she took advantage of the distraction and dug her fingers
into the collar of Megan's jacket and started dragging
her toward the shadows along the side of the clinic.
Even though Megan was delirious with pain, she must
have realized what Lana was up to, because she started
kicking weakly with her right leg, trying to push herself
across the ground.

They made it less than ten feet before someone
grabbed Lana by the hair and savagely jerked her back.
She tried to spin around and claw at whoever was holding her but stopped cold when she felt the hot barrel of
a weapon against the back of her neck.

"Get inside!" Boyd yelled, using Lana as a human
shield as he dragged her backward toward the shattered
glass doors of the clinic.

Lana prayed they'd leave Megan, but one of the other
hunters hoisted her up, bringing her with them. Another
grabbed their injured companion and brought him, too.

Lana wasn't surprised when the shooting from the
darkness immediately ceased. Jayna and the other werewolves weren't trained SWAT officers. They weren't
going to risk hitting her and Megan.

Moments later, they were inside the clinic, the hunters
fanning out and gathering up Lacey, Triana, Saunders,
and the other doctors and nurses, pushing everyone
against the wall to one side of the main hallway. Dr.
Saunders immediately dropped to a knee to check on
Megan. She was still conscious but pale.

"Her leg is broken," Dr. Saunders whispered to Lana.
"Her hip, too, I think."

"Hey!" Seth shouted from inside the lab where Zane was resting. "That werewolf we shot at the cop's house is in here. He's full of tubes and wires, and covered with cooling blankets. I think he's in cryogenic suspension." Seth poked his head out the door. "Should I kill him?"

Lana's stomach plummeted, sure Boyd would give Seth the okay, but then another voice sounded from the far end of the building. "There're more of those damn freaks outside this door. I can't see them, so I can't tell how many, but I can see the glow of their fucking eyes."

"Keep an eye on them. If they come out of the trees, shoot them," Boyd ordered, then looked at Seth. "Don't do anything with the werewolf Popsicle. We might need him for something."

"Hey, Boyd. Jesse is bleeding pretty good over here."

Lana turned to see one of the hunters down on one knee beside his injured buddy. The guy had gotten shot in the shoulder, and while it was bleeding profusely, unfortunately, it didn't look bad enough to kill him.

"Hey, you—lab coat boy," Boyd grunted, bending down to prod Dr. Saunders in the back with the barrel of his weapon. "Get over there and look at Jesse—now."

Dr. Saunders didn't take his gaze off Megan. "I'll take a look at him as soon as I'm done here."

Eyes narrowing, Boyd put the barrel of his gun to Megan's head, eliciting a weak growl from the small werewolf. "How about I put a bullet through her head, then you won't have to bother with the freak at all?"

Dr. Saunders looked up, anger clear on his face. He was about to do something stupid—Lana just knew it.

"Take care of Jesse," Lana whispered. "I'll look after Megan."

Dr. Saunders continued to glower at Boyd for a moment, but then nodded at her before standing up to move over to look at the injured hunter.

"Smart girl," Boyd said to her, giving her that emotionless grin of his. "I'd hate to have to kill you before it was time. Not that you have a lot of that left anyway."

Lana tried not to flinch at the blatant threat. Instead, she glared up at him. That only seemed to piss him off, and she thought for a moment he might hit her—or worse.

But then she heard a quiet buzzing sound, and Boyd turned away, pulling a cell phone out of his pocket. He looked at the number on the screen, then moved a little farther down the hallway for privacy. Like that mattered. She could still hear him just fine.

"What the hell happened?" a harsh male voice demanded on the other end of the line. "I gave you the address of the clinic where the injured SWAT officer is being treated—the same place I told you the female werewolf would probably be—just like you asked. The plan was for you to slip in and kill them both, then get out of there. Now 9-1-1 calls are coming in about a major shoot-out and a possible hostage situation. How did you screw this up so badly?"

Boyd's face twisted. "How did I screw it up? Maybe you should have mentioned they had werewolves on the perimeter guarding the place. I doubt they're stupid enough to try to come in here while we have their friends as hostages, but you need to do something to help get us out of this damn place."

The man let out a short laugh. "I don't think so. You getting trapped in there is not my problem."

"It will be your problem if they arrest us and I start talking," Boyd warned.

"I don't think there's very much chance of that. Something tells me SWAT isn't going to be too interested in arresting you when they show up. They're more likely to kill you on sight, considering you injured a member of their pack. If you want to get out of there, you're going to have to shoot your way out."

"We've got no problem with that," Boyd said coldly. "We've already confirmed our new ammunition will put these things down with a single shot. But it'd help to know exactly how many we're dealing with."

"I have no clue," the man said. "But you should probably assume you'll be dealing with the entire SWAT team full of those monsters."

Boyd didn't say anything for a while. "A whole SWAT team full of freaks, huh? That's like music to my ears, since it means there's more of them to kill."

——————

"This is a revolver," Max told Kari, showing her how the snub-nose .38 worked. "There's no safety on it of any kind, so if you squeeze the trigger hard enough, it will fire. But there are only six bullets in it, which means you'll have to make them count."

Max tried to talk slowly as he showed the beta werewolf how to open the cylinder and reload the weapon. Staying calm was tough at the moment, since everything around him was barely controlled chaos.

A good portion of the SWAT Pack was at the compound now, loading up and getting ready to head for the research clinic any minute. Gage was putting all his eggs in one basket, taking everyone with him and gambling that all the hunters were going to be there when they arrived, instead of some of them attacking the compound. But before they left, they were handing out weapons to any werewolf who felt they could safely use them. Max knew it was insane, but they didn't have a choice. Once he and his pack mates left, the compound would be unguarded except for a ragtag collection of werewolves who barely knew each other. There were women and children here. They couldn't leave them defenseless.

Max's hand trembled as he demonstrated how to load the revolver again. He was so worried about Lana he could barely think straight. Somewhere on the compound, he knew Remy and Alex weren't doing much better. The hunters had all three of their mates, and no one had a clue what they were going to do with them. Lana could be writhing in pain on the floor of the clinic right now from one of the hunters' poison bullets.

The thought made him almost hyperventilate.

"I've got this," Kari said, reaching out to put a gentle hand on his arm. "Go save that girlfriend of yours."

Max nodded gratefully. He was more than ready to get the hell out of there. It had only been five minutes since Jayna had called from the clinic, but it seemed like a frigging lifetime. He and his teammates normally rolled out of the gate within sixty seconds of getting a call, but with the need to arm and instruct the werewolves staying behind, it was taking a hell of a lot longer.

He was about to bail but then noticed Kari was no longer looking at him. Instead, she was gazing at someone behind him. He frowned as he picked up Coletti's scent. He turned to see the IA detective standing there with a baffled look on his face.

"What are you doing here?" Max asked. "Are Mrs. Wallace and her kids okay?"

The man continued to look around for a moment, at everything from the SWAT cops obviously loading up for a major operation to all the civilians running around the compound like their hair was on fire.

"They're fine," Coletti said, finally looking at him. "Well, as fine as they can be after what went down tonight. I was coming over to tell you they're settled in again over at the Safe Campus, but I guess you're a little busy right now."

"A little," Max said. "So maybe we can talk later?"

Coletti took a quick step back as Brooks rushed past, carrying two big, wire-bound crates of ammunition for the team's M4 carbines. In them were over six thousand rounds of ammunition. The detective's eyes widened in surprise.

"What's going on?" Coletti asked in what could only be defined as a suspicious voice. "I heard over the radio there was a minor hostage situation at a clinic over near the medical center, but dispatch wasn't calling for more than a couple cruisers to establish a perimeter."

Max opened his mouth, not sure what the hell he was going to say, praying it would be convincing, whatever it was. He didn't have to find out because Coletti chose that particular moment to notice Kari standing there with a .38 revolver in her hands.

"What are you doing here?" Coletti asked. "And why are you carrying a weapon? Where the hell did you even get that?"

Max expected the beta to freeze up, but instead, Kari calmly slipped the small weapon into her coat pocket and looked at Coletti.

"Vince, there's a lot going on that you don't understand," she said. "But I'm carrying this weapon to help protect the people at the compound…and myself."

Coletti frowned. "From whom?"

Shit. They so didn't need this right now.

"We really don't have time to explain everything," Max said. "It's complicated and you probably wouldn't believe most of it. You're going to have to trust us."

Max made to step around him, but Coletti put a hand on his chest. Max let out a low growl, the tips of his fangs brushing his tongue. Since the situation at the Wallace house tonight, he'd felt more in control of his inner wolf than he ever had in his life. His fangs weren't out because he was losing it. They were out because he was too worried about his mate to play nice anymore. At least they weren't hanging over his lower lip yet. Gage would go nuclear if that happened. But Max took a perverse sense of pleasure in seeing Coletti take a step backward.

"My team and I have hostages to rescue," Max said. "Your only options are staying to help protect Kari and the rest of the people left at the compound, or getting cuffed and shoved in the trunk of your own car until it's all over with. Your call."

Coletti looked like he was going to go for option three—fighting—but Kari reached out and took the detective's hands in hers, tugging him away from Max with a strength that obviously caught the man off guard.

"Vince, this isn't something I can explain in five seconds, but I swear it's all being done for the right reasons." She looked up at him imploringly. "You don't need to trust Max, but I need you to trust me. Let Max and his teammates go. The time they're wasting could mean people dying."

It looked for a moment like Coletti might argue. There was a part of Max that wished the IA detective would. He really needed to vent some stress right then, and taking his anger out on Coletti would work just fine.

But then Coletti nodded. "Okay, we'll play this your way, Max. But after this is over, you're going to tell me everything."

Max snorted. "You say that now. But after I've told you how the world really works, I'm guessing you're going to wish you'd never asked."

———

"Maybe we should wheel that half-dead werewolf out here and use him to block the door," Seth said casually as he wheeled an empty gurney out of the OR and positioned it with the others already blocking the exit.

From where she sat on the floor, Lana's heart tightened in her chest. She'd been worried the hunters would harm Zane the moment they found his comatose body. Frankly, she was surprised they hadn't disconnected the cryo-equipment already.

Boyd considered Seth's suggestion for a moment, then shook his head. "Nah. We don't have enough extension cords to keep him plugged in, and I don't want to smell rotting werewolf when he starts to thaw out."

Seth and the other hunters laughed, as if that was the funniest thing they'd ever heard. Lana bit back a growl—and her tongue. If she said something to piss off the hunters, they might take it out on Megan, Triana, Lacey, or Dr. Saunders.

The five of them were sitting against the wall across from the OR. At the far end of the hall, the cool evening air came in through the shattered windows of the front doors. The flashing lights of the police cars in the parking lot danced on the walls around them.

Seth threw a glance in Lana's direction as he walked past, eyeing her with an expression that made Lana's skin crawl. It was like he was fantasizing about how much he was going to enjoy killing her—or worse. She had no doubt that if she and the others didn't currently have value as hostages, they would already be dead.

"That man is a psychopath," Saunders muttered under his breath to her. "He wants you dead, and he wants to be the one to kill you. When the shooting starts, make sure you know where he is. He'll be coming for you."

All Lana could do was nod. As far as she was concerned, all of the hunters were unhinged. The men had spent the past thirty minutes barricading the doors and windows of the clinic, talking about how many werewolves each of them was going to kill when SWAT got here. They were even making bets about it. The notion they might not make it out of here never seemed to enter their minds, even though none of them had mentioned a getaway plan beyond shooting their way out of the building.

"Who's Boyd talking to now?" Triana asked softly.

Lana glanced over at the leader of the crazy men. He was standing over by the OR, his cell phone to his ear again. She was getting better at shutting out other noises and picking up only the sounds she wanted to hear and was able to immediately latch on to Boyd's voice, as well as the lower, gruffer voice of the man on the other end of the phone.

"It's that same older guy he was talking to a little while ago," Lana said, focusing to pick up exactly what the man on the phone was saying. "Boyd's still trying to convince him to send help."

While Seth and the other hunters had been busy talking trash, Boyd had been calling people. After speaking to the first man who'd somehow known Lana and Zane were at the clinic, Boyd had turned his attention to getting some backup in here. The half-dozen calls he'd made were to people Lana guessed were other hunters. It terrified her to think there were that many of them out there, but she was thrilled when none of them had been willing to ride to the rescue after finding out Boyd and his crew were surrounded by the police.

That's when Boyd had called the older guy. While she couldn't be sure, Lana got the feeling from the respectful way Boyd spoke to him that the guy was his boss.

"I'm telling you, we've struck the mother lode here in Dallas," Boyd said. "I can't believe you don't want to take down an entire SWAT team full of these werewolves. I thought a major hit on a full pack was what you've been looking for all along. We can finally teach these freaks a lesson."

"That's exactly what I've been looking for," the man on the other end of the line agreed. "And I would have been thrilled if you had come to me with this information several days ago, before you alerted this pack to our existence and splashed your faces all over the internet. Not to mention got trapped at some damn clinic."

"I'm sorry about that." Boyd ground his jaw, as if he hated having to apologize. "But our source in the DPD didn't give us any indication there'd be any other were-wolves here besides the female we were after and the injured cop. If I had known this was a major research clinic full of doctors and nurses guarded by werewolves, we would have come in with a different plan."

"Uh-huh," the older man scoffed.

"Look, I'm not making excuses," Boyd snapped. "I can only work with the intel I have at hand."

"I'm not interested in any of that. I want to hear about the clinic. What kind of research are they doing there?"

Boyd must have realized that he'd just stumbled over something the old man actually cared about because he grinned. "It's a frigging werewolf hospital. They have the cop we shot with wolfsbane ammo in some kind of cryo-suspension. He should have died yesterday, but they're keeping him going. They have doctors and nurses and loads of special equipment."

"I don't care about the equipment," the man said. "I'm interested in the doctors and nurses and what they know."

Boyd's smile broadened, as if realizing he had the old man where he wanted him. "I was thinking they could help us advance our weapons program. With the proper motivation, of course."

There was silence on the other end of the line as if the man was considering that. "Could you get those doctors out of there if you had assistance?"

Lana's heart plummeted. She didn't like where this was going.

"Hell yeah," Boyd said, that arrogant tone coming back into his voice. "If that assistance gets here soon."

"I can have people there in an hour. Can you come up with a way to delay this SWAT team of werewolves for that long?"

Boyd shot Lana a look of pure malice. "Oh, I think I can come up with a way to discourage them from coming in for a while."

While she didn't have werewolf hearing, Triana must have realized something bad was going to go down because she cursed and leaned in toward Lana slightly. "I have no idea what they're talking about, but the way he looked at you can't be good."

"It's not," Lana agreed softly, watching as Boyd put his cell phone back in the pocket of his jacket.

Heart racing, she turned to look at the broken windows in the doors. "Max, if you or any of your teammates out there can hear me, you need to get in here now," she whispered. "Something really bad is about to happen."

Lana strained her ears, hoping Max or one of his teammates would whisper something in return, but Boyd interrupted.

"Hey, werewolf girl," he said as he came toward her. "Come here. I have something special planned for you."

Crap.

"Max," she whispered hoarsely. "Hurry!"

Chapter 15

"ALL TEAMS, READY ON MY MARK," GAGE SAID OVER THE radio as Lana's urgent plea echoed in Max's ears. "We go in five…four…"

The terror in Lana's voice had frozen Max solid, but Gage's countdown broke through that ice, forcing him to move. On the east side of the roof of the clinic, Max snapped into his rappel line alongside Remy and Brooks, then braced his feet on the edge of the roofline and waited, heart pounding.

"Three…two…one…*go!*"

As one, all three of them kicked away from the edge of the roof, dropping their ropes behind them at the same time. Since the clinic was only a two-story building, it wasn't going to be much of a rappel. One jump away from the building, a long slide down the rope, then they'd be crashing through the front doors. On the west side of the building, Alex, Trey, and Diego were doing the exact same thing through the back doors.

Max and his teammates had slipped onto the roof ten minutes ago. It would be their jobs to get to the hostages and protect them, while Gage and the rest of the SWAT team went in through the side windows of the clinic and took out the hunters. Gage had deliberately put Max, Alex, and Remy on hostage rescue, knowing that's where their heads would be anyway.

The ground came up fast between Max's feet as

the rope slid through the carabiner clip at his waist. As he glided toward the building in a graceful swing, he yanked the slack end of his rope around behind his right hip, jerking his body to a rapid halt. The momentum of his swing carried him inward, and a moment later, he crashed through what little glass was left in the main doors.

Brooks and Remy hit the floor right beside him, weapons coming out as they kicked the gurneys in front of the door aside and dove forward to cover up the hostages. Max would have done the same, but he caught sight of Boyd dragging Lana kicking and struggling toward the operating room.

Max took off after them with a snarl, ignoring the gunfire erupting in the entryway of the clinic and the burning stench of the hunters' poison as it hung in the air. He stayed low to the ground as he moved, his feet churning as he closed the distance between him and Lana. Out of the corner of his eye, he saw Gage's team come in through the windows. One of them went down immediately, but Max didn't see who it was.

Ahead of him, Boyd backed through the swinging doors of the OR, Lana firmly in his grasp. The hunter must have caught sight of Max coming his way because he turned and fired a few rounds in his direction. Lana shoved her shoulder into the man's chest, throwing off his aim, and the bullets hit the floor in front of Max, shattering violently and spreading more of the poisonous mist, but he kept moving, ignoring the sting of the stuff against his skin and in his nose.

He was moving at full speed when he hit the swinging double doors, slamming through them. He dived to the floor and rolled, expecting a shower of poison bullets to come his way, but nothing happened.

Max came up, his weapon ready, but Boyd and Lana were nowhere in sight. The room was dark except for the light over Zane's bed and those blinking on the monitors around him. Not that Max needed lights. His nose told him everything he needed to know.

Lana was on the other side of Zane's bed. Max had learned in New Orleans that hunters used a spray to mask their scent, so although he couldn't smell Boyd, he knew the asshole was with her.

He discovered he was right when Boyd popped up behind Zane's bed, a squirming Lana grasped in his arms. The hunter had his weapon to the side of her head and a hand clasped over her mouth. Blood oozed between the man's fingers, where Max's soul mate must have bitten him.

Boyd ignored that, grinning at Max with a sick smile. *Shit*, Max thought. Boyd was going to kill Lana right in front of him, then take him out after forcing him to watch the woman he loved die.

Max charged, his fangs and claws coming out. Boyd's eyes widened as Max crossed the distance between them in the space of two heartbeats. Max wondered how many times—if ever—the hunter had faced down an alpha. Judging by his reaction, the answer was probably never.

Cursing, Boyd swung his weapon on Max. Lana shoved her elbow in the man's ribs as he fired the MP5 submachine gun, knocking his aim off a little, but Max was too close for it to make a difference.

He felt the initial sting as the small 9mm rounds from the MP5 hit him as he leaped across the bed in the center of the room and Zane's comatose form. One hit him in the left side of the rib cage, one to the right of the sternum, and another in his right shoulder. He ignored the immediate bloom of burning pain that followed, knowing what it was and also knowing there wasn't anything he could do about it.

Boyd tried to adjust his aim when he realized the first few shots that hit Max weren't going to stop him, but by then, Max had cleared Zane's bed and slammed into both Lana and the hunter. Max hated running into her so hard, but he didn't have a choice. He needed to get Boyd away from her. He accomplished that, sending Lana tumbling as he landed on Boyd and rode him to the ground.

The hunter tried to twist the barrel of his weapon around and get it pointed at Max's head, but Max wasn't going to let that happen. The pain of the poison coursing through his chest was already becoming unbearable, and his body was starting to shake. He didn't have much time to end this.

Max reached out and grabbed Boyd's right forearm, clamping down as hard as he could, then twisting so the man would drop his weapon. There was a snapping sound, then a roar of pain as the hunter's arm broke. Boyd punched Max in the face with his free hand, trying to push Max off him.

Max ignored everything—the fire roaring through his chest, the tremors breaking out all over his body, even the asshole punching him in the face—and focused on what he needed to do to make sure Boyd never hurt anyone he loved ever again.

Grabbing Boyd by the hair, Max yanked his head to

the side, then darted forward and sank his fangs into the hunter's neck. He'd never done anything like that before, but he didn't question the need now.

When Boyd was dead, Max pushed away from him, rolling onto the floor as his body started to convulse uncontrollably.

Lana was at his side in a heartbeat, screaming and crying as she pulled his upper body into her lap. She put her face close to his, and while he could see her mouth moving, he couldn't hear what she was saying. All he could hear was the thrum of his rapidly weakening heartbeat.

But he didn't need to hear what she was saying, because her face said it all.

"I love you, too," he tried to say, but nothing came out.

Max opened his mouth to try again, but the pain was suddenly too much, and his whole body began to spasm.

Lana's eyes went wide with terror, and at that moment, all Max could think was that he wished she didn't have to see this.

———~~~———

Lana had known everything was going to crap when Boyd grabbed her and dragged her away from the doors. Then Max and the other SWAT alphas were swinging into the outer hallway, bullets flying everywhere, and for a moment, she allowed herself to believe this was all going to work out okay.

Then Max had smashed through the OR doors and Boyd had shot him.

From that moment forward, time had slowed to a crawl as Max had leaped over Zane's unconscious form and slammed into her and the hunter. They'd all gone down in a heap, and by the time she'd scrambled up, it had only been to see Max ripping Boyd's throat out.

Lana had barely reached his side before the poison-induced convulsions hit, twisting Max's body so savagely she thought he might break his own spine. She'd seen where he'd been hit, and she knew it was bad. Trey had said it just the day before.

What happens the next time we tangle with the hunters and they put a poison bullet through a werewolf's chest? He or she won't live more than a couple minutes—if that.

Tears streaming down her face, she pulled Max into her lap and shouted for help even though she heard occasional shooting and fighting still going on outside the OR. But she couldn't sit there and watch Max die. There had to be something she could do.

"I love you, damn it," she told him. "Don't you dare leave me!"

She pressed her hand to the wound in the center of his chest, hopelessly trying to stop the bleeding even as her palm stung from the poison pumping out of him along with his blood.

"Please don't leave me, Max. I love you."

She babbled the words over and over, praying it was enough to help him live. He tried to respond, but no sound came out. His heart pounded faster and faster. He wasn't going to last long.

Then Trey and Alex were at her side, yanking Max out of her arms and rolling him over to check his back.

"Two of them went through and through," Alex said, his voice tight. "The one in his chest is still in there."

Lana watched through her tears as they flipped him over onto his back and went to work, shoving forceps

and probes into the wound, coming out with fragment
after fragment of the poison-filled hollow point before
flushing the wound with saline.

Max was already unconscious but still convulsing.
His heart was starting to slow. He was dying.

Lana didn't know why they were still bothering
to clean the wound. The poison was already in him.
Nothing they were doing was going to save him.

"Go help the others," Alex said to Trey. "I've got this."

Others had been hit? This nightmare couldn't get
any worse.

Trey took off at a run. Then suddenly, Dr. Saunders
was at Max's side, his face calm, his movements sure.
For a moment, Lana tried to convince herself the doctor
could help, that he could get Max cooled down and into
a hypothermic coma before he died. Then she remembered that the research clinic had only this one small
OR, and Zane was already using the only equipment
capable of putting a werewolf under.

But as Saunders shoved a syringe needle into the top
of a small vial of a familiar-looking yellow liquid, she
realized he wasn't thinking about putting Max into a
medically induced coma. He was going for something
more permanent—and risky.

"We don't have much," the doctor muttered as he
drew back on the plunger of the syringe and began to fill
the barrel. "But it will have to do."

Lana stared in disbelief. "We haven't tested the antidote. It could kill him."

Dr. Saunders pulled the syringe out of the vial, then
looked at her. "He's dying already. This is the only
chance we have to save him."

Lana knew he was right but still dreaded giving Max a drug that could make the short time she had left with him even shorter. Dr. Saunders was right, though. This was the only way to save Max.

She blinked back fresh tears and held out her hand for the syringe. "Let me," she whispered. "If someone has to give it to him, it should be me."

Dr. Saunders hesitated, then handed her the needle. He guided her hand as she slipped the syringe in between Max's ribs and straight into his heart. Then she slowly pushed the plunger—and prayed.

Nothing happened. Max's heart rate continued to drop and his body continued to spasm.

"Should we give him more?" she asked.

Dr. Saunders shook his head even as he started filling four more syringes. "If it's going to work, the amount I gave him will do it. If I give him more, I won't have enough for Gage, Hale, and Diego—or Zane."

Saunders gave two of the syringes to Alex, then both men were up and moving, heading to help the others.

"I'll get Gage," the doctor said. "You take Hale and Diego. If the antidote works, we'll try it on Zane last."

Alone in the room now, except for a comatose Zane, Lana leaned forward and rested her forehead against Max's shoulder, still praying as she tried to come to grips with the fact that they might lose more pack members tonight.

She reached down and grabbed his hand, not having a clue whether he knew she was holding it but doing it anyway, just in case. Then she knelt there, waiting for the next beat of Max's heart to be the last. As she listened to its unsteady thump, she replayed every second she'd spent with this amazing man over the past week. It was difficult to believe it had only been seven days since they'd met. Seven beautiful days she would always remember as the best of her life.

She found herself smiling as she remembered meeting him at the award ceremony and how he'd immediately attracted her attention with his witty charm and devastating smile. Everything from there had been a whirl of emotions and experiences she couldn't imagine ever forgetting. There'd been the flirting over pizza, the trip to Austin, their first night of perfect lovemaking at his place, the afternoon spent with Terence and his sisters, that crazy night he'd told her she was a werewolf, and then the night she'd shown up at his place after getting away from the hunters and learning Max had been right all along and that she really was a werewolf.

Her smile broadened as she relived that moment she'd shown up at his door, flashing her claws and telling him he'd been right. They'd torn each other's clothes off and made love up against the door. She actually laughed a little when she realized she hadn't worried one bit about protection at that point—or at any point over the next couple hours they'd made love over and over. She absently wondered if a child would come out of that crazy night of passion. She hoped so, simply so she'd have something more of Max to remember.

Lana was still daydreaming about that possibility when she felt a hand lightly trailing up her back and into her hair. Her breath caught in her throat when the hand she was holding gripped her fingers tightly and the

chest she'd collapsed against bore a heart beating strong
and steady.

She jerked her head up and looked at Max, shocked
to see his eyes open and clear of pain, a warm smile
spreading across this face. She opened her mouth to say
something, but no words would come. Her body was
full of so many emotions right then, she couldn't think
clearly enough to talk.

"Hey there," Max said, his expression turning serious.
"I hope you're not crying over me. I'd die if I thought
for a second I'd done something to make you unhappy
enough to cry."

Lana was about to tell him that of course she'd been
crying over him, but instead, she threw herself forward
and buried her face in his neck, crying even harder now.

Max held her, murmuring meaningless words that
meant the world to her all the same. She squeezed
him back until she was finally able to believe he was
alive and going to make it; then she lifted her head
and shouted for Dr. Saunders, telling him the antidote
had worked.

Turning back to Max, she leaned down to kiss him
long and slow on the mouth. "Don't you ever do anything like that again, understand?"

Max smiled up at her. "Wouldn't dream of it," he
whispered softly, tugging her down for another kiss.

Chapter 16

"LET ME KNOW WHAT YOU THINK OF THIS," BROOKS SAID with a grin as he slid two plates in front of Lana. "Max asked me to come up with something special for you since I had grill duty today."

She looked up and was momentarily distracted by the sight of Brooks standing there in a pair of shorts and a muscle shirt. And man, was there a lot of muscle there to fill out that shirt. She loved Max with every fiber of her being, but that didn't mean she couldn't appreciate a fine-looking man when she saw him.

She forced her attention away from Brooks—who insisted he was dressed like he was on the chilly November day purely because it was so hot over by the grills—and leaned over to smell the food. She let out a little moan of appreciation. "This smells amazing. What is it?"

"Two grilled portobello mushroom burgers with Cajun spices and a little onion jam on the side, along with grilled sweet potato wedges spiced up with lime and cilantro."

Lana glanced at Max, who shrugged and shook his head. "What can I say? The big man has some mad skills with the grills."

Lana laughed and picked up the mushroom burger, taking a bite. "It's awesome!" she said around a big mouthful of tasty goodness. She knew talking with her mouth full was poor manners, but it was *so* good.

Brooks grinned again. "Glad you like it. You need anything else, let me know."

Giving them a nod, he headed back to his grills over by the volleyball court, where he'd spent the better part of the afternoon working hard to feed all the people attending the monthly SWAT cookout. Team mascot, Tuffie, and Lacey's dog, Leo, sat beside him, patiently waiting for their specially made plates of food.

"That does smell damn good," Remy said from the other side of the table, where he sat with Triana. "Can I have a piece?"

Lana cut off a piece from the back side of the burger and passed it over to him. Remy took a bite with as much gusto as she had.

"I can't believe what I'm seeing," Diego murmured from the other side of Max as he dug into his bloody rare steak. "A Cajun werewolf eating mushrooms instead of meat. Your family would probably disown you if they found out."

Remy chuckled and licked his fingers clean. "My family would eat cardboard if you put Cajun spices on it."

Lana laughed along with everyone else at the table. "I'm glad so many people were able to come today."

Max looked up from his barbecue chicken and around at the compound. "Yeah. We've never had this many people here before. Though I have to tell you, these events are usually a lot louder than this."

"I can't say I blame anyone for not being in a partying mood," Remy said, the jovial expression gone from his face. "The wounds are still a bit raw for everyone."

Lana couldn't argue with that. This was her first cookout, but even she'd noticed the event seemed a bit subdued. That was understandable. Although the Pack had been lucky to make it out of the recent encounter with the hunters in one piece, it was too soon to be laughing and joking.

Thankfully, Gage, Diego, and Hale had completely recovered from the wounds they'd sustained during the fight with Boyd and the other hunters. In fact, unless someone had told her, she'd have been hard-pressed to know how close they'd come to dying that day. Dr. Saunders had tried to give her and the others much of the credit for the antidote, but Lana knew whom to thank for saving Max's life.

Since he'd been shot three times in the chest, Max's recovery had taken longer than the others. Two weeks later, he was still moving a little slower than normal. Last week he'd gone up to Alaska with her for Denise's funeral, and that had nearly worn him out, but he was getting stronger every day, and Lana had no doubt that he'd be back to his old self soon.

On the bright side, Max no longer seemed to have any issue controlling his inner werewolf. Maybe it was an outcome of saving Terence and his family, or maybe it had come from saving Lana. Either way, his fangs and claws hadn't made a surprise appearance since that night.

Unfortunately, there wasn't much of a bright side when it came to Zane, which was probably the biggest reason there was a dark shadow hanging over this entire event. Yes, they'd all lived through the hunter's attack, but one of their kind had paid a steep price.

Zane was supposed to be at home on bed rest for at least another week, but he'd insisted on coming to the cookout. He'd never missed one before, and he said he didn't intend to start now, arm in a sling or not. While the antidote had cleared the poison from his body, the stuff had still been in his system for nearly two days, doing an unimaginable amount of damage. Something as simple as getting out of bed was a chore for him at the moment, but yet here he was.

It was the injury to his arm that had everyone worried, though. The antidote couldn't replace muscle that was no longer there, and even though Dr. Saunders was hopeful the werewolf gene might allow some muscle regrowth to occur, the fact was no one knew if it would.

Zane wasn't handling the possibility of being disabled very well. And Trey—who essentially believed he was responsible—was handling it even worse. The medic hadn't left Zane's side all day unless it was to grab more food for his pack mate.

Not everyone at the cookout was feeling down, though. At the far picnic table, Coletti was sitting with Kari, their heads close together, grins on their faces. Max had told Lana about what had happened between Coletti and the beta werewolf at the compound right before the SWAT team had left to raid the clinic. No one seemed to know what Kari had said to the man, but afterward, the detective hadn't asked Max for any of those details he'd been demanding earlier.

Brandy was there, too. She'd finally accepted an invitation from Chris, and now they were sitting on a bench on the other side of the volleyball court, talking. Lana could have eavesdropped but refused, especially since they were obviously having a good time together.

Terence and his sisters were on the volleyball court,

playing with Megan, her human boyfriend, Zak, and some of the other kids. Megan was completely healed now and seemed to have a calming effect on the recently traumatized kids.

Their mother wasn't smiling as much as Terence and his sisters, but she was trying to put on a good face for her children's sakes. Lana hoped Eileen and her kids became regulars at the SWAT cookouts. They fit in here.

Lana was absently nibbling on her sweet potato fries, thinking she and Max should take the Wallace kids to a Cowboys game, when Gage and his wife, Mac, came over to their table and sat down.

"I was hoping your mom and dad could make it today," Gage said to Lana.

"I was hoping so, too," she said. "Dad is doing much better, but there's no way his doctor was going to let him out yet, even if all he'd do was sit at a picnic table."

Gage nodded. "I can understand that."

"Everything is okay between you and your father now, right?" Mac asked. "Your dad is on board with you and Max being together?"

Lana smiled and reached out to take Max's hand. "Yeah. Max and I have been hanging out with my parents almost every night. Dad finally got around to apologizing for how he treated Max—and for hiding my werewolf nature from me. We're really good now."

"I'm glad," Gage said, then glanced at Diego. "How're you feeling? Any long-term effects from the poison?"

Diego shook his head. "Not really. My ab muscles are still a little tender, but it's fading fast. I'll feel a hell of lot better when the son of a bitch who shot me goes to trial."

Diego was talking about Seth, the only hunter who'd

made it out of the raid alive. He was currently in Dallas County lockup, awaiting arraignment.

"Seth Oliver's looking at the death penalty for the attempted murder of the deputy chief, not to mention shooting you at the clinic. That's a given," Gage said. "But I might as well tell you the latest news before you hear it through the grapevine."

"What?" Diego asked warily.

"There are least six other states that want to question Seth relating to his possible involvement in a series of unsolved homicides. Bottom line, the guy will probably avoid the death penalty for years because he'll be traveling around the country, getting charged with other murders."

"You're kidding me, right?" Diego said.

Gage shrugged. "I wish. Then it wouldn't hurt so much."

Remy took a swig of beer. "You think Seth is in contact with the other hunters out there?"

Gage shrugged. "We have to assume he is because he sure as hell is never going to tell us voluntarily."

The SWAT commander should know. Everyone on the SWAT team except for Zane had paid Seth a visit in jail, trying to get the man to crack, but no luck yet.

"How long do you think it'll be before more hunters show up?" Max asked.

Gage sighed. "Based on what Lana overheard, we know Seth and his crew were nothing more than hired killers on a leash. The man pulling the strings is still out there, and we don't have a clue who he is or what his motives might be. It's a safe bet they'll try again at some point, especially now that they know exactly who and where we are. My concern is that next time, we won't see them coming until it's too late to do anything about it."

"But we have the antidote to their poison," Triana pointed out. "And Dr. Saunders said he's going to start giving small doses of the drug to every werewolf in town to help build up some kind of resistance to the poison. Like a vaccination."

"And that's a good thing," Gage said. "But there's nothing to say they'll use the same poison the next time they show up. I'm worried about the weapon program Lana overheard them talking about. Something tells me they may have more than poison bullets in their bag of tricks."

Max cursed. "Great. Now we have to worry they might have something even worse than wolfsbane the next time we tangle with them."

"That may be the least of our problems," Gage muttered.

Diego stopped, his burger halfway to his mouth. "It gets worse?"

"If you consider the possibility of someone in the DPD knowing about us and actively working with the hunters to kill us to be worse, then yes," Gage said.

Lana and Max had been talking about the same thing since the night at the clinic. The man who'd told Boyd she and Zane were at Dr. Saunders's clinic had to be high up in the DPD organization. Very few people had known Zane was injured, much less where he was. The thought that there was a cop out there working with the hunters was absolutely terrifying.

Gage and Mac hung out at their table for a little while longer, but Lana could tell the SWAT commander's mind was a hundred miles away. No doubt he was worrying about protecting the rapidly growing pack from the hunter's next attack.

"He blames himself because he didn't see this coming," Remy said quietly after Gage and Mac had left to talk with some omegas and betas at another table.

Triana frowned. "That's silly. He did everything he could."

"I know," Remy agreed. "But he holds himself to a higher standard than that. The werewolves in his pack got hurt. He's going to be beating himself up about it until we stop these hunters for good."

Lana and everyone else at the table were still trying to figure out what they could do to help Gage carry some of the burden of protecting the Pack when the sun started going down. Beside her, Max looked a little worn out. Since he'd never admit it, she had to make certain decisions for him.

"Why don't we head home?" she suggested softly, leaning in close. "I'm beat."

Max gave her a look that told Lana he was onto her, but he didn't call her on it. Instead, he smiled and kissed her. "Then let's get you home."

She and Max made the rounds of the compound, saying good night to everyone, then walked hand in hand out to his Camaro. As he started the engine and drove out of the parking lot, heading toward his apartment they were now sharing, Lana realized he was more quiet than usual.

"Hey," she said. "Are you feeling okay? Should we stop in and see Dr. Saunders?"

He shook his head. "I'm okay. I'm was just thinking about stuff."

"What kind of stuff?"

He shrugged. "About how crazy it is for us to be trying to have a relationship while we're wondering when the hunters are going to show up and try to kill us again."

Lana reached over and grabbed his hand, squeezing it hard, something that was a lot easier to do now that she had access to all her werewolf abilities.

"You can stop wondering right now," she said firmly. "I just got you back, and I'm not wasting a second of our lives together worrying about what may happen with those hunters. If they come back, we'll deal with them."

Max didn't say anything for a while, but then he looked over and smiled. "I'm glad you feel that way because I've been putting a lot of thought into not wasting time either."

"Oh yeah?"

"Yeah," he said, turning his attention to the highway again. "What would you say if I told you I wanted to get married?"

Lana's heart did a little happy dance. She'd learned enough about the legend of *The One* over the past couple of weeks to know it meant that Max and she were going to be together for life. After almost losing him to the hunters' bullets, she realized she wasn't interested in waiting around before starting that life. It was nice to know Max felt the same.

"I guess that depends," she said coyly, "on whether you're actually asking me to marry me or simply talking hypothetically."

He suddenly pulled over to the side of the road, stopping in the grass. Cars sped by them at seventy miles an hour, but Max ignored them as he turned to look at her.

"I'm definitely asking." He grimaced. "I'm sorry if this isn't as romantic as it should be, with a ring and everything, but if I learned anything from going up against the hunters, it's that things move fast—even when you've found the person you're going to be with for the rest of your life. I don't want to waste a second of the life we have together, Lana, so yeah, I'm asking you to marry me. And if you say yes, I'm completely okay with heading to the airport right now. We can be in Vegas by midnight, have a diamond on your finger an hour later, and be married by the time the sun comes up."

She laughed and leaned over the console to kiss him. "The answer is yes, I'll marry you, Max. And while a whirlwind wedding in Vegas would certainly do the trick, how about we slow things down just a little and see if we can set up something local? I don't need much, just my parents, my friends, and the Pack. I want this moment to be perfect for both of us, okay?"

He tipped her head back and kissed her hard enough to make her almost change her mind. Then he pulled back and flashed her a grin.

"Okay, that's the plan then. We get married as soon as we can pull everything together. A Christmas wedding, maybe. What do you think?"

Since it was almost Thanksgiving, that would give them a little more than four weeks until Christmas. She smiled. "I think that sounds good to me."

Max suddenly turned serious again. "One thing, though."

"What's that?" she asked.

"You have to be the one to tell your dad. He's just

now starting to like me, and if I tell him we're planning to get married already, he'll probably shoot me."

Lana laughed and kissed him again. "Don't worry. I'll handle my dad. You just figure out where you're taking me on our honeymoon."

"I can handle that," he murmured against her mouth. "Anywhere with you will be perfect."

Acknowledgments

I hope you had as much fun reading Max and Lana's story as I had writing it! Now we finally know why Deputy Chief Mason has always looked the other way when it comes to his SWAT team!

While this story is a work of fiction, the issue of domestic violence is a very real problem today. If you or anyone you know is affected by domestic violence, please visit thehotline.org for help.

This whole series wouldn't be possible without some very incredible people. In addition to another big thank-you to my hubby for all his help with the action scenes and military and tactical jargon, thanks to my agent, Bob Mecoy, for believing in us and encouraging us and being there when we need to talk; my editor and go-to-person at Sourcebooks, Cat Clyne (who loves this series as much as I do and is always a phone call, text, or email away whenever I need something); and all the other amazing people at Sourcebooks, including my fantastic publicist Stephany, and their crazy-talented art department. The covers they make for me are seriously drool-worthy!

Because I could never leave out my readers, a huge thank-you to everyone who has read my books and Snoopy-danced right along with me with every new release. That includes the fantastic people on my amazing Street Team, as well my assistant, Janet. You rock!

I also want to give a big thank-you to the men, women, and working dogs who protect and serve in police departments everywhere, as well as their families.

And a very special shout-out to our favorite restaurant, P.F. Chang's, where hubby and I bat storylines back and forth and come up with all of our best ideas, as well as a thank-you to our fantastic waiter, Andrew, who takes our order to the kitchen the moment we walk in the door!

Hope you enjoy the next book in the SWAT series coming soon, and look forward to reading the rest of the series as much as I look forward to sharing it with you.

If you love a man in uniform as much as I do, make sure you check out X-Ops, my other action-packed paranormal/romantic-suspense series from Sourcebooks.

Happy Reading!

About the Author

Paige Tyler is a *New York Times* and *USA Today* best-selling author of sexy, romantic suspense and paranormal romance. She and her very own military hero (also known as her husband) live on the beautiful Florida coast with their adorable fur baby (also known as their dog). Paige graduated with a degree in education but decided to pursue her passion and write books about hunky alpha males and the kick-butt heroines who fall in love with them.

Visit Paige at her website at paigetylertheauthor.com.

She's also on Facebook, Twitter, Tumblr, Instagram, tsu, Wattpad, Google+, and Pinterest.

Also By Paige Tyler

SWAT: Special Wolf Alpha Team

Hungry Like the Wolf
Wolf Trouble
In The Company of Wolves
To Love a Wolf
Wolf Unleashed
Wolf Hunt
Wolf Hunger

X-Ops

Book Her Perfect Mate
Her Lone Wolf
Her Secret Agent (novella)
Her Wild Hero
Her Fierce Warrior
Her Rogue Alpha
Her True Match
Her Dark Half
X-Ops Exposed

Don't miss Paige Tyler's action-packed X-Ops series:

> "The chemistry is scorching hot."
> —*RT Book Reviews* for *Wolf Hunt* ★★★★

SHE'S ALL THE WOLF HE'LL EVER NEED...

When SWAT Officer Max Lowry meets Lana Mason, he falls fast and hard. He's positive she's *The One.* And Max's favorite part? Lana's a wolf shifter too, so they can skip the awkward reveal and head straight to the happily ever after. There's just one problem: *Lana doesn' know that she's a werewolf.*

To make matters worse, hunters with intent to kill have tracked Lana to Dallas. Max has to figure out how to keep Lana safe, show her who and what she really is—and just how much she means to him.

Readers are hungry for Paige Tyler's SWAT series:

> "I don't think I will ever get enough of Paige Tyler's Special Wolf Alpha Team."
> —*Night Owl Reviews* Reviewer Top Pick
> for *To Love a Wolf* ★★★★★

> "I love the SWAT series, I love Paige Tyler, and now multiply this tenfold!"
> —*Fresh Fiction* for *To Love a Wolf*

EBOOK EDITION ALSO AVAILABLE
SOURCEBOOKSCASABLANCA.COM
SOURCEBOOKS CASABLANCA

Romance $7.99 U.S.
ISBN-13: 978-1-4926-4237-4

50799

9 781492 642374